"Who's there?" she asked. Her voice emerged roughly, jolting through the fear, and then there was the black silence once more, so heavy it weighted the ear drums. The footstep came again, closer this time, and suddenly, out of the blackness and the quivering silence there emerged a pale figure, ghostly at first, then taking form. She stood in a void, as though certainty had switched the fear off, then a hand brushed her arm, the fingers gripped, curled round her flesh, and at that moment between herself and her attacker, against the background of his white garment, there was the flash of a knife.

THE BHUNDA JEWELS

ANNE WORBOYS

ace books

A Division of Charter Communications Inc.
A GROSSET & DUNLAP COMPANY
51 Madison Avenue
New York, New York 10010

THE BHUNDA JEWELS

Copyright © 1980 by Anne Worboys

An ACE Book

First Ace Printing: May, 1981

2 4 6 8 0 9 7 5 3 1
Manufactured in the United States of America

You will not find the town of Kodapur or the village of Tarand on a map. Nevertheless, they exist under another name. The rope sacrifice is still carried out in villages of the Himachal Pradesh where the inhabitants can afford it.

My thanks are due to Penelope, Lady Betjeman, who gave me in a few short weeks a unique view of India. Also to Kranti Singh and particularly to Chumba, who dragged me up that last impossible precipice.

Chapter One

It was there, as she had suspected. A small, white tombstone announcing the fact that Ashley's father had been born in 1920 and died in 1947. Jane was momentarily shocked. She had not thought of him as being so young. The dust and dirt of thirty years had been cleared from the inscription, roughly, with fingernails, or a twig. That gave her the clue to Ashley's presence here in Kodapur. Jane stood looking down at the stone, tense and disturbed. Jasper Edward Carlyon. Her mother's first husband. Torn to pieces in the Hindu/Muslim riots, Louise had said. Now, because it was suddenly real, she shivered.

Something deep inside Jane shifted painfully. She had once seen a neighbour's son in their village cemetery, hands in pockets, shoulders hunched in the rain, staring down at his father's grave. And yet, Ashley did not seem the type to travel six thousand miles to make a pilgrimage to the father he had never known. She and her half-brother had both been upset by their mother's death, but it seemed now that Ashley had been more deeply disturbed. She had sensed it at the time, and standing here looking at the rubbed stone, the feeling redoubled itself. There was something she did not know. Ashley had spent a great deal of time in Louise's sick room that week before she died. What had their mother told him that she had not told Jane? Louise's past as the daughter of an Indian Army colonel was open enough, but something happened during her first marriage. It had been whispered that she had an affaire with an Indian prince. How could one, as the wife of an Administrator?

Jane had travelled from Delhi all the night before last and

7

most of yesterday. Nobody had told her an Express, in Indian terms, was not a fast train. That on a long journey one arranged to travel by Mail. None the less, she had journeyed well by Indian standards to the point where she had had to change to a bus, which was awful, jammed in with a hundred Indians in a vehicle built to carry forty or less. She had tumbled out of it dishevelled and desperate after three hours of swirling, choking dust as they rattled across the bare plains. But on the train she had been in a first-class compartment, with a clean bed roll and a hand basin (that was certainly not clean) at the end of the carriage. But the tap worked, which was all that mattered.

Jane's carriage had a toilet, though it didn't bear thinking about. (She could hold her breath to a slow count of forty.) Watching Indians erupting from their third-class carriages at each station like lemmings at the sea's edge, scrambling down from the roof in a mêlée of bony shanks and draped white cotton, jamming themselves in the windows, she had known a sense of privilege that was different in both essence and sentiment from the sanction of vindicable right with which her ancestors had swept across those dusty plains.

The taxi driver had told her there was only one hotel in the town. He meant there was only one suitable for a respectable English girl. This meant Ashley should be staying there. It was up on a hill looking across this wide river where the ramshackle outer reaches of Kodapur began. The driver was a Sikh. Jane understood most of the taxi drivers were Sikhs because they were born mechanics – born bad mechanics, Louise used to say, and bad drivers into the bargain. But they were magnificent to look at, with their long hair and black beards rolled up in bright turbans, and they were taller than the average Hindu. This one drove with tremendous style, if dangerously, his rattly old car leaping over the rough stones, shying away from a donkey drawing a cart and pulling up so precipitously in front of a flock of goats that Jane had to put out a hand against the front seat to stop herself flying forward. The sun had gone down by the time she arrived but heat struck upwards from the road and the goats leaping and darting past had sent clouds of dust puffing through the open windows, so that later when she looked in the hotel mirror a thin veil of grey had dulled her golden hair and hidden the petal freshness of her skin. The smell she had first noted in Delhi was more pronounced in Kodapur. Sitting in the stifling heat of the back of the car she decided she had placed it, and it was less acceptable. Dust and urine. Ugh. She had known from her mother and grandparents about India's smells; knew she had to get used to them.

But Ashley was not at the hotel which appeared at first glance to be still in the process of being built. Bare concrete walls, partially laid tiles, idling workmen in white overalls more interested in Jane's arrival than in their work. Only the reception area was beautiful, gaudy with brochures and plate glass. That little oasis could have been lifted straight out of an airways office in London's West End. The manager was large and well-fed with the pallid skin of the indoor Indian. His name was Mr Arun Prakash. There were two Englishmen here, he said, but neither was called Bellamy. Jane's own father, when he married her mother, had adopted the child Ashley and changed his name.

It was midday now and in the British cemetery the heat was dreadful. Jane raised the brim of her hat to wipe the perspiration from her forehead. As she was about to turn away from the grave a movement in the distance caught her eye. She paused, narrowing her eyes against the glare.

There was a man crossing the river below. A white man? He wore a small hat with a brim, rather like her own. Indians wore Ghandi caps, or turbans, or pillboxes. She waited, nails digging into the palms of her hands, lower lip caught between her teeth. To meet her half-brother across his father's grave, she realized unhappily, was an intrusion of privacy in dubious taste, yet if this was Ashley, she must

9

wait. And now it was not only because she needed his signature on legal papers. There was a poignancy about the sight of that cleared inscription that cut through everything she had known, or thought she knew, about Ashley. Perhaps he needed her.

Dr Clive Retford picked his way across the stepping stones of the wide, rocky river that looped and curled its way round the town, warily avoiding the chalky blue water still cold from the snow mountains. A lammergeier circled slowly overhead, then winged away. On the shore he turned. The dark-skinned old waif with the smashed, syphilitic nose, filthy sari and bare feet who had followed him all the way from the clinic like a faithful dog, was still there. There was a vulture on the gatepost ahead, watching her, scraggy neck stretched, brooding evilly. Clive gave the crone a few annas then hurried up the slope and came through the cemetery gateway between the drooping ashokan trees. Slowly and thoughtfully, he walked along the path where the babies slept beneath their miniature tombstones. There were always more small tombstones in the British cemeteries because so often the white babies came on earth for only a little while to point up what needed to be done. That was one of the comments Clive's father had made, influencing him, though unintentionally.

He saw Jane and stopped in surprise, his eyes lighting up as he took in the heart-shaped face with gentian blue eyes, the fine, silky hair puffing out palely from her shoulders that were broad for a girl except that her height brought them into proportion. The delicately cut, firm but sensitive mouth.

'Er – hello,' he said.

She straightened, smiled. 'I thought you were someone else.' The voice was faintly resentful as though, in spite of the smile, she could not overcome her disappointment. 'I dare say there are masses of English in Kodapur,' she added.

'I don't think so. A few hippies down at the Ashram and two of us at Savakar's.'

'I'm at Savakar's. I'm Jane Bellamy.'

He introduced himself. 'What are you doing in India?'

She could not say she was looking for her brother who had inexplicably disappeared the day after their mother's funeral six months ago, and recently, equally inexplicably, had indicated his whereabouts by sending her a coloured card with the postmark of Kodapur and a diverting picture of the god Shiva. So she said, 'My mother's first husband was British Resident here.' She added diffidently, 'That's his tombstone.' Clive glanced at the inscription, then sharply back at her. Louise Carlyon's daughter! Arriving here only days before the Bhunda!

'You've heard of him?' Jane asked. They had never talked of Ashley's father at home. Not even her grandmother, who liked to reminisce. She wondered if Clive was going to make some enlightening comment, but he seemed to put aside whatever was in his mind. He said in a measured, oddly deliberate manner, 'It's curious the way we're drawn back. My ancestors plundered the country for over a hundred years. I owe it a frightening debt. We're all riddled with guilt.'

She gave him a second, more searching look, smiling faintly, uncertainly, at his assumption of her role in India's misery. He had longish, dark hair swept back loosely over the ears, a slim, lithe body and frosted grey eyes within spiky dark lashes. The nose was high-bridged, the mouth set firmly above a hard jaw. 'The East India Company made my family rich in the latter part of the nineteenth century,' Clive said. 'To have been born, as my antecedents were, with a silver spoon of an underprivileged country in their mouths was, in my view, to be given a sacred trust. But they took it all out of India and squandered it at home between the wars. I'm a doctor. I'm trying, in my own way, to put back.'

Even feeling he was tilting at windmills she was oddly touched and humbled by his vision. 'I wish you luck,' she said. Her grandmother, Lady Bellamy, widow of a General, wore rings given her by enormously rich Maharajas who had seemed, at one time, able to hand them out like trading stamps. The Bellamys had played polo, raced horses, enjoyed a houseful of servants. Could it be said they did not put much back? With an automatic, defensive reaction she turned and glanced again towards the grave.

'What are you doing here?' she asked.

'I was sent out two years ago by the World Health Organization,' he replied. He told her the sick people who squatted so patiently in the clinic courtyard waiting for attention as sharp winged black vultures circled, needed help more quickly than the sparse Indian staff could provide.

'And what can you do? You, I mean.'

He smiled, glanced out over the river, fumbled in a pocket as though looking for cigarettes. 'What can I do?' he repeated the question as though it was all too familiar. 'It's what I'm determined to do,' he answered. 'Overcome the problems of filth and disease.'

She smiled wryly. 'In India?' Immediate memories crowded in. Beggars in the dust. Children's faces crawling with flies. Stinking garbage strewn by pariah dogs round the streets.

'Somehow,' he said, 'I'm going to get a sanitary educational programme going in Kodapur.'

'I wish you luck,' she said again.

'And as soon as possible, a fully equipped, fully manned hospital.' He said it less with confidence than with determination and sincerity. He had found the cigarettes. He offered one to her.

She shook her head. 'I don't. Well, not often.' She watched him as the match flared, invisible in the white glare of midday. He had a very open face; a good face. The smoke hung motionless in the still air.

'Where will you get the money?' she asked. They had begun to walk up the hill.

'Ah!' The look he shot her was suddenly strained. 'That's the sixty-four dollar question.' He turned to look back and she stopped beside him. So he was one of those illogical, optimistic dreamers. He did not look it. He looked stern in a resilient way; tough.

'The river is beautiful,' she said.

'Yes, but don't be tempted to wander down and climb over the rocks. They're Kodapur's open air public lavatory.'

'Ugh!' With her background she knew all about the hygienic complexities of the Indians who said the British were dirty because they sat in their own bathwater but refused to either build toilets or obey the late Mahatma Ghandi's injunction to carry a small trowel to bury their excrement.

'Are you on your way to the hotel? It's far too hot to be out walking. Besides, it's lunch-time.'

'Yes. Yes, I suppose I am.' She fell into step beside him. 'What a quaint place Kodapur is! I came across the market this morning. Oh! So many big-eyed, beautiful children!'

He added dryly, 'And so many diseased ones. We're getting the pill going. It's slow to take.'

'Yes, that's the answer, isn't it. But not really the answer. You've got to change their thinking. They've a need for those children—' She stopped, looked up at him and laughed. 'There, you've got me on to their problems, and I'm only here on a brief visit. I just want to look, and — maybe I'll think about it later. There's nothing a visitor can do. Except make oneself miserable.' He did not answer. 'I'm sorry,' she apologized. 'I shouldn't have said that.' A moment later she added, 'The dogs bother me.' She laughed wryly, engagingly. 'How typical of an Englishwoman to worry about the dogs! But they're so evil.'

'Not enough love. And not enough food.'

'Yes.' She took a little skipping step, suddenly light hearted at having one of her own countrymen to talk to. 'Up in the market I saw the most wonderfully placid, doe-eyed woman sitting cross-legged with a diamond in her nose.' Jane clapped her hands together. 'How marvellously eccentric, to go back to London with a diamond in one's nose!'

Clive laughed with her. He liked her gaiety and recognized it was good for him. He was not seeing enough of the lighter side of life. It was too long since he had even met an English girl. 'How do you like the smells?' he asked. 'Can you take them in your stride?'

'Some of them. I'm surprised at the lack of perfumes. Blossom smells. Fruit. There's a fusty, dusty India smell that rather intrigues me. It's everywhere, in the air and the earth and in the grubby garments of the people one passes in the road. Actually, you know,' she said, remembering, 'it's the smell that one gets when one wanders into those little boutiques in the West End of London that sell Indian clothes. Much diluted there, of course.' His heart lifted, lightened. He was remembering how India had excited him before its filth, its squalor and the need of it took him in its vice.

They came up over the brow of the hill. There was a ramshackle little gate in the stone wall that shut off this remaining bit of England in a State now free. A flock of small, bright birds landed on a bush close at hand, twinkling in the sunlight, twittering and cheeping and stirring the leaves, bringing the plant to life.

'That great expanse of dirt in front used to be a parade ground,' Clive told her, 'in the days of the British Raj.' Heat flared up from it as from a grill. 'Let's skirt it. We'll find an occasional bit of shade that way.' A pair of kites swung in from above, planed in a great circle and disappeared. They followed a track edged by dry little bushes, an occasional fig, some pipal trees, and neem. Even in the brief shade there was little respite from the heat.

'What are you going to do here?' Clive asked. 'Have you got friends?'

Again, she found herself shying away from the truth, not

quite knowing why. He was going to think her devious when Ashley turned up, yet even telling herself that, she continued to hold back.

'Not really. I know an Indian. I might trip around. Go to Simla, perhaps. My grandfather had a bungalow there. We've got watercolours of it. It was beautiful. I'd like to take tea in the Mall. Just to sit there at a little white-clothed table letting my imagination fly back!'

'To the days when the Indians weren't allowed in?'

She caught the dry wryness of his tone and shot him a sharp look. 'To the Mall?'

'It's full of Indians now.'

'Yes,' she replied uncertainly. 'Yes, I'm sure it is. It's another world. My mother and grandmother used to talk of balls at the Residency—'

'It's a university now.'

'Yes. I'm sure that's better,' she agreed quickly. 'But what's wrong with ghosts?' A careless ecstasy that came with what she had known of India from her family flooded up through her, and he watched her face, enchanted, in spite of himself. 'Imagine the men in those wonderful dress uniforms and the ladies in silks and satins, being pulled along the roads in their little *doolis*. Every *dooli* had its own lamp, so there were bobbing pin-sized lights in the darkness like big glow-worms. And it would be all silence except for the shush-shush made by the Indian's bare feet in the dust.'

'I don't believe the British were meant to come here for that sort of thing,' Clive said quietly. 'I believe they were meant to break up the princes into tiny pieces and feed them to the poor.'

She came down out of the clouds with a shock. He saw her stiffen, noted her sensitivity and was touched by it. But it did not stop him saying what he had to say, just in case . . . 'Do you know that while the ordinary people of India starved, the Maharaja of Patiala kept five hundred polo ponies and a harem of three hundred and fifty women? Did you know that?' She was silent, suddenly desperately ashamed of her ill-considered reference to the man-drawn *doolis* of Simla. To Clive, the soft sound of bare feet in the dust meant not only that the Indians could not afford shoes, but that they were being used by the British as beasts of burden. 'The Nizam of Hyderabad used to use the famous Jacob diamond, all two hundred and eighty carats of it, as a paper weight,' Clive told her. 'His cellars were ankle deep in precious stones. We didn't do anything about it.'

She smiled at him, though a little uncertainly. 'I don't see what the British could have done.'

'As the law stood, they possessed the power to remove a ruler if they had a good enough excuse,' he told her. 'What better excuse than that they were exploiting their own people? But we allowed the most outrageous behaviour, so long as the princes remained loyal. I'm here for revenge,' he said.

She had never heard anyone talk like this. He was tearing the fairy-tales apart. She scarcely knew how to reply. 'What do you mean? What sort of revenge?'

'A revenge of the soul.' He turned his head to gaze out over the scraggy treetops into the painted blue sky. 'An atonement,' he added. 'I believe we're sometimes offered opportuni— no, situations. Situations that can turn into opportunities, if we recognize them. There is such a situation here, at the moment, in Kodapur. You could help,' he said. He watched her carefully, very carefully, for a reaction. She looked faintly puzzled but he could not tell if it was assumed. 'With your background, you ought,' he added. 'It depends where your heart lies.' They stopped because an old man was lying across their path. He was dressed only in a dirty loin-cloth. Bony arms were bent so that the hands could shield his face. The dry skin, burned by the sun, was drawn from jutting bone to jutting bone, sagging like a dark, creased curtain between. There seemed to be not an ounce of flesh on the ancient body.

'See what I mean?' said Clive. His voice was quite straight-forward, as though the pity in him had run its course and eaten itself away.

'That's India,' said Jane, not because she did not care, but because her mind was on the enigma of her brother, and anyway, Clive's concern made her feel uncomfortable and helpless.

'It bloody ought not to be India,' he replied, startling her with the force of his feelings. 'A hundred years is long enough to remedy anything, if the heart's in the right place. You mentioned you had an Indian friend.'

'Actually, he's a friend of my cousin. I'll look him up.' She had not wanted to call on Gopal Behera. It smacked of inter-ference. But perhaps he knew something of Ashley's where-abouts. 'You mentioned the ashram. My cousin Helen was living there last year.'

That faint suspicion Clive had about her being interested in the Bhunda withdrew fractionally. Perhaps the family were merely trailing back in the natural order of things, out of sheer curiosity. His tolerant smile was touched with a trace of cynicism. He'd had white girls from the ashram in his clinic often enough. Poor, pathetic, vulnerable creatures in their long, tatty skirts; with their long hair and embroid-ered headbands; their fanatical worship of the swami; and their dysentery.

'She wasn't a hippy, but she might have become one if this Indian boy hadn't rescued her. He's the victim of an arranged child-marriage. He has been to England, but he's back here now to try to sort something out.'

Clive's eyebrows rose but did not ask the question that sprang automatically to mind. 'The Indian is very family orientated. The children revere their parents. He's got a job ahead of him if he's having to tell his father a mistake's been made. His father will have chosen the bride.'

She nodded. Gopal was sweet but the Bellamys did not want an Indian relative any more than the Beheras wanted an English one. If Gopal fiddle-faddled long enough, Helen, they all hoped fervently, might meet someone else in London. Anyway, that was not her problem. Jane's problem was Ashley. But she could not very well, under the circumstances, tell Clive for the only facts she knew about his disappearance made him sound very odd. She was certain there was an explanation. She asked diffidently, 'Is Savakar's really the only hotel in the town?'

Clive glanced at her in surprise but she turned her head swiftly away, reaching at some drooping leaves, crumbling them in her fingers. 'Why? Aren't you comfortable?'

'Yes, yes. Perfectly. I just – wondered.'

'Kodapur's very much off the beaten track. There's nothing here to attract visitors. Savakar's caters for Indians of standing, and all visiting foreigners.'

She felt suddenly enormously depressed. Perhaps Ashley had been and gone.

Chapter Two

The thin boy with the bright face and black velvet eyes who had carried her bag upstairs the evening before was waiting in the hotel foyer. Jane asked quietly, turning her head so that Clive would not hear, 'Has Mr Bellamy turned up?'

He cocked his head on one side, frowning. 'Turn up, Memsahib?'

'Sorry. I mean, has anyone else booked in?'

'No one book in, Memsahib. Only Dr Retford, you and Mr Hills, here, Memsahib.' Barry Hills. She had seen the name in the visitors' book.

She went despondently up the stairs in Clive's wake. Her accommodation lay along an open veranda that overlooked a rough, rocky slope decorated with scraggy fig trees, Coca-Cola tins, some bamboo and a few stained newspapers. Hearing her footsteps, Clive turned, smiling. 'Ah, they've put you on the same floor as me. I'll see you in a few moments for lunch.' He went with a light step into the room next door, looking pleased.

Shooing the flies off the bedcover, Jane sat down trying to decide what to do, staring blankly through the open door into the inexplicably vast, white-tiled bathroom. She did not want to call on Gopal. It was going to evoke unwelcome complications. She eased her blouse away from her hot neck. She would have liked a shower but the conditions were daunting. The water was so cold it must come from the snow-fed river that ran round the town and, there being no shower curtain, the spray swept across the inadequate little outlet pipe set laughably close to the wall in a level floor. By the time she had finished her ablutions last night the flood had reached the door.

Her thoughts returned inevitably to the enigma of Ashley. Ashley, here in Kodapur, visiting the grave of the father he had never known. Her half-brother was an unknown quantity, it was true, but she was certain, now she came to consider it, he was not as unknown as that. Thrown out of Oxford for failing his prelims, he had had no trouble in finding a place at Dublin University and holding it through to a third class degree. 'Blarneyed his way in, no doubt,' his stepfather, Jane's father who openly disliked him, had observed cryptically. Without a drop of Irish blood, Ashley had an Irishman's wildness and his gentle charm. He had toyed with Marxism. He had been a bus conductor for some reason obscurely concerned with the rights of the workers. Writing for one of the raggier national Dailies, he had persuaded them to print some fringe libel. From the ensuing court-case Ashley had emerged unscathed but Louise had been upset, Bernard angry. 'I did it for the money,' Ashley had said innocently with that faint, familiar wickedness showing through. He had not received a penny, in the end, and lost his job into the bargain. 'You can't win 'em all,' he had said, shrugging as the protagonists picked up the pieces. Jane did not begin to understand her half-brother. Perhaps she never would. But if he needed help, she wanted to help him. That scraped tombstone had been a shock. But no, he simply was not the type to travel six thousand miles to visit his father's grave. She glanced automatically at the suitcase where she had left the papers that must be signed before Louise's estate could be finally wound up. The papers that were her excuse for being here. The solicitors were angry about Ashley's disappearance. They did not know him as Jane did.

There was a tap at the door and Clive put his head round, asking pleasantly, 'Ready?'

She snapped out of her reverie and stood up. 'I don't think I'll have any lunch, after all. I'll go off and see Gopal.'

'Gopal?' There was a question implicit in his sharp repetition of the name.

'My cousin's friend. Gopal Behera.'

'Oh.' That was a surprise.

'Why do you say "Oh!" like that?' She looked up at Clive with her head on one side, half smiling. 'Do you know him?'

'No. I've seen him around. I know of him. Hadn't you better wait until it's cooler?'

She made excuses. She was too anxious about Ashley to enjoy eating. 'It'll be curry, won't it? Awfully hot.'

'Not necessarily. But I'll admit the interesting part of these meals are the hot bits.'

'Mm – I'll find a bit of fruit. I'm really not hungry.' And that was true. Yesterday, she had felt she was starving to death. On the train she had merely eaten a few bananas, some biscuits and drunk Coca-Cola. There were plenty of stalls on railway stations and the smell of boiling sweet-meats in the air had been achingly tempting but she had not been prepared to risk food bought in public places. Now, with the good food of Savakar's at hand, anxiety had dulled her appetite.

'Do you know the way?' Clive asked.

'Yes. It's apparently on the slope behind the market. I'm to ask directions from there. Quite a lot of Indians, it seems, speak English.'

'Oh yes. Perhaps you'll have a drink with me before dinner.'

'Thank you.'

'See you later, then.'

When Clive entered the dining-room the other English-man, Barry Hills, was already there. He looked up but Clive merely nodded and went to a table on the opposite side of the room. He had decided, when Hills first arrived at Sava-kar's, it would be better not to strike up a friendship. When Clive disappeared in a few days' time the fewer people who noticed the better. He sat down hoping Jane, when she went outside, would be put off by the heat and might, after all, turn up to join him at lunch. When she did not come his thoughts wandered inevitably back to his original suspicion.

It was mighty odd that she should arrive just a few days before the Rajah was due to set out for the Bhunda cave.

The sun was burning hot. Jane pulled the denim hat from her bag and jammed it on her head. Her shining hair bounced lightly on her shoulders. Her sunglasses were new, bought specially for the trip, enormous, blue rimmed to match her eyes and they killed the glare stone dead. Slim-hipped in her jeans, she swung off long-leggedly down the steep drive that curved between soft green eucalyptus and acacia trees. From the road below came the clip-clop of a donkey's hoofs and two buffaloes wandered past pursued by a ragged urchin brandishing a stick. Down here she was less aware of the sun's burning rays than of the heat rising stiflingly from the broken tarmac, and the dust enveloping her, bringing with it the inescapable scents of animal dung, frying food from the wayside stalls, charcoal smoke, spices, old smells of an old town without sanitation.

She stepped into the road in order to avoid two pi-dogs settling their differences in the wayside dust. Some women head-loading baskets of animal fodder looked at her curiously and she thought, Oh God! I see what Clive means. How lucky I am to be me! The women's bodies were strained forward against the weight. One could develop a burning conscience in twenty-four hours, here. She hurried through the disorderly traffic, stepping aside to avoid a flock of goats, a meandering buffalo. A turbanned taxi driver, temporarily held up, leaned out of his window and spat with precision, just missing the goat boy's foot and Jane formed a wry mental note to keep alert.

She made her way along beside the baked earth of the parade ground and across the ramshackle bridge, then up a slope to a triangular stretch of dry grass over and around which lay the hubbub of the market. The heat had slowed her up. She flicked her hot hair away from her neck and wiped a tissue across her brow. She dawdled through the market looking at the thin silver jewellery with pale, inset stones; at the little tailors sitting cross-legged on the ground behind their hand machines; she smiled at the ragged children jamming tiny work rooms. Some men in turbans and grubby dhotis sitting placidly smoking hookahs, squatting on the ground watching her idly, suddenly came alive, putting their heads together, whispering.

One of them jumped up, threw her a suspicious glance and scuttled across to a stall exhibiting some startling posters of Indian gods. A tall young Sikh in a red turban spoke to him, they both shot a quick glance at Jane, then the old man crept away and the Sikh came forward to meet her. He walked arrogantly, swinging his hips, his eyes unfriendly.

'You wish to buy picture? God Kali?' He indicated a highly coloured poster showing the multi-armed monster woman, fierce consort of Shiva.

'No, thank you.'

'This?' He held up another poster depicting Durga, dangerous and beautiful on her tiger.

'I really don't want to buy anything,' Jane said apologetically, wondering at his aggressive manner. 'Perhaps you could tell me where to find this house.' She pulled Gopal's address out of her pocket.

The Sikh glanced down at the paper. 'House is half-way to top of hill. Turn left,' he snapped, and moved away.

'How will I know the house?' she called after him. 'There's no name or number.'

'Big house. Two veranda and carved wood door. Babul tree in garden.'

'Babul?'

'Like umbrella. You will see.' He disappeared like a wraith through a slit in the sacking that formed the walls of the stall. Faintly unnerved by the incident, she spun round. The old man regarded her malevolently from his cross-legged position on the ground. She moved swiftly away. Were the

English no longer welcome here? Surely, if that were so, Clive would have warned her.

Beyond the tightly packed perimeter of the town the houses on the hill spread out a little and grew larger. Between them grass grew rampant, short where animals had been kept, long where they had not. There was an occasional fig tree and here and there a tethered goat chewing fast in that alert, sharp-eyed way goats have. The earth road was pitted with dry rivulets and rough with stones. Even wearing flat-heeled sandals, Jane stumbled. She turned left as instructed. Several hundred yards further on where the houses were square, double veranda-ed and roofed with grey stone tiles, she could see the umbrella-shaped tree. A crow landed too close, wings creaking, and Jane jumped half out of her skin. It cocked its head as though scrutinizing her and cawed harshly. G-rah-h. G-er-r. She flapped her hands at it. 'Go away, you unfriendly thing.' Three others came out of the sky, landed in a little circle with the original bird who had ignored Jane's protest and they hopped together, scary black ogres staring inquisitively. 'Go away, you silly asses.' Crows at home were nothing like their size and not self-consciously fierce, not hostile like these. And they never came so near.

The Behera house stood back a little way up a rough dirt path that ran through a wild garden. Mattresses and bed linen were spread in squalid disarray over the upper veranda rails, and below a middle-aged man slept on a kitchen chair, his long, bony sandalled feet thrust out before him, head sunk into his chest. It was a welcome picture of warm domesticity after her unpleasant experience in the market and Jane went through the gateway with a spring in her step. The crows escorting her cawed raucously. G-rah-h. G-er-r. Her footfalls crunched faintly on the weed-strewn path and the man's eyes opened.

'Mr Behera?'

At that moment an aggressively big bosomed woman in a

24

white sari with a great deal of black hair piled on top of her head came like a hurricane through the front doorway, crossed the veranda and descended the steps at a run, furious black eyes snapping within sockets that were wrinkled like dark crêpe. Jane took an instinctive step backwards, confusedly wondering if she had come to the right house. The woman raised one arm exposing a fleshy midriff where the sari separated into skirt and blouse and pointed imperiously down the road. 'Go away,' she shouted insultingly.

Oh lord! Jane smiled, though her knees were suddenly weak with fright. 'Mrs Behera?'

The woman made a sound half-way between a moan and a threat.

'Ay-ee-ee!' Even at several yards' distance, Jane felt the physical sensation of a push. Behind her one of the crazy crows squawked. G-rr. G-rr.

Battling with an hysterical desire to laugh and an equally strong temptation to run, Jane said, 'I am sorry to bother you. I'm looking for Gopal.'

The Indian woman's anger exploded. 'This is my home,' she shrieked in startlingly faultless English. 'You have no right to come here.'

Help! This was ludicrous. Impossible. Jane retreated another step. The man on the veranda was rocking his head in his hands. Holding the vanishing smile firmly on her face, Jane said entreatingly, 'I want to see Gopal. I want to know—'

'How dare you come to see Gopal!' the woman screeched, half out of her mind. 'You will not see him. He does not wish to see you. He is married and you will please stay away. Go back to your own country.' She advanced upon Jane, a mountain of aggressive flesh in a filmy white sari. 'You do not belong here,' she declared, waving those fat brown arms.

Helen! Of course they thought she was Helen. Damn that too clear family resemblance! Controlling her physical fear

25

of the woman Jane shouted, 'I only want to ask Gopal about my brother.'

'Go. Go!'

The situation was no longer funny. Jane backed a few more paces and shouted at the top of her voice, 'Mrs Behera!' bringing the encounter to the level of a street brawl.

Already two dark heads had appeared in a gap in the overgrown hedge and in the road outside an old man wearing an untidy white turban paused to stare. Suddenly there were running footsteps on the wooden boards of the upstairs veranda. 'Gopal!' she cried in an explosion of relief. By his side and deferentially a fraction behind him, stood a shy young Indian girl.

Gopal's emergence brought Behera Senior out of his chair with the speed of a man half his age and Jane realized he was coming right at her. Turning to run in very real fear, she shouted, 'I want to talk to you. I'm at Savakar's.'

'Wait! I'll come down.'

His father stopped, swung round. The mother seemed suddenly transfixed. Then Gopal emerged from the door and everything came to life again. His father burst into a torrent of abusive Hindi. Gopal answered calmly but when the old man shouted back he, too, lost control and suddenly the two of them were engaged in a violent quarrel. Jane hurried through the gateway and out into the road. At least Gopal knew she was here and could follow. Everyone stayed at Savakar's. She wiped a hand across her brow. Whew-w! Then Gopal broke away. As he hurried up the path his big, black Indian eyes shed their anger and softened with pleasure. Jane saw with horror what was going to happen and tried to side step, but the Indian boy took her hand in his and kissed her affectionately on the cheek.

'Jane, how lovely it is to see you. I did not know you were coming. Why did you not write?' Without waiting for a reply, he indicated his furious parents with an apologetic gesture. 'I am of course very sorry for this. My mother is kind and gentle but she does not find it easy to accept English girls.'

'She must think I'm Helen.'

He said unhappily, 'I will talk to her.'

Jane was still backing away. 'Is Savakar's really the only hotel in the town, Gopal?'

'The only one suitable for you.'

'But I want to know, is there another? You see, I think Ashley is here. Is there anywhere else he could possibly be staying?'

'Ashley in Kodapur?' Gopal's huge eyes widened further in astonishment. 'Oh no. Ashley is not here, Jane, I would have known.'

Mr Behera shouted abusively in Hindi. Gopal turned with a placating reply. Jane moved further away. She did not want to look back at the angry faces, nor at that young girl on the veranda. Gopal turned, saw she had walked on and hurried after her. 'Why would Ashley come here?' he asked. Suddenly he was defensive, as though sensing the disapproving Bellamys were about to surround him.

Jane said evenly, though her heart was pumping furiously with shock and anger, 'That's your wife on the upstairs veranda, isn't it?'

'Yes. That's Puniya, Jane.' He looked at her with big, uncertain eyes.

She could see the Indian girl still, kohl-eyed, mouth drooping. She was too young to be hurt like this. Jane said tartly, 'You're living with Puniya. Don't think I'm interfering, Gopal. As I said, I came to see if you could throw any light on Ashley's whereabouts. But it's only fair to end Helen's suspense if – I mean – perhaps it's time for her to face up to facts.'

Gopal's soft eyes were heavy with hurt. 'Facts? You mean, I would not go back? Jane! I couldn't treat Helen like that.'

She had a feeling of having come up against a wall of

resilient, but none the less impenetrable, cotton wool. 'I had better go,' she said bleakly. Puniya was Helen's business, not hers. The elder Indians were following, step-by-step, their eyes baleful. They, too, had reached the road.

'I will come to the hotel.'

'All right.' She flipped the hat back on to her head. The sun was a furnace. The girl on the upper veranda was crying. 'Please go back,' she said. She looked past Gopal to his father. At that moment, whether deliberately or from custom she could not tell, Mr Behera spat.

'I am sorry,' said Gopal miserably. 'It does not mean anything to an Indian. It is rude of my father, of course, and he will apologize, but it does not mean anything.'

Jane swung round abruptly and strode off down the road. As Gopal fell behind fear overtook her. A cumulative panic that came from the sinister old man in the market, the hostile Sikh who had given her directions, and a ludicrous memory of Ghandi saying if all the Indians spat at the same moment there would be a lake big enough to drown thirty thousand Englishmen. She tried to laugh but fear caught at her throat. She had to find her brother and get out. There was something very wrong here.

Chapter Three

All through lunch Clive mulled over Jane's arrival and the more he thought about it the more sinister the possibilities became. The timing was too pat. He rose from the table, pulled his hat out of his pocket and went, still obsessed with the problem, to collect his gear from the Sikh rogue, Rudrapal Singh. A slippery customer, but Clive had to trust him because he was the only gunsmith in the town and he did have his ear to the ground. Clive wasn't naïve. He knew there was nothing magnanimous about a spy. It was a simple arithmetical fact that working for opposing factions brought in twice as much money as working for one side.

He entered the rough little lane that turned off the almost equally rough street. The smells were more flagrant than usual today because the sun was still high. He hurried past the place where the gutter full of rank slops and ancient garbage crossed the lane, holding his breath, averting his head. There was a tiny shrine at the side of the road. Through its arched doorway he saw that the god with the strange dead face had a fresh wreath of marigolds garlanding its neck. There was no time to clean up the rubbish and filth, but there was always time to find flowers and make wreaths for the gods. He gave a sharp little sigh that was exasperation overlaid with despair and amusement in almost equal parts for the people he had come to love and to know as their own worst enemies.

He walked carefully, avoiding treacherous stones and the dried up water channel that meandered downhill as though out of control. Turning left by the old cloth shop he went on past the ramshackle, tin-roofed shacks and stalls selling betel paste, sweetmeats and small cakes. Filthy children stared at him, then gathering confidence advanced towards him, holding out their hands for money. He gave them a few annas as he always did and as always immediately regretted it for another dozen of them leaped in from nowhere, swarming like flies. He brushed them away, pityingly, but also roughly because this was India and you could not let it swamp you.

Outside the gunsmiths a man in a loincloth, wizened and old and squat, sat huddled against the mud wall smoking a hookah. He watched Clive through bleary, heavily lidded eyes. Rudrapal Singh was at the back of the shop deeply engrossed in low voiced conversation with an Indian in a pink turban. He looked up alertly, his fierce bearded face relaxing into a smile and said in a voice that was patently a warning to his visitor, 'Ah! Here is the doctor.' The other man turned round. Clive knew him and his presence brought a sharp reaction. The fellow had been to the clinic for treatment for a knife wound that had festered. His name was Kumar Singh and – Christ! – he was brother-in-law to Gopal Behera! Clive's nerves tightened. Jane, daughter of the one-time Louise Carlyon, had gone to see Behera. She had said – oh so bloody innocently, he thought with a flash of anger – that the Brahmin boy was in love with her cousin and Clive's mind had automatically swung to the immigration trick because it seemed so obvious. And was, of course, so common. Behera was known to want to settle in England. The visitor nodded his beautiful pink turban gravely, slid off the counter and went quietly out of the shop.

Rudrapal Singh beamed. 'My cousin.'

Cousins! With every Sikh in the country called Singh it had not occurred to Clive to connect these two. He nodded grimly. 'I have everything ready,' the gunsmith told him. 'You want to take now?' He tossed the packed tent on to the counter. 'Arrive from Delhi yesterday.'

'Yes. I'll take them. You managed to get the cartridges all right?'

Singh produced a small box from under the counter, fingering it lovingly. 'All okay, Doctor.' He smoothed the black beard that was brushed upwards and tucked into his blue turban along with his hair. 'Is said Bellamy girl is here,' he remarked conversationally.

Clive had been looking at the gun. His head came up sharply. 'What's that to you?'

Singh looked pained. 'You pay me for information. Is information.'

'She's staying at Savakar's. If you really want to earn some good money, find out why she's staying there where I can trip over her every time I move.'

'To see Gopal Behera?' The Sikh put his tongue in his cheek, a sinister old rogue trying to look droll.

'I'd like a reason that's less obvious,' he said.

'Oh, is very obvious, Doctor. She go to house today. One hour ago. Kanshi Behera moved Gopal's wife in. Is time to consummate marriage, you see. But Gopal have this English girl. He want to go England.'

Clive frowned. 'How do you know all this?'

'Is cousin. Sikh girl, Puniya, my cousin. Sister of young Kumar you see here. He tell me.'

'She's not the girl,' Clive asserted positively. 'Jane Bellamy, who is here, is not Gopal's girl.' He was certain of that. Absolutely convinced.

'Ay-ee!' The gunsmith rolled his strange blue eyes towards the ceiling. 'Is Bellamy, Doctor. My cousin tell me girl is Bellamy.'

'Yes, that's her name. Gopal's girl is her cousin.'

'Cousin, eh?' Rudrapal Singh sneered good naturedly.

'You mean, this girl is the one Gopal Behera is involved with?'

'Of course.'

'You're wrong.' Clive dug in his pocket for some rupees. What was he getting so steamed up about? Only a little while ago he was suspecting Jane of being interested in the

Bhunda jewels, and commonsense told him he had better not lose sight of that suspicion. Just because she was pretty, it did not mean she was innocent. 'If you get any more information, let me have it,' he said shortly. He picked up his purchases and went out, angry and disturbed. Opposite, the black walled *chaikhana* with its enormous brass pots of rice and curried vegetables was doing a good trade. He noticed the pink turbanned Sikh who was so unfortunately the relative of both the gunsmith and Gopal Behera was standing idly before it. Why was the man staring at him? Why were all the men loafing around looking at him? His flesh crawled. Then, determinedly, he shrugged the question away. When you had nothing to do you might as well stare at a white man as a pot of curry.

He went back up the filthy street carrying his pack with the tent inside and the gun tucked well out of sight. Perhaps he had better have a word with Jane about the Gopal Behera affair. It would be only civil to warn her the Brahmin boy's wife was a Sikh, with all its attendant implications. In a hundred years of rule the British had not been able to get through to the bone marrow of the true Punjabi Sikh. They had been killing each other before the British arrived and they went into the next round at Partition. A Sikh could, and still would, remove a human head with one slice of his *kirpan*, the long curved sword they all wore. And he ought to underline, too, what he had mentioned to her in the cemetery this morning. That an arranged Hindu child marriage was not to be lightly broken. Even if Gopal's private and mischievous intention was eventually to have his young Sikh wife join him in England, the girl's family might not want her to go.

Commonsense told Clive he ought to mind his own very serious and important business, bearing in mind his original suspicion about Louise Carlyon's daughter turning up here a week before the Bhunda. That sweet, innocent face came up disturbingly in his mind's eye. Keep your head out of the clouds, he told himself sternly. There is far too much at stake.

Deeply engrossed in her unhappy thoughts, Jane retraced her steps down the hill, warily skirted the market, crossed the bridge and made her way along the busy road beside the parade ground which would eventually lead to Savakar's hotel.

Oblivious to the rumbling and roaring of the traffic, she jumped as a horn blasted close by and swinging round saw one of those Tata diesel trucks lumbering up close behind her. She jumped back out of its path, flashing an indignant glance at the driver grinning at her behind his gaudy fat windscreen goddess. Suddenly a taxi emerged from a lane and the grin left his face. The car whisked in from the off-side, bringing the truck to a swerving halt with a screech of brakes, sending up a great cloud of dust. Through the burgeoning brown haze Jane saw, just in time, that one of the vehicles taking avoidance tactics had swung sharply in her direction. Instinctive self-preservation sent her into a flying leap, then a helter-skelter run up the bank.

And it was from there that she saw Ashley. Sitting in the back seat of the taxi like a young potentate, his dark hair falling softly across his tanned forehead, totally unperturbed by the disturbance, he was smiling quietly to himself.

'Ashley.' Jane leaped down the bank. 'Ashley! Ashley!' Her voice was drowned by an earsplitting blast from the lorry driver's horn. She fell back as the great vehicle lumbered forward and the traffic leaped away. 'Ashley,' she screamed, waving both arms in a maniacal effort to attract his attention. 'Ashley!' The taxi merged with all the other vehicles and disappeared.

Jane swung round in a frenzy of despair. 'Taxi! Taxi!' There were taxis everywhere. A ramshackle, clattering vehicle drew up beside her. She wrenched open the door and flung herself into the back seat. 'There's a taxi in front of that big truck,' she gasped as she recovered her balance. 'Please follow it. Please catch it.'

'Catch, please?' The turbanned driver, bright-eyed in the rear vision mirror, requested an explanation.

'I want to talk to the passenger. I want to talk to the man in a taxi out in front.'

'Okay. Okay.' She sat forward in the seat, straining to see. The driver was doing his dangerous, suicidal best. He swung out, narrowly missed another vehicle, sustained a shout of abuse with fastidious calm and pulled in once more to the side.

'We catch him.' He rolled the new word round his tongue. 'Catch. Catch,' he repeated with satisfaction.

'Please hurry.' She meant, desperately, forget the English lesson and concentrate on driving. She took some rupees from her bag, allowing herself to bounce closer to the door as the car jerked its way from one strategic position to another. They were bound to be caught in a traffic block as they approached the bridge.

She was ready to make a dive but, maddeningly, the traffic swept on, down the slope and across the river. Here, on the opposite side the road split at right angles.

'There it is!' Jane exclaimed excitedly. 'Quickly, slip in behind that taxi and blow your horn.' But they were too late. Their quarry had sped away along the river bank. There were too many horns. They blasted on every side and no one took any notice. Suddenly the driver jammed on the brakes. Even as she crashed agonizingly up against the back of the seat in front, Jane saw that Ashley's taxi, she was certain it was Ashley's taxi, had swung left. They lurched to a precipitous halt. The driver jumped out. Someone was lying in the road. A crowd had already begun to gather.

On shaking legs and feeling miserably guilty, Jane climbed out of the car, automatically rubbing a painful shoulder. It was an old woman lying in the road. Someone helped her to her feet. 'Is she all right?' Jane asked anxiously.

The driver nodded, dug into his pocket and producing some rupees pushed them into the woman's hand. Someone started to protest. 'Is all right.' The Sikh gave his victim a cursory glance, adjusted his elegant turban and opened the door with a flourish, signalling to Jane to re-enter. 'We lost your friend, is it not?'

The woman, surrounded by a concerned little crowd, was tottering away. No one, after the initial shock, seemed to bear the driver any ill-will. Jane climbed unsteadily back in. 'The taxi we were following turned left, just ahead,' she told him.

Her driver shook his handsome dark head. 'No road. Only drive to Rajah's old palace.'

'Are you sure?'

'Sure. Sure. Rajah's old palace.'

'You mean, the palace he doesn't live in any more?'

'Not. New palace now. Rajah in new, small palace.'

And yet, she could have sworn Ashley's taxi had turned up that drive. 'Does anyone live there?' she asked.

'No one live. New palace, I say.'

'Is it open to the public?'

He shook his head. 'No understanding.'

She made a snap decision. 'Turn in at the drive.'

'You go palace? In taxi now?' The Indian was astonished.

'Yes.' Of course she could be wrong. The accident had shattered her concentration, but she still had a very certain feeling the taxi bearing Ashley had turned left. If the place was deserted she had lost nothing.

'Mm.' The driver flung her another startled look. 'Okay. Okay. I go.' The engine cackled to frail and noisy life. The gears were engaged, and with a succession of crazy leaps they shot forward as though out of control.

Chapter Four

The gates at the head of the drive leading to the palace had indeed, at one time, been grand. Now they stood open, dusty and rusted, on a forest of overgrown shrubs and palms. All the way up the rather steep and twisted drive it was the same. Shrubbery rose in a dark green, suffocating mass, sometimes to twenty feet on either side. It encroached on the rutted asphalt and spewed little trailers out into the air. And there, as they swung round the last corner, was the building. But there was no taxi in sight. The driver pulled up, switched off the engine and turned inquiringly to Jane. She had rolled down the window and was frowning at the palace façade. Half a dozen white marble pillars formed a porch in the grandest style, though cracked badly, and the shallow flight of chipped steps was cracked, too. There were enormous double doors in some dark wood, ornately carved, with leopard head knockers. On either side of the porch were tall rounded windows, curtainless, one of them indecorously stained with a white trail of birds' droppings.

'Maybe mistake,' suggested the driver. 'You go back now?'

'No. I'm going to have a look round.' The place seemed deserted. She paid the man, waited until he had gone, then went hesitantly and with growing curiosity up the steps. Standing on tiptoe, supporting herself by one of the pillars, she peered into the room on the left of the door. A vast and ornate chandelier hung from the ceiling and she glimpsed the corner of a gold-framed portrait. The place was as silent as a tomb. Then suddenly the door swung open and she took a quick and guilty step backwards. A small, grave-faced Indian stood before her. He wore a forage cap with khaki coloured jacket and trousers. His white shirt tails flapped laconically outside of them. His long, bony feet were bare.

'Memsahib?'

She pulled herself together and asked in a startled voice, 'Is Mr Bellamy here?'

'Mr Bellamy, Memsahib?' The servant looked at her with a buoyant glimmer of a smile and then, as though a lifetime of training had come to his aid, the look fell away.

'I am Jane Bellamy. I'm looking for my brother. Is he here?'

The Indian turned, gesturing to her to follow. She stepped into a large marble hall with a domed ceiling from which the paint hung in flakes. There was no furniture. A wide staircase with heavy banisters curved its way to the upper floor. The servant went through double doors into the room she had seen from the porch. Jane followed, uncertainly. 'Did you understand me?' she asked. He nodded, muttered something incomprehensible then left, closing the doors after him. Jane had a breathless feeling of having slipped into a void from which there was no escape.

It was a vast, L-shaped room that would easily have contained a party for two hundred people. At the extremities there was a domed ceiling, similar to that in the hall. Those enormous rounded windows she had viewed from the front were repeated at the side, stark and unfriendly without the softening influence of curtains, and not particularly clean. There were acres of glowing peacock blue carpet woven to the curious bulbous-ended L of the room's shape, and edged startlingly with a border of apricot, pink and gold flowers. It glowed against the marble whiteness of walls and ceiling. In the main part of the room, as though lined up for some splendid and noble committee meeting, a dozen gilt and tapestry chairs stood elegantly in an egg-shaped ring. A mini-throne with leopard head armrests broke the ring where it stood back a little, importantly. Slumped incongruously near the inner wall lay an ancient sofa, its springs gone, its loose cover sagging. The only other piece of furniture was a low coffee table that would have looked more at home in a fourth rate boarding house.

What on earth was Ashley doing here? But even as she asked herself the question, a possible explanation was flowing up through her mind, unacceptably. Their mother, it was said, had an *affaire* with a Rajah. Was Ashley audacious enough, irresponsible and impertinent enough, to stir up that old scandal after thirty years? She shrugged away contagious guilt. If Ashley was here, then it was his muckraking, not hers. And she must find him. She sat down cautiously in one of the gilt chairs, then feeling nervous stood up again. There were half a dozen flamboyant portraits on the walls, one of which dominated the room. It must have been fully twelve feet tall, a glowing and crude vision of a young Indian prince in dress regalia. Sail-shaped hat topped by an egret plume, buttoned coat, tight trousers and a jewelled sabre. Behind him, a forest and within that a badly painted tiger, its belly low, its cat's eyes gleaming with the over-zealous application of titanium white. There was another of a youngish and rather beautiful woman wearing a ruby and emerald necklace. Of course the stones that made it up were genuine, they had to be, but strung together like that with glittering, finely wrought gold, it was so gaudy it was almost bizarre; plethoric with over-charged brilliance; vulgar, magnificent and larger than life. She could scarcely take her eyes off it. It must be worth a king's ransom.

The remainder of the gallery appeared to consist of portraits of the same boy at different stages of his life. As a child he was undeniably beautiful, his eyes black and lustrous, his skin smooth and brown. As a young man he was handsome if perhaps a trifle fat, but in maturity he was magnificent. Sensual sculptured lips, blazing eyes, heroic bearing and a stiffly waxed, arrogantly upturned moustache.

She jumped violently as the door opened and a smallish dark man entered. Before she could take a step he was standing before her, his hands outstretched for hers. She had never seen a man move like that before, fast and stealthily, so that one was not aware of his strides, only of his being there, and of being mesmerized by his eyes. He was the subject of the portraits, that was boundlessly clear, except that now he was thinner and his hair was heavily streaked with white. The moustache he had worn as a young man had given way to a small goatee beard with side whiskers and the lips had lost some of their sensuality, but the portrait painter had not lied. Incongruously it seemed to Jane, and in spite of the temperature, he wore a tweed suit with collar and tie.

'Louise's daughter! "Jane Bellamy" can only be Louise's daughter!'

Fascinated, Jane stammered. 'Y-es. Er, y-es.'

'She wrote me she was going to marry a man called Bellamy. And the resemblance is there.' Holding her hand, he pushed her away a little, gazing delightedly into her face. 'How very kind of you to come and see me all these years later! My servant who opened the door knew your mother. And he recognized you. Imagine that! He remembered what Louise looked like over thirty years! He came straight to me saying, "The Memsahib's daughter has come. Jane Bellamy." ' His tongue lingered on the words, his eyes roved over her face, examining it closely, nostalgically. 'How is Louise?' His accent was Oxbridge, his English perfect.

Weak at the knees, Jane managed an uncertain smile. 'My mother died six months ago.'

The Rajah was silent, secret; still with those mesmeric eyes on her face, he was away in a world of his own. Even with her hand in his, Jane had a strange and uncomfortable feeling of having been not only discarded, but forgotten. Her mind swung back to Ashley. He was not here, she realized with a sick and sinking feeling. She was the audacious one, impertinently digging into Louise's past.

'Have you met my brother?' she asked. 'He's here, in

Kodapur.' After that ardent welcome she could not say she had called accidentally.

'You have a brother, too? You must bring him to see me,' the Rajah said graciously but she saw he could do without Ashley. There would be no reliving the past with her brother as with a girl who reminded him of Louise. He indicated that she sit in the chair to the right of his throne-like armchair. He seated himself. The past was still there, consuming him. A servant came through the door carrying a tray. He brought the table over and set out the cups and saucers.

'I'm glad you're pleased to see me. I was a little uncertain about coming,' Jane said, unable any longer to contain the silence that was crammed with her own embarrassment and the mystery of Ashley's disappearance. Now that Louise's affaire with the Rajah had leapt from myth to reality, now that she was actually face-to-face with him, she found herself faintly shocked. Her mother had been auburn haired, delicate. There was something gross, sexually raw about this man. Something at once hypnotic and faintly repugnant. He smoothed her hand. Then the servant went, padding silently across the thick silk of the carpet in his bare feet.

'Would you like me to pour?' she asked.

'Please do.' He sat back, watching her, gratifying himself with her English beauty. With the memory of Louise. 'And then we will talk. You like muffins?'

'Is that what they are?' It was a relief to laugh and let the tension slip a little. 'I've never tasted them. I've never even seen one.' Her grandmother talked about having muffins in the nursery. Jane picked up the teapot. It was made of heavy brown china and, astonishingly, there were chips round the spout.

The Rajah said, 'I'm only camping here. I always come back when my wife goes to visit her people. You must allow us to entertain you in our new palace when the Rani returns. There, you will be graciously received with silver and good china.' Jane held a cup out to him, noting with a mixture of surprise, amusement and distaste that there was a tannin-streaked crack down one side.

'Why do you come back here?' she asked him.

'Why?' he repeated. 'I suppose because this is where I was born and where I expected to live out my life. I can't come to terms with what has happened.' He paused a moment, then added softly, 'I try to keep the palace warm, as it were. These chairs—' He paused, his hands caressing the leopard head arms, 'would not fit into my new palace, so they had to stay. The world is a duller place without us princes,' he said.

'I'm sure it is,' she agreed.

'When we were at our grandest we rode in a gilt howdah on an elephant. Its saddle cloth was cloth of gold. Your mother rode in my howdah,' he said, his black eyes wistful. 'Did she tell you about it?'

Not wanting to say Louise never spoke of him, that he had been merely a rumour in the Bellamy family, Jane shook her head.

'We had elephant fights and tiger shoots. At one time I had enough tiger skins to carpet this room.' When she did not answer he looked at her sharply. 'You're about to tell me you don't approve of killing wild life,' he stated aggressively.

The very normality of his remark put Jane at a kind of ease. 'Why should you want to kill an animal as beautiful as a tiger?' she asked.

'Because it is a difficult and dangerous feat. Why do Englishmen climb Mount Everest? To shoot wild animals is the same sort of challenge. One could send servants out to kill them if it was merely for the skin.' He added, looking at her shrewdly, 'I can see you're a girl of spirit, Jane. You would have enjoyed a tiger-shoot. Such a spectacular it was! To ride out on an elephant to shoot a tiger! Ah!' The Rajah of Kodapur sank back into the past, dreaming. A past, Jane thought cryptically and with a faint touch of distress, where it seemed his luxuries really had included making love to the

41

British Resident's wife. She felt desperately uncomfortable. The dead, she thought, were entitled to take their secrets with them to the grave. Where had Ashley gone? 'Would you like another cup of tea?' she asked to break the silence that was prickling at her nerves.

'No, thank you. Pour one for yourself, my dear. This is a thirsty country, outside of the monsoon.' Those very dark eyes were thoughtful once more, considering her. 'It's strange that you should have come now when I'm about to set out to attend a Bhunda ceremony. I last saw your mother at this time of year. We attended the Bhunda together.' His eyes lifted to the portrait of the Indian woman in the magnificent necklace and Jane thought with renewed awe as she followed his look: rubies like pigeon's eggs. It was something she had heard somewhere and half forgotten. 'We returned to Kodapur the day the Pakistan/India divisions were announced,' the Rajah said. 'You know what happened then.'

'India was split up between the Moslems and the Hindus. Would it be true to say they made the Moslems into Pakistanis?'

He smiled at her, tolerant of her youth, accepting, because she was who she was, that the shattering of his life should be a confusion in her English mind. 'Yes,' he said, 'they drew a line right through my State. Right through the centre. I believe your mother's husband had a hand in that,' he added bitterly. 'You never knew him, so I can say it to you without offending.'

'But how could he?' she burst out. 'A man called Sir Cyril Radcliffe drew the partition lines. A man of enormous integrity.'

'Carlyon was a friend of Sir Cyril,' the Rajah replied, as though that proved his guilt and sealed his misconduct for all time. 'Anyway, they're both dead.' He reached convulsively for her hand and held it tightly between his own. She waited for the emotional shock her coming had brought to subside. She did not want to talk about Partition. She

42

knew the Indians blamed the British for what happened. She did not want to think, either, about the British Administrator who had been torn to pieces in the ensuing riots. Ashley's father, who had been a mere shadow, had suddenly, unacceptably become a tortured reality. 'You attended this Bhunda with my mother?'

The Rajah's eyes were reflective, now. 'I'll tell you a little bit about it.' He leaned forward, looking into her eyes. He had let go of her hands but one of his lay embarrassingly on her knee. 'Did you know I wanted your mother to stay with me?'

Oh God! Where was Ashley? This must be what Louise had told her brother on her death bed! Jane felt cold inside. Was it the Rajah's fault that Ashley's father lay in that British cemetery over the river? Ashley had driven in at the palace entrance, then disappeared. She was certain of it. More certain, now. 'Why did Louise not stay?' she ventured.

'There are always many reasons why, when a woman makes a monumental decision. In our case they were incorporated in the wishes of Louise's father, your grandmother, and their friends. And the Begum, my mother.' His face darkened. 'Oh, yes, she had to do with it,' he said, and again he seemed to have jumped back in time in that disconcerting way, reliving something too private for telling. 'But I like to think the real reason was the timing of Partition. Romance is for the good times, Jane,' said the Rajah. 'When people are being slaughtered and in danger of being slaughtered, no one believes in love. It can be buried with impunity, or at the very least, shelved until life becomes normal again.' He sighed. 'It was a very long time after Partition before life became normal again for me. Not until the Moslems in Western Kodapur had driven out or killed their Hindu neighbours and burned and pillaged their homes. And not until the Hindus in Eastern Kodapur had done the same to their Moslems.' Then he underlined what she had heard from Louise. 'The Punjabi Sikhs – we are very close to the Punjab here – are a quarrelsome lot. They live with a hand on their kirpans.'

'Kirpan?'

'It's a very sharp, curved sword they all wear.' His fingers had moved from her knee to her wrist. 'Why are you trembling?' he asked concernedly. 'I didn't mean to upset you.'

When she did not answer he added, 'I wasn't going to say any more. Only that, by the time the country had simmered down, Louise was home in England.' And then, with sweet, sad words almost bizarre in their unexpectedness, 'If one is to capture an English lady, one must do it while the magic of India is on her.'

In spite of herself, Jane found she was looking at him with compassion. 'You mean, they never come back?'

'Oh yes, they have been known to come back,' he replied, 'but you must understand they come fresh from the green lawns and cool air of England. The first sight of the dream is filthy docks – I'm talking of the past you understand – or even when they fly there's a railway station they must go to which is smelly and dirty and crowded. Some of the beggars, as you will already know, are not a pretty sight. And then, a long hot train journey. Twenty-four hours or more to think. All that time to compare the roasting, dusty plains and filth they're passing through with the clean green they left behind.'

'You mean, they depart on cloud nine and return with a clear head?'

'Yes,' he agreed settling back in his great chair and staring at the floor, 'as you say so succinctly, Jane, they come in re-injected with good British commonsense. There was none of that in my relationship with Louise. A real romance is not based on commonsense. Our love affair would have lived if she had stayed.'

Jane shifted uneasily. 'You were going to tell me about the Bhunda.'

'Oh yes.' His eyes had returned, as though compulsively,

to the portrait of the woman wearing the necklace. 'It's a rare sort of celebration. It's held in the little villages of the Himalayan foothills once every twelve years if the village can afford it. Basically, it's a sacrificial ritual with processions and feasting.'

'Tell me all about it. I'm really very interested. Who goes?' He smiled at her, not knowing she meant: Don't talk about Louise. She had no right to know. But more than that, she did not want to know. The implications were frightening.

'Invitations bearing the golden temple seal are sent out in Sanskrit to the gods and to people connected with the temple,' the Rajah said. 'There can be thousands of visitors, and the host village supports them.'

To the gods! The ready laughter on Jane's lips died as he continued gravely and she turned away to hide the colour in her face. It was confusing, this so thin veneer of Englishness in him.

'There are also musicians and members of royal houses and their retainers to look after.'

'Thousands of people, in one village?' she asked incredulously. 'Where do they all sleep?'

'Of course you understand they don't expect a room and bath. You've seen how Indians sleep, on the hard ground. Or perhaps in open-fronted shelters erected for the purpose. At Tarand the great god Situ-Rama, who has been locked away since the last ceremony, is brought on show with three pieces of jewellery that are in his cave with him.'

'Jewellery?'

The Rajah's eyes went back to the portrait, back to the ruby and diamond necklace. 'People make sacrifices,' he said.

Jane's startled eyes had followed his. 'You mean, they would give a very valuable – you mean – you *didn't*—'

He smiled at her. 'If one wants a favour of the god, one must pay for it. Yes, Louise and I carried that necklace my

45

mother is wearing in the portrait to the Bhunda and I gave it to the god.' She could not believe it. He must be mad! But he did not look mad. He looked quite serious and perfectly sane. 'It was a sacrifice.'

'Does that mean you would never get it back?'

'Never,' he stated authoritatively. 'Never, never will that necklace come out of the cave, unless of course one of the goldsmiths chances to pick it up and bring it out with the god to be put on show for the duration of the ceremony. Only for four days. Then it would go back again afterwards.'

'Does your mother not mind? I mean, I presume it was hers.'

He shook his head. 'It was a part of my estate. Of course she wore it. A man does not wear such things. But it was never hers.' He said the words matter-of-factly with centuries of male dominance in the weight of them. And then he added, sadly, 'Twelve years ago, when the cave was opened for the last Bhunda ceremony I regret to say my mother did try to bribe the goldsmiths to bring the necklace out. But no Hindu would do such a thing. Woe betide a Hindu who attempts to remove a present given to the god.'

'Why did you sacrifice it?' Jane asked with awe. Such an insane gesture! Such waste!

'It is usual. I had asked a favour of Situ-Rama.' There was a slyness now in the Rajah's smile. 'Louise used to wish on a star. An English habit?'

'Perhaps.'

'She would never tell me her wishes. She said they would not come true if she divulged them. So—' and again came that sly smile, 'I must not tell you the reason for sacrificing the necklace.'

Had he wished for Louise to stay? No, because she had not stayed, and now she was dead. 'Did he grant your favour?' she asked tentatively.

'Yes.'

'And my mother knew you gave the necklace?' Jane

asked, thinking of Clive, feeling outraged enough to want the Rajah to say, after all, Louise had not known.

'Yes.'

She couldn't believe it! An Englishwoman standing by while he made that barbaric, futile gesture. Burying underground, as though it was trash, a necklace that, liquidated, could produce enough money to put this old palace to rights! To build Clive's hospital. She shook the anger away. Her mind had begun to spin off in a different direction and it did not include the paltry satisfaction of criticism. 'Where is the god hidden?' she asked soberly.

'Behind seven doors guarded by seven serpents.'

Now she saw how Louise had been trapped. Such a preposterous fairy-tale, told as it was deadpan, would have sent her romantic mother off on a divine plane of ecstasy. 'Go on,' she said. She had to know all about it, now.

Chapter Five

'It all starts months beforehand,' the Rajah told her. 'The villagers must gather sacred grass to the sound of music. Then it is twisted into a cable a quarter of a mile long. At the time of the Bhunda ceremony it is brought out and strung across a ravine, fastened at the bottom end to a post near a temple and on the other side of the valley, higher up, to a tree or peg.'

'Like a clothes line? Why?'

'You will remember I said this is a sacrificial occasion. After the festivities and the religious ceremonies, the victim is given the rites of a dying Hindu and then is taken up to the opposite side of the valley and put on a wooden saddle on this rope. The saddle is let go and he rides swiftly across to the temple.' Jane saw a certain wistfulness in the Rajah's eyes and recoiled inwardly. This man was a savage!

'The sacrifice was outlawed by the authorities,' he said, 'in 1868 when the victim's saddle stuck and the excited crowds jerked the rope so hard to loosen it that the rope broke. At the last moment now,' he added regretfully, 'they have to change the man for a white goat. The goat is tied to the saddle. Mark you,' he smiled, 'they would still use a human if he volunteered and they thought they could get away with it.'

Jane brushed a hand across her forehead, brushing the idea of a human sacrifice from a mind that would not contain it. 'Does the goat ever survive?' she asked accusingly.

'Of course. It survived when Louise and I were there. Naturally, being English, she was concerned for the animal.' He added almost apologetically, 'A handwoven grass rope is bound to have some roughness.'

'You mean, the saddle stuck that time, too?' Louise could not bear even to see a pheasant shot, Jane remembered painfully.

'Your mother reacted very strangely,' the Rajah told her evading her direct question. His eyes had glazed over as though again he had flown back in time. 'There was a curious expression on her face. She put a hand to her middle and thinking she was going to be ill I tried to lead her away but she wouldn't go. She stood there looking terribly frightened and saying, "It seems to be happening to me." '

'What? What was happening to her?' Jane was sitting on the edge of her chair, nerves tingling.

He did not seem aware of the question. 'She asked me to hold her until the feeling went. Perhaps that's why she didn't come back,' the Rajah conjectured. 'Perhaps she thought she was having a premonition, and was afraid.'

'A premonition of what?' Jane, Louise's daughter, asked sharply, nervously. 'I mean, you couldn't put an Englishwoman on the rope! You've said you're not allowed to put an Indian on it. What do you mean?' His eyes were hooded. 'Well, anyway, it didn't happen,' Jane stated flatly. 'Louise didn't come back, and now she's dead.' She felt angry with the Rajah for upsetting her, and angry with herself for being upset. 'How did they get the goat down? Did the crowds break the rope again?'

'Feeling doesn't run so high among my people when an animal is involved,' he replied, startling her again. 'It was freed to complete its journey.'

'Upside down, I'd guess, and in a pretty anguished state, poor creature.'

'Why do you say that, my dear?'

'You said Louise reacted strangely. No Englishwoman would like to see an animal subjected to that sort of thing.'

'She insisted upon the goat being brought down quickly and carefully, and then she led it away.'

'Why? Why did she have to lead it away?'

49

'You must understand,' the Rajah explained, 'that India is still a primitive land. The British touched, as it were, only the tip of the iceberg.'

She shivered. 'You mean, the crowd could get out of hand? Louise might have been killed for saving the goat?'

Before he could answer the door behind them opened precipitously and Jane swung round, startled. The Rajah also turned in surprise. An Indian woman stood in the doorway. Involuntarily, Jane rose to her feet along with her host. She knew immediately the woman was the subject, perhaps even forty years earlier, of the portrait featuring the fabulous ruby and emerald necklace the Rajah had given so audaciously to the god. She stood there in her rich, red silk sari, her eyes widening as though she had expected to see someone else and was consequently lost for words.

The Rajah greeted her with respect rather than affection, his palms pressed together in the ritual gesture of *namaste*. '*Amma!* Welcome!' But now his personality seemed quenched, like a bonfire in a downpour. Jane stared at the Indian woman, too fascinated to realize she was being rude. With the deep-set, dark penetrating eyes, the high-cheekboned, powerful face, the way she held her head, the Begum seemed to fill this big, empty room even over and above that vast, chocolate box portrait of her son.

"*Amma*, may I present Miss Bellamy, Louise's daughter,' her host said. His eyes glinted with what looked suspiciously like a touch of mischief, but if he expected a reaction he was disappointed. Only the muscles of her jaw line tightened. Jane went forward and the Begum extended a heavily ringed brown hand.

'How do you do. You are here on holiday?'

'Yes.'

'I will not stay, my son,' she said, turning back to the Rajah. 'I am on my way to see my guru.' The Begum's English was good, but unlike her son, she spoke with an accent of which she had never tried to rid herself. She did not like the British. She used their language merely as a convenience, preferring to speak Urdu or Hindi. She resented her son's insistence that they speak English in his homes. She also resented his mocking, 'It was you who had me educated as an Englishman,' and his re-formed proverb, 'You do not take a horse to the water and then refuse to allow him to drink.' It had not been her decision to have her son educated at Harrow, but now that his father was dead she was not averse to circulation of the rumour that she had always been the one with her hands on the reins.

The Rajah's face had closed as his mother spoke. The tension between them was tight as a cable. Embarrassed by the silence neither the Begum nor her son seemed in a hurry to break, and by this woman's intense stare, Jane said uncomfortably, 'This is my first visit to India. I'm quite overwhelmed by it. I wish I had the opportunity to see this palace in its grand days.'

Without moving, the woman appeared to relax a little. 'Ah! When the State of Kodapur was ours. Y-es.' She scrutinized the heart-shaped, intelligent young face before her, searching in a paroxism of anxiety for Louise, trying to remember specifically what she had looked like and failing to produce anything more clear than a fine white skin, vibrancy that danced through the room, and an aura of delicate gold. This girl, as far as she remembered, was certainly superficially like the hated Louise who had so nearly destroyed her son's marriage; who had gloatingly carried off the necklace because she, the Begum, had stood by Carlyon, trying to break up the wicked affair.

'There were peacocks out there,' said the Rajah, waving an arm towards the uncurtained window. 'Of course, those trees have grown up since. If one were to clear them away one would find all the trappings of a beautiful garden. Statues. Ponds. Flights of steps. A pergola . . .'

The Begum was not listening. She had turned towards the portrait and her eyes glittered as they rested on the long-lost necklace that was about to come so miraculously into her hands again. At the same time her mind was scrabbling back through the recent past. This girl who did not seem to carry the essence of Louise seemed all the same very familiar. Wasn't she the girl Swamiji had befriended last year? The young woman who had accepted his hospitality and his teachings and then allowed herself to be carried off, to everyone's consternation, by that young Brahmin who was already married to the Singh girl? Had she actually been Louise's daughter? Louise's daughter, returning at the time of the Bhunda! Why had her son kept the girl's identity a secret last year when she was at the ashram? And now, the Begum thought feverishly, why was he producing her? The Swami never bothered with surnames. He probably never knew who the girl was. And if he had, it might not have meant anything to him. He was a comparative newcomer and Louise had left thirty years ago.

'. . . isn't that so, Mother?' The Rajah called her that now, wanting to displease her because he was angry about her association with the guru.

The Begum was suddenly aware that they were looking at her. She had not the slightest idea what had been said. She smiled at them as she would not have smiled had she known her son addressed her in the hated English style. 'I thought Mr Hills was with you.'

The Rajah's face fell, comically. 'I forgot! Rafiq told me Miss Bellamy was here and I came to greet her, leaving Mr Hills in my study. Oh my goodness! I forgot all about him!' He turned to Jane, explaining, 'I am taking an Englishman to the Bhunda with me. We were finalizing arrangements.'

The Begum said swiftly, 'Don't worry. I want a word with him. I will tell him you've been detained.'

'I'll go,' said Jane, but the Begum gestured to her to sit down. 'Please stay.'

'Send Mr Hills in,' the Rajah suggested, 'when you have finished talking to him.' He turned back to Jane. 'You've met

Barry Hills? He is at Savakar's.' She shook her head. 'Then I will introduce you.'

The Begum went down the hall and turned right into her son's study. It was empty. She clapped her hands in the arrogant, imperious way she still had as an inheritance from the old days and Rafiq, the little Hindu servant, appeared. 'Where has Mr Hills gone?'

'He has left.'

'When? How long ago?'

'When the girl came.'

The Begum stood there chewing her lip, her eyes speculative, faintly suspicious. To be fair, Hills had not known she wished to see him. And why should he wait indefinitely for the Rajah? She swept the tail end of her sari up over her head and glided back across the hall. It had taken her thirty years to get her own back on Louise. It was poetic justice that one of Louise's countrymen should be the instrument by which she was to regain possession of the necklace. But Louise's daughter! Her breast heaved with the enormity of the Englishwoman's devilishness. This daughter must have come last year to spy out the land. And now, she was back, dead on time, for the opening of the cave.

The Begum knew she must move now, and move fast. The car was waiting outside. 'The ashram,' she snapped as she ran down the steps. 'And hurry.' The car swept down the drive, shot into the mainstream of traffic narrowly missing a rumbling buffalo cart, then headed off, in a stream of reciprocal abuse, towards the barren cantonment that was the holy man's quarters.

The Rajah had made no attempt to see the Begum off. As she disappeared, closing the door firmly behind her, he said unhappily, 'My mother is involved with a guru.' He rubbed a hand across his forehead and then his face, as though in an ineffectual effort to wipe away the irritability. 'It's not that the disciples grow fond of these people. They become mesmerized by them. My mother has been out of reach since she has known this man. I believe him to be unscrupulous. I believe he uses her to his own ends. Without her knowing it, of course. It's strange, because she's such a strong person, and yet I believe she is under his domination.'

There was nothing to say to that. Gopal had thought the guru unscrupulous, and certainly it had sounded as though Jane's cousin Helen was under his domination when Gopal took her angrily away. But Jane did not want to talk about Helen and the problem of her being in love with the Brahmin boy. She said she must go. The light had long since failed and the big, uncurtained windows looked on to the early night. Very much to her surprise, the Rajah would not allow it. 'You are to meet my English friend, Barry Hills.' He glanced at his watch, then clapped his hands. A servant came in, silent in his bare feet. The Rajah spoke to him in Hindi, frowned, asking a question, then turned back to Jane.

'Mr Hills has gone,' he told her. 'But never mind, I was rude to leave him like that. Everything flew out of my head when you were announced. I will apologize to him tomorrow. Now, you and I will have a drink together.'

'It's very kind of you, but it's already dark. I really ought to go.'

'I will send you back to Savakar's in my jeep,' he replied kindly, making it impossible for her to depart without discourtesy. 'You will be there in good time for your meal.' His servants brought whisky in toothglasses on a kitchen tray, not asking her if she liked it or indeed wanted to drink at all. 'So you have a brother,' he said, his eyes caressing her face in that way that made Jane feel uncomfortable, knowing he was looking at her resemblance to Louise. 'Is he older than you, or younger?'

'He's my half-brother. His father is buried in Kodapur.' The Rajah's eyes were hooded and again that frightened suspicion swept through Jane, the feeling that the Rajah had something to do with the death of Ashley's father. 'Does he, too, favour your mother?'

'Ashley? No. He's dark.'

'Ashley? Louise called him Ashley?'

'Yes. You look surprised. It is an English name. Have you not heard it before?'

The Rajah drank his whisky at a gulp. 'It is not that I had not heard the name,' he explained, 'although I must confess I had not.' His eyes were glittering strangely. 'It is usual to call a male child after the father, especially—' he paused, carefully choosing the right words, it seemed, '—especially in the circumstances.'

'Perhaps Louise didn't like the name Jasper.' Perhaps she had not liked her husband, Jane wondered not for the first time. Her mother had seldom spoken of him, and never willingly.

The Rajah said, 'You will bring Ashley to visit me? Why do you hesitate? Do you think he might not want to come?'

'No. No, it's not that. It's simply that I haven't been able to find him.' She told her host then about Ashley's coming alone to India, omitting the strangeness of his precipitate departure after Louise's funeral. Of the post card sent from Kodapur. She said she had glimpsed him in the back of the taxi.

The Rajah shook his head. 'You were mistaken, my dear. He has not come to visit me. I would welcome him most warmly. The day after tomorrow I go to Tarand for the Bhunda ceremony. Perhaps you and Ashley would like to accompany me.'

'Really?' Her eyes lit up. 'I'd love it. And so would Ashley, I'm sure. If I can find him.'

He squeezed her hand. 'Then find him, my dear, and we will all go together. It will be a wonderful nostalgic experience for me. And you shall see India, the real India, as I showed it to Louise.' The servant left to collect the jeep, the Rajah apologizing as he led Jane to the front entrance. 'When Louise was here we had five Rolls Royces. And so, her daughter rides in a jeep!' He lifted his hands in a gesture of amused distaste.

55

'I like jeeps. And I've never been in a Rolls Royce. What you don't know you don't miss. What on earth did you do with five of them?' *And* an elephant with a howdah, she would have liked to add, if she had known him better.

The Rajah looked vague. Then there was a crunching of tyres on gravel and the jeep came round the corner. It pulled up in the little oasis of light beneath the pillared porch. They shook hands. Jane climbed into the jeep and with an ear-splitting crash of gears they set off down into the blackness of the drive. 'You will hold on tight,' said the Indian driver. 'The brakes will not be good.'

He spoke with such an absence of concern that Jane glanced at him sharply, nervously. One accident today was enough. They swept away at an alarming rate. As they spun round the first corner only narrowly missing the trees, a protruding, flexible branch brushed Jane's shoulder. She gripped the seat with both hands. The next corner was coming up too fast. She gave a little shriek of genuine alarm. This man was crazy! 'Stop. Please stop!' She was remembering the drive was a long one, running downhill all the way to the busy thoroughfare that lay high above the rocky river bed.

'Is all right,' replied the driver soothingly, swinging round on two wheels.

'Please stop,' Jane ordered him peremptorily. 'I want to get out and walk.'

'Is too dark to walk, Memsahib.'

She reached across him, swinging the steering wheel so that the vehicle spun sideways, made a half-hearted effort to climb the low bank, then bounced back, its tyres nudging at the soft earth. 'Tell the Rajah I'm very grateful for his kindness,' she said shakily as she climbed down, 'but I think he should have those brakes attended to.'

The driver protested. It was too dark. It was not safe for a memsahib to be walking here alone. Certainly it was pitch black except for the jeep's lights, two golden beams shafting into the trees. Jane could not see the driver's expression but she could tell by the way he sat scratching his head, making no effort to start the engine again, that she had placed him in a very awkward situation.

'I'll be perfectly all right,' she said briskly. She thanked him and set off. She was unprepared, though, when she had turned the next corner and left the lights behind, for the intense blackness of the night. It crept in from the trees, enfolding her, taking away her judgment, playing tricks with her feet so that she stumbled, directionless. She had expected to hear the roar of the engine in reverse, or to have its light flood round her as the driver shot past to turn on the road below. But there was nothing.

Her feet scuffed into soft leaf mould and at the same moment a spray of leaves brushed across her eyes. Stifling a scream she turned sharply and strode downhill, hands outstretched before her, her soft shoes making a spongy, crumbling sound on the asphalt. Once, she slipped where the gradient fell sharply, and nearly fell headlong. The blackness was frighteningly dense, the drive suddenly too steep. She stopped. There was a movement in the trees close at hand. The crack of a twig, then another. Jane froze. What kind of animals lurked in this Indian garden? A footstep. A man's step. The driver, genuinely concerned for her safety?

'Who's there?' she asked. Her voice emerged roughly, jolting through the fear, and then there was the black silence once more, so heavy it weighted the ear drums. The footstep came again, closer this time, and suddenly, out of the blackness and the quivering silence there emerged a pale figure, ghostly at first, then taking form. She stood in a void, as though certainty had switched the fear off, then a hand brushed her arm, the fingers gripped, curled round her flesh, and at that moment between herself and her attacker, against the background of his white garment, there was the flash of a knife.

Chapter Six

Jane jerked violently away and began to run wildly, crazily. She tripped and plummeting through terror found her wrists and hands buried in the soft debris at the edge of the drive: pain came where the asphalt had scraped her knees, pain clouded by panic as she lay spreadeagled. Then came an automatic reflex movement that was self preservation, and she had gathered herself up like a small animal, knocking against a tree trunk and coming blindly, drunkenly, erect.

Pain hid, now, behind the urgency of escape. The footsteps pounded and crunched on the rough surface behind her. Not thinking, not caring if she fell again, cornered by darkness into sobbing frustration because there was a way out that she could not find, Jane ran wildly, hands up to protect her face from the soft smash of leaves, feet charged to swing herself aside each time they struck. A stumble, arms flailing. A twig in her face. Eyes tightly closed against the smaller danger of mutilation by some innocent, benevolent tree. She headed into the greenery at the opposite side of the drive, swung back and somehow found her bearing once more by the slope of the ground beneath her feet, the ease of body projection. Her pursuer was near now, closer than before, though her own footfalls and the singing terror in her ears disguised his exact whereabouts. Only his nearness again came through. The threat of him.

When she felt the touch of his hand again it seemed a part of her fevered imagination. And then there was a grip of hard fingers and she screamed, wrenched herself down and away, swung left then right and almost fell as the asphalt surface dropped sharply once more. Unbelievably, then, out in front there was the blessed assurance of a wisp of light.

She raced towards it and suddenly there was the faint noise of traffic in her ears, the jangle of a bullock cart and then, across the entrance in lamplight, the muddled to-ing and fro-ing of pedestrians.

Jane reached the road, ran to the sheltering light of a café and stopped, gasping for breath. Shaking uncontrollably, she brushed away the black soil and grit from her elbows. A trickle of blood came with it. Fear began to give way to a sense of outrage. A sad old man with leathery skin sitting cross-legged on the pavement looked up and muttered something, holding out his hand. She moved away, her eyes returning to the drive's entrance. The beggar leaned forward, half rising to his feet, extending a leprous arm partially clothed in a filthy cotton drape. Jane moved further but he came after her and she had to keep going, glancing behind until she saw him reluctantly stop, muttering to himself.

She was now some distance from the drive leading to the palace but she could still see the entrance. She started to cross the road. It would be easier to see from the river side. Then she saw the beggar had guessed her intention and was propelling himself, bent double and leaning on a stick, in and out among the cars and carts. She hesitated, turned back quickly and to her dismay saw the entrance was already obscured by a bullock cart trundling slowly along the road. Beside the cart where the people walked through there was no pavement, a group of young men jostled one another in passing. With a shiver of very real fear she realized that anyone wanting to come out undetected had been handed his obscurity on a platter. Her pursuer might now be coming towards her and if so she would not be able to identify him.

Fear cut through her like a knife, but the sense of outrage persisted. Her eyes moved mesmerically over the little crowd behind the bullock cart. There were three turbanned men, one young and two middle-aged. They all wore pale shirts with light trousers. The turbans of two of them were loosely wound and a rather grubby white. One was taller and wore pink. She could not tell if they were together or if they had merged to allow the cart to pass. As they came nearer she saw they all wore knives at the waist. Behind them came a slender woman in a dirty sari, and two boys. The woman paused to hold out an emaciated arm, her beautiful black eyes pleading. Jane turned uncomfortably away. A little cascade of stones came funnelling down from the high bank above and Jane jumped. But it was probably only a goat inadvertently pulling up a plant by its root as it fed. The soil on these mean hills was no match for the weight of stones, rocks and pebbles it was supposed to hold back.

She crossed the road and made her way towards the bridge. The river was a black canyon, silent against the shriek of horns, the clatter of carts and rattle of loose boards as the cars crossed. She hurried on to the road that led towards the hotel, up the slope and by the side of the parade ground. At the top of the short rise that led from the bridge she paused, her heart sinking as she realized she had left the last street light behind. Ahead lay darkness, not that black, uncompromising darkness of the Rajah's drive but a pale kind that would entice her in then shroud her as it would shroud anyone following her. She hesitated, half turned, then with a great surge of relief saw a taxi pulling up only a few yards away. A man emerged from the back seat and was preparing to pay the driver. She ran the short intervening distance. The passenger was still counting out coins.

'Savakar's?'

The driver nodded. The back door was standing open. She stepped in with a quick sigh of relief.

What happened next was afterwards a blur in her mind. Except for the thrust. That was the man's mistake. If he had not been so anxious: if he had allowed her to settle herself in the corner, then jumped in after her, he would undoubtedly have had her like a cat a mouse. But he could not resist a sharp push. She fell with a gasp of horror against the opposite door, its shining chrome handle coming up against her hand. With her system adrenalin-charged, her mind honed finely to the scent and touch of danger, in a split second she was out again in the road and running, with a despairing sense of disbelief, swerving between the cars, the bicycles and the meandering sacred cows. Somewhere in the back of her mind was the knowledge that whilst her assailant could mingle undetected by her in a crowd of his own kind, Jane herself, with her hair and her short skirt, would be flagrantly exposed.

With no clear idea of what she was looking for by way of salvation, for even an English crowd might stand back from public brutality, she reached the opposite side of the road and headed back towards the river. By the time she came upon the enclosed challenge of the bridge with its special danger from racing wheels, slap-happy drivers, and the taxi that may have turned back and already be pursuing her, she knew she dared not cross. There was a small, steep bank leading to a well worn track that ran down beside the bridge towards the river bed. She leaped blindly over the edge.

She landed on hands and knees in a welter of stones and dust. Picking herself up, blinking the dust out of her eyes and coughing it from her lungs, she felt her way towards the bridge. If the roar and clatter of the traffic, heard from the pedestrian path, was overwhelming, from beneath it was a vile abuse. Small stones fell like shrapnel as Jane clambered over the rocks that projected from the bank. It was like fighting her way through a sandstorm. The rocks themselves were coated not only with the suffocating powder but also with rubble that bit into her hands. She could not hide here. She clambered forward in the darkness, coughing uncontrollably, slipping and sliding until suddenly, with a gasp of relief she emerged on to the open river bank. Rough, dry plants scraped her skin with their needle sharp leaves as she slithered forward. Battling with a panic stricken desire to hide, she kept going until she came to a place where the bank sloped very steeply and the trees grew taller and more dense. She raised the drooping branch of a sturdy bush and crept inside, wriggling herself into the embrace of a fork with her back against the trunk. Hidden in the depths of a foliage darker than the outside night, she waited with a kind of desperate acceptance, knowing if her pursuer found her here, there would be no getting away.

And then the dreaded sounds came, very faintly through the local silence that surrounded her hiding place which was outside the rushing and rattling and klaxoning of the cars on the bridge. There was a patting sound as of bare feet on rocks, the rattle of a dislodged stone, and then she froze as she heard the jagged intake of breath and an angry, subdued muttering. Cold beads of sweat stood out on her forehead. He moved on, cat footed, with only his heavy breathing to mark his presence, and then that faded.

Five minutes passed. Perhaps ten. The nerve-splitting strain eased. There was a smell coming up from the river, penetrating her curtain of leaves. Jane wrinkled her nose distastefully. It was a vile smell that was suddenly wafted closer by the faintest of breezes. And then she remembered what Clive had told her. This river valley where it ran by the town was its open air lavatory. She moved for the first time, only a small movement to take a tissue from her pocket and place it over her nose but a small stone became dislodged and rattled a few feet, then stopped.

She shrank back in terror as she heard movement again, this time from below. Footsteps crunching on loose stones, the grunts of her pursuer clambering back over rocks. Or was he her pursuer? He could be a local man going down a well-known path to relieve himself. Carefully, very carefully, Jane inched forward, parting the leaves with one hand.

Her eyes had grown so accustomed to the exceptional blackness within the upturned bowl of the bush that the light outside seemed brighter than it actually was. She saw a figure in dark trousers, wearing a sleeveless pullover over a white shirt with rolled-up sleeves, and with a pink turban on his head. He turned slightly and instead of looking at his face she found her eyes riveted by the shining hilt of a curved sword at his hip. His fingers touched it tentatively as he looked about him. He had not the air of a man who returns to civilization after an innocent sojourn down the river bed. He was at once stealthy and businesslike as he fingered the sword. Besides, one of the men she had seen at the head of the drive was wearing a pink turban. Slowly and very, very carefully, Jane released the handful of leaves she had been holding. It was only the faintest rustle that could have been made by a mouse or a bird but he heard it and was immediately on the alert. Jane scarcely dared breathe, knowing he was waiting for her to betray her position. Then, mercifully, a stone broke away some distance above them both and he went to investigate.

He had exceptional patience. He must have stayed there for twenty minutes or more, as a cat waiting for a bird to abandon pretence of death and give him his deathly game. Then, with a grunt and a sigh, he moved and she heard him clambering back up the path until the noise of him merged with that of the traffic. Fighting an almost overwhelming temptation to run, Jane waited a long time before making her move. Stretching out her legs slowly, and carefully unwinding herself, she crawled stiffly forward and inch by inch parted the leaves. She could see nothing in her immediate vicinity. Shifting her aching body slowly, she edged through the outer foliage. There was no movement. Nothing. Intuitively, she sensed the emptiness and a feeling of wary safety crept in.

She stood up, nerves jumping like crickets at the inevitable shush-shush of the leaves sliding into place, at the equally inevitable crunch of earth against stones beneath her feet. There were no other sounds. No movement. She took a deep breath and clambering forward faster than was safe, she reached the little dry earth path that ran on to the road. She scrambled up, looking round swiftly, heart hammering. She was at the edge of the traffic that was heading away from the town. There was a taxi just emerging from the bridge. The interior light was on. It was empty. Nervously, she scrutinized the driver's face. He was bareheaded, one arm crooked on the open window, his face young and dreamy. Dreamy! That looked like innocence. Like safety. She darted towards him. He braked when the traffic slowed to a stop. She slipped through the cars and ran towards him.

'Could you take me to Savakar's, please?'

He shook his head. 'It is the end of my work. I go home.' His eyes were on her untidy, dusty hair. Belatedly, she brushed it back from her grimy face, felt the leaves and twigs in it and knew she must look a sight. 'Is not far to Savakar's,' he said.

'But it's dark. Please take me,' she begged, and his hand moved forward to the gear, 'Please. *Please*. You must be going past the bottom of the drive. Please take me.' His patent innocence was a magnet.

'Yes, yes,' he said at last, impatiently. 'Is all right. Please to get in.' She opened the door and collapsed thankfully into the seat. The driver, looking back over his shoulder in careless disregard of the traffic as he accelerated, remarked interestedly, 'You have accident?'

'Yes,' she replied. 'Yes, I have had a small accident.'

'What happen please?'

'I fell. I was – er – climbing over rocks.'

He laughed. 'Climbing over rocks, eh? By yourself, eh?'

She glanced away, expressionless, aware that he was watching her in the mirror. 'Tell me,' she said stiffly, 'is it safe for an Englishwoman to walk alone at night in Kodapur?'

He shrugged. 'Of course. Safe, yes. Why not?'

She did not answer. They were speeding by the darkness

64

of the parade ground. There was not much farther to go. With a scream of the horn the driver swung into and sped up the steep winding drive. With a theatrical flourish he slewed round in a tight circle flinging her against the door as he came to a stop before the glass entrance. 'Thank you very much. I am most grateful.' She clambered out and for the first time saw in the pale light over the door the sight she had presented to him. Filthy jeans, a torn and dirty blouse exposing her breast, wild hair. No wonder the driver had been surprised!

There was no one in the foyer. She sped up the stairs and along the veranda. Clive was standing at the rail outside their rooms and ludicrously, as he looked up and she saw astonishment grip him, she remembered: He said we'd have a drink together before dinner!

Chapter Seven

On Clive's return from the clinic he went out to the veranda and instead of settling to read, stood looking down the steep hillside with its straggly bushes, its stones and dirt and bits of rubbish. A tin can came flying through the air then bounced like a rubber ball until it hit a tree trunk. A vulture wheeled by, circled, lowered its wings and went to investigate. Clive glanced at his watch, lit a cigarette, smoked it half-way through then flung it away and a moment later lit another. Jane. The gunsmith Kumar Singh. Gopal Behera. He could not bring himself to believe that they were all actually implicated. All the same, he had been unable to concentrate on his work at the clinic this afternoon. And now, why had Jane not returned? What was she doing out this late?

Down below a door banged and there was the sound of running footsteps. He leaned, without much curiosity, over the balustrade. The Englishman Barry Hills was coming out of the foyer and making for his room like a bat out of hell. The doctor frowned. He glanced out over the town. The sun, a vermilion ball blanketed in thin blue mist had gone down now leaving a savage sky. In another moment it would be dark and Jane had still not returned. He looked at his watch again and went restlessly into his room, threw the book on the bed scattering the thin flies and wondered if he would pour himself a drink. It might help to take his mind off the bogeymen.

He brought two glasses from the bathroom, put them down side-by-side and took a bottle of whisky from the cupboard where he had hidden the gun. He poured himself a small measure then took it outside. He was leaning on the veranda rail gazing into the distance, his fingers tap tapping with a jerky movement on the glass when another door banged below. With nothing better to do he leaned over the rail again. Barry Hills, carrying a pack, was hurrying through the glass door that led to the foyer. With a quick, nervous movement Clive put the glass down, strode out on to the landing and hurried down the stairs. In the foyer the tall, dark haired Englishman was standing at the desk.

'Have a good journey, Mr Hills,' said Prakash. The boy with the shining black eyes picked up the pack that was very similar to the one Clive had thrust under his bed not two hours earlier, and walked to the revolving glass doors.

With his nerves honed finely to disaster, Clive felt suspicion cut into him like a knife. He walked across to the man he had been so carefully avoiding since his arrival at the hotel. 'Are you leaving?' he asked, pointedly, superfluously.

'That's right. I'm joining one of those Himalayan foothill treks. There's an English party up in the Kulu Valley. I had a message this afternoon,' Hills replied. He seemed anxious to get away.

'Are you coming back here?'

'Perhaps. Who knows? I rather doubt it. I'll probably go off and have a look at the Western Ghats, or Nepal.' He spoke carelessly, flipping the names off like facile little lies. 'I must go. My car's waiting.'

'So long, then.' Clive followed him to the door and stood, hands thrust deep into his pockets, looking thoughtfully out into the courtyard. It was an Ambassadore car Hills had hired. The sort of car Clive himself had hired for tomorrow. The driver was opening the boot to put Hills' gear inside. He had already flung himself into the back seat as though anxious to get away. The driver jumped in, revved the engine noisily and the car sped off.

Clive swung round and crossed to the desk. Of course people went trekking from the Kulu Valley all the time. And Hills looked the type. Strong, athletic, lively.

'Yes, Doctor?' The clerk gave Clive his attention.

He rattled the annas and rupees in his pockets, trying to think of an innocent trick question.

'You want something, Doctor?'

'I was wondering if there's any mail for me.'

'No, Doctor. No mail today.'

'No mail?' His heart plummeted, and it was not because he had expected a letter. 'I must have been mistaken, then. I thought Mr Hills said he had a message. Perhaps by telephone.'

The clerk shook his head. 'No messages today.'

Clive turned and went slowly with shoulders hunched back up the stairs to his room wondering if he was an innocent abroad, a jumpy ass, or a bloody fool.

It was more than an hour later that Jane, filthy, her clothes torn, came running through the glass door on to the upstairs veranda.

'What on earth! Good God!' exclaimed Clive. The tears were too close. At the sight of his shocked expression her face crumpled. 'What happened to you?' She began to cry. He took her arm. 'Come into my room,' he invited her concernedly. She sat on his bed while he quickly took a bottle of brandy from his cupboard. 'Drink this. What happened to you?' he asked again.

'I was followed by an Indian. Chased. I ran under the bridge and hid in the bushes. That's how I got in this mess.' She looked down tearfully at her filthy clothes.

He put a towel under the tap and was bathing her scratched forearms with great gentleness. 'All this time? You've been under the bridge all this time? You've been gone since midday.'

'No. No, I went to see Gopal. But – oh dear,' she laughed in an overwrought way, 'his family chased me off. I think they must have imagined I was my cousin Helen. And Gopal's poor little wife was there. It was a quite horrific experience. I couldn't get through to them. But, my God, nothing to what's – oh dear! I am a mess!' The tears began to fall again. 'I'm not often like this, honestly. Really, I'm quite tough. But my nerves seem to be shattered. Oh God, it was horrible!' She brushed the tears away, blew her nose on a tattered tissue. 'You're awfully kind.'

'Just sit quietly while I do this. It doesn't hurt, does it?'

'No. No, really.'

He looked queerly down into her face. 'Did you see who it was chased you?'

'An Indian. I didn't see him properly.' She shuddered. 'He had a knife.'

'They all carry knives.'

'You mean, it might have been merely attempted rape?' She grimaced, trying to laugh and produced a cracked little cough. 'It wasn't funny. I've never been so panic-stricken in my life. Merely rape!' she repeated turning the words over shakily. 'Can't a woman walk round this town alone?'

'I don't know that it's wise, at night. You haven't told me how it happened? Where were you?'

She hesitated, then her wits came into play, swinging her mind right across the earlier part of the afternoon, excluding the awfulness of Louise's indiscretions and Ashley's strange behaviour. 'I was getting into a taxi. He jumped in after me and I shot out the other side.' She described how she ran under the bridge.

Clive listened gravely, eyes narrowed, the suspicions flooding through him. She was talking in a stagey fashion, holding something back. She *was* involved. The apprehension in him hardened to anger and underneath there was the sharp cut of disappointment.

'Don't bother to put that stuff on,' Jane said as Clive took up a small bottle and a piece of cotton wool. 'I feel a lot better now.' She gave him a wan, warm smile. 'I must have a shower,' she said. 'I'm filthy. Anything you dab on will only wash off. That damn cold water again!' She had recovered. The brandy had done its work. She rose. 'You're awfully

69

kind,' she said again. 'I'm very grateful. There's nothing like having a doctor in the house.' She smiled at him, again, ruefully. His face was unexpectedly grim. He had a strange, aloof look that he had not worn before. At the door she hesitated. 'I – I'm sorry I forgot about – about – we were going to have a drink,' she ended uncertainly, still watching his eyes, deep lashed and all at once a rather steely grey.

He shrugged, relaxed a little and gestured towards her empty glass, his half-filled one. 'It wasn't quite as planned,' he said cryptically. 'See you when you've cleaned up. I've asked the dining-room to hold our dinner.'

'Great. Give me half an hour.' She went out of the door and he stood staring after her, his face grim.

Chapter Eight

It was only the faintest sound, like that of a mouse, but Jane's nerves were on edge. She had slept lightly, only just over the edge of consciousness. The noise came again. Sh-shush. It was coming from the outside wall. The window? She had left it open last night. It might be only the sound of wind sighing in trees. Sh-shush! Her eyes were growing accustomed to the darkness, now. She could see the faint outline of the window. Such light curtains would not lie still in a breeze! The small hairs on the back of her neck seemed to stand on end. Sh-shush. There it was again, a live sound like something scraping softly on the outside wall. She crept out of the bed and went towards the window, her bare feet silent on the tiles. Yes, there was something there. Perhaps a small animal in the creeper. And then stark fear shot through her as she realized there could be no creeper up the outside walls of such a newly built hotel. Taking care not to disturb the curtain, she leaned cautiously forward. The night was ink dark, with a faint scent of flowers. The sound came again, that same soft scraping sound and with it a scent that was not of flowers. A scent she had noticed in the market yesterday. Dried sweat overlaid on the dusty, musty odour of the Indians' clothes.

In a frenzy of alarm she reached up and pulled the window sash. To her horror, it did not move. Exerting all her strength, adding her weight, lifting her feet off the ground, she dragged at the wood. Then something touched her thigh and she leaped back with a small scream. A hand had come over the sill. There was a grunt as of a body shifting its weight. Jane swung round, stubbed her toe on something in the darkness, floundered across the room and scrabbled for the light switch. She saw then that the intruder was heaving himself up. He was nearly waist-high against the open window. In another moment he would have swung his rump round on to the sill.

Looking desperately for a weapon, Jane's eyes encountered the holdall where she kept the duty-free Scotch she had brought as a present for Ashley. She picked it up and turned back, raising the bag high above her head. She saw the helpless look of horror on the dark face, the grimacing mouth. Forgive me! Oh God, do I have to do this? She brought the bag down, closing her eyes as it made contact. There was a groan, a slithering sound, and she opened her eyes sickly to see an arm sliding back into the night. There was a crashing of small branches, a dull thud, a low chatter of distressed voices, and then silence.

Jane looked down at her hands. The whisky had poured through the opening of the bag spattering her with slivers of glass. The shattered bottle fell with a subdued clatter into a pool of its own making and with heart thumping she backed away from the still open window, crossed the room and with trembling hands unlocked the door.

'Well!' said a quiet voice. Before she recognized it she cried out in alarm and jumped back. There was a low powered globe in the veranda ceiling. Clive wore a thin dressing-gown. His long, brown legs and feet were bare. 'What's going on?' he asked.

Jane said, her voice coming in torn little strips, 'Perhaps you'd like to go – and have a look. I think – I've killed a man – who was trying to get in through my window.'

He hurried past her and peered out into the darkness. Pitch darkness. He reached for the sash.

'I couldn't get it down. That's why I had to hit him.'

Clive tried again. He punched the sash with his fists, eased the cord, and eventually the window gave way. He locked it and went back to Jane. 'There's nothing to see. The moon's behind a cloud. Great Scott! What's happened to your hands?'

She held them out, covered in glass. 'I hit him with a bottle of duty free whisky I'd brought for Ashley.'

He began to pick little slivers of glass out of her hands. 'Did you see him?'

'Not really. He was Indian. In a—' she gasped. 'He was wearing a turban, too. The man who chased me tonight wore a turban. Clive!' Fear gathered round her, crushing her with its tightening, suffocating fingers.

He made a little pushing gesture towards the bathroom. 'Run the cold tap over them. If there are any bits left they'll wash away. I'll have another look when you've got rid of the blood.' She retreated, instinctively obeying him.

'I hit him with a bottle of whisky. I told you that. God! What a thing to do! I'd bought it duty free. It was lying there on the floor, in a bag. If I hadn't had it – oh God! To be killed with a blow from a bottle of—' She went into the bathroom turning her back sharply because she was gabbling, the words tumbling repetitively, senselessly over one another. She was afraid he would laugh. Or she would laugh. And she may have killed a man!

Clive could see right through her nightdress and he knew, as a doctor, it should have left him unmoved. Her soft, rumpled fair hair was falling forward over her face as she held her hands under the tap. She had small, beautiful breasts and a rounded belly. She obviously hadn't a clue he could see her nakedness. And now there were big, slow tears rolling down her cheeks. He felt sorry for her and he wanted to say something kind, but he had to watch himself, now. He said cautiously, alert for her reaction, 'Ashley won't be too pleased about losing his whisky.' And then he waited for the shock to appear on her face when she realized she had given away her brother's presence here.

But she only brushed a hand unselfconsciously across her eyes and said, 'He doesn't know about it. They're bleeding furiously. What am I going to do?' She gave a little wail of distress.

Clive followed her into the bathroom, took her wrists and

held them under the tap, peering closely at the skin. 'They're only very minor lacerations,' he told her reassuringly. 'They're not as dramatic as they look.' He picked up a small towel, wrapping it round them. 'Come to my room and I'll put something on them.' He saw a thin gown lying on the bed, picked it up and draped it round her shoulders. 'Better have this on,' he said gruffly, 'just in case someone turns up.' He saw her colour flare and wished he hadn't embarrassed her. She would have realized in her own good time.

'Thanks. Well,' she added defensively, 'you are a doctor.'

'That's right,' he replied in his crisp medical voice. 'You see one naked woman, you've seen the lot.'

'How long have you been here? In this hotel, I mean,' she asked as they went into his room. 'All the time you've been in Kodapur?'

'Yes.' He was taking his medical box out of the cupboard. She saw the gun and her eyes dilated.

'Has anyone broken in?'

'Not that I know of.'

'Why have you got a gun there?'

Instinctively covering up, he pushed the cupboard door shut with his foot. He said lightly, 'You should ask, after your experiences!'

'What does one do now? Call the police?' She had started to tremble again. 'I may well have killed him.'

'In your place,' Clive replied, busy with his bandages, 'I'd clear up the glass and leave it at that unless you get a complaint. The body isn't lying in the garden.' She lifted her head, eyes startled 'How do you know that? It's dark.'

'Didn't you hear the chatter of his friends? They would take him away, wouldn't they?'

'Yes, I did, now that you remind me. Yes, they would cope. Is that what wakened you?'

'Hold out your hands.' He bandaged them deftly. 'I wasn't asleep. Yes, they're okay now. They'll settle down and there won't be much to show in the morning when the bleeding has stopped. The cuts are very superficial. Now do you think you'll sleep, or shall I give you a dose of something?'

'Sleep?' She rubbed a hand distractedly across her forehead. 'Clive, someone's trying to kill me.'

'Why would they?' He asked the question very seriously, looking into her face. 'Have you any clue?'

'Why would they?' she echoed. 'There's no reason. And whoever it is, it's someone who knows I am here.'

'Anyone would know you were here.' And he repeated the statement that made a mystery of Ashley's presence. 'White people stay at Savakar's.'

'But they wouldn't know what room I have, unless they had inside information.'

He did not answer immediately. Then, 'Who knows you're in Kodapur?' he asked, watching her face to see if she was going to tell the truth.

'No one.'

'Gopal Behera knows.'

'Yes, of course.' Her breath caught as she remembered the frightening experience she had at Gopal's house that morning. And of course the Rajah knew, and his mother, and his servants. She was suddenly very confused, very frightened.

'Who's Ashley?'

'My brother.'

'You didn't mention him before.'

'No. I – er – I couldn't find him. I was – er – I was looking for him this afternoon when that Indian came after me.'

He rested both hands on her shoulders and looked into her face. 'Are you quite sure there isn't something you'd like to tell me?'

She glanced down at the floor, 'There's nothing. I mean, only something rather private I'd prefer not to talk about.'

Clive said gently, 'There's something bothering you. Can't you tell me?'

'I can't,' she whispered distractedly. 'I honestly can't. It's frightening, but it's awfully private. It's about Ashley, and the Rajah and—'

Clive said gently, 'Perhaps I can help. You seem to have got yourself into some sort of a queer hole. If it's any assistance my family were here at Partition, too, and I know about your mother and the Rajah of Kodapur.'

'Oh God!' She burst into a wild sort of laughter. 'Does everyone know, then?' Without waiting for a reply, she added soberly, 'I'd laugh about it. I could laugh about it, but I've discovered today – at least I think I've discovered today, I mean I suspect – oh hell! I'm such a shivering mess I can't even talk straight.'

He sat down beside her and put an arm round her. 'Take it easy now. What did you think you discovered?'

'That old Kodapur might have been the cause of Ashley's father's death.'

He started visibly. 'Ashley's father?'

'Yes. That tombstone with Jasper Edward Carlyon on it in the British cemetery is over the remains of Ashley's father.'

'Oh.' He said it oddly, flatly, and his eyes fell away. 'Oh, I see.'

'But that's nothing to do with me.' She looked down at her trembling hands. 'Oh, dear, I'm starting to shake again. Can I have another brandy?'

'Sure.' He took her glass and poured a measure.

'Thanks awfully. This is becoming a habit. Perhaps I should tell you about what happened this afternoon. If you can make anything of it, I'd be grateful.'

Clive sat in the chair watching her face as she talked. His own expression was grave. She did not say she suspected Ashley was here for revenge but he could read it behind her troubled, muddled sentences. He did not see how he could tell her the truth, even though he was horrified at the suspicions she entertained. He consoled himself by thinking they might easily be put right at any time. But the other –

that was something else – and a responsibility he did not care to take.

At the end she asked wanly, 'What do you make of it?'

He shook his head. 'I agree, there are no clues. It could be a ruffian with a penchant for white girls.'

'He'd be a very determined ruffian who went to the trouble of finding out which room I was in. Are there a lot of hangers-on around Indian hotels?'

Clive nodded. 'Sweepers and such like. Everybody's children. It wouldn't be difficult.' She felt a faint brush of relief. 'I'd better give you something to make you sleep.'

'Clive, there's something.'

'Yes.' He paused in the act of rising.

'Don't laugh. But I wanted to tell you, just in case there's a possibility. I mean a loophole. I mean – well, the Rajah is going to a village in the Himalayan foothills the day after tomorrow. It's called Tarand. They're going to open a cave where there's a necklace hidden. I've seen a picture of it. I mean, there's a portrait of the Begum Kodapur wearing it at the palace and I'll swear it's worth a million – I mean, it's the most flamboyant thing I've ever seen. Don't look like that, it's true. And the hell of it is, my mother had a hand in this. That's why I'm telling you. I feel, not guilty, of course, but concerned. Louise and the Rajah gave this necklace to the jolly old god as a sort of bribe. He'd asked a favour. And he says it's never to come out of the cave. But I wondered, could an Englishman like you rob the cave? I mean, that necklace would build your hospital, if you could get hold of it. And it doesn't belong to the Rajah. He should have given it up at Partition in exchange for his pension. Why are you looking at me like that?'

Clive leaned over, put both hands on her shoulders and kissed her gently on the mouth. 'You lovely girl,' he said softly.

She felt the hot colour flood into her cheeks and her foolish heart leapt then pattered on too fast. Brimming with excitement, and something warmer than that, she sat up very straight, her head raised, eyes sparkling, 'You would have a go? I'd come with you. I mean, actually he has invited me, and Ashley if I can find him, to go along with him.'

'Did he now?' Clive asked sardonically. 'That's interesting. Actually, I did know about the jewels – er – necklace. It's – er – fairly common knowledge in Kodapur. I mean, there's a rumour tossing around ever since Partition, that the Rajah may have got away with some of his treasures. But they're no use to him. If he dug them out he couldn't liquidate them and neither could he take them out of the country. I thought you were here to have a go yourself,' he said, smiling.

'Me? You must be joking. You mean, you thought Louise had told me?' He nodded. 'Oh, I see. No, she never talked to me about – well – about any of this.' Their eyes met. She said soberly, 'Are you?'

'After the necklace? No,' he replied, quite categorically.

One hand flew to her mouth stifling a horrified gasp and all at once the excitement had gone. She looked up at him, appalled. 'My god! Clive, the awful truth has dawned on me. I've just realized, that's what Louise told Ashley when she was dying! That's why he's here.' She crumpled. 'He couldn't!' She looked away from Clive seeing in her mind's eye Ashley's handsome face, remembering things about her half-brother that she would rather not tell anyone. 'He must be going to follow the Rajah to the cave.'

Clive said gently, laying aside his own thrusting fear, 'That explodes the theory that Ashley's here to revenge his father's death.' He was glad to be able to point it out and take that weight off her mind. And it was not going to make any difference to him. Ashley was a fact, and at least she had done him a favour by spelling out her brother's presence here.

'Yes, it does, doesn't it. But stealing the necklace, would be revenge.'

The necklace! He wondered whether he ought to tell her

the truth. And then he wondered just how fond she was of this brother of hers. She could be a help, but she might also be a bad hindrance, if she was loyal. And he was pretty certain she was a loyal sort of girl. 'What type of a man is your half-brother, Jane?' She looked at him mutely, not wanting to answer. 'I have to ask you this. Is he the sort of chap who would take the jewels for a good cause?'

She glanced away, her face tight. 'I can't answer that, Clive.'

'Do you have any influence with him?'

'No, I don't think I have. But—' and she looked up at him, her eyes full of pain, '—I do love him very dearly.'

He had his answer. He glanced at his watch. 'It's nearly three. We had better finish this tomorrow. It is tomorrow. I'll give you some pills.' He poured some boiled water out of a covered jug and took tablets from a bottle. 'Swallow these. They should ensure a bit of shut-eye.' He escorted her to her room and stayed clearing up the mess until she was asleep. The tablets were quick acting. As he went quietly out he took the key from the door and locked it on the outside. He took his gun and a torch, then went quietly down through the hotel. There were two dhoti-clad Indians apparently asleep curled up in chairs in the foyer, and the young man who helped in the office, dressed in westernized clothes, stretched out on a sofa. There was more room here than in their shanty homes and Prakash would be grateful for unpaid night watchmen.

The moon was behind a cloud. With his gun cocked in his right hand, he held the torch in his left, shining it again. There was track down each side of the building. He brushed the bushes aside, crossed a steep bank and stood looking down at a flattened shrub directly beneath Jane's window. There was no body. He might have survived, Clive felt. The bush would have broken his fall.

Chapter Nine

The clinic, it seemed, was at the poorer end of the town beyond the bazaar. The streets were narrow, packed tightly with tiny shops that sent out steam and savoury smells to mingle with that of animal odour, over-ripe fruit and bidi tobacco. A legless beggar sitting in the dust looked up, brushed a posse of flies from his face and held out a hand, palm upwards.

Jane took a coin from her purse and gave it to him. Though she had always known about the poverty of India she found herself emotionally ill-equipped to accept it. No wonder Clive felt as he did. A small child defecating in the gutter saw her gesture and as though summoned by some secret telegraph suddenly they came running in their dozens with matted hair and streaming noses, filthy little hands up-turned. She hurried off, jolting over the pitted dirt track between the shanties and poor little shops. The children fell behind. Here the noise of traffic came again. The revving of engines, the shriek of horns, the bleat of a goat, the abusive cry of a taxi driver beaten to a small space. A dark skinned water carrier went by bent double beneath the weight of the enormous metal can sloshing noisily on his back.

She found the clinic easily enough. Two decent looking oblong buildings, their low roofs tiled with slabs of thin grey stone, with a dusty courtyard between. Behind, a raggedy garden, a broken fence and a goat chewing busily under an old apple tree. Upwards of twenty Indians squatted in a line in the dust, their big, beautiful eyes calm with the patience of the underprivileged for whom there is, anyway, nothing else to do, and nowhere to go. It was dreadfully hot in the sun. She went through the yard and seated herself on the prickly dry grass beneath the apple tree. The goat looked at her with interest but did not move away.

It was a full hour before the yard had fed the patients through the clinic and emptied itself. Clive emerged carrying his hat in one hand. She jumped to her feet, calling 'Hi!'

He swung round in surprise. She stepped over the broken fence and came up beside him. 'I came down to meet you because I reckoned if there were any questions to be asked by the management about last night I'd rather have your moral support.'

He smiled. 'I am glad you didn't run.' They fell into step together. 'No sign of Ashley?'

'No. Clive, I'm scared silly about what happened last night '

'Have you any more theories?'

'No new ones. Only the fact that I do look like my cousin Helen,' she said broodingly. 'Gopal's parents were so absolutely awful to me when I called at their house yesterday. Hysterical.'

'Perhaps there's been trouble there, and you got the backlash. If he wants to go and live in England, with or without his wife, the family may be hostile to the idea. Indian familes are very close.'

They were hurrying along the busy road beside the bridge. She had to raise her voice over the sound of the traffic. 'What do you mean, with or without his wife?'

'You must know how the Indians operate. It's a parliamentary issue and the papers have been full of it for ages. One of them gets into England then gets visas for all his relatives.'

'You mean, he might use Helen?' Her eyes widened.

'I don't know your friend Gopal. He may be genuinely in love with your cousin and genuinely want a divorce. But if you're fond of her this is something you could do for her. Find out what his motives are.'

'Yes,' she replied soberly. 'I see. Thanks. Well, I hope he comes to Savakar's because I'm not going back to brave what I came up against yesterday.'

'There's another thing. Gopal's wife is a Sikh.'

'Meaning what?'

'Meaning the chap who chased you wore a turban. In case you don't know, Sikhs are forbidden by their religion to cut their hair and beards, so they tuck them under a turban.'

She caught her lower lip between her teeth. 'They're the warlike ones, aren't they, easily incited to bloodshed.' In 1947 Pakistan had been given, disruptively, to the Moslems, India to the Hindus. In the vicious holocaust that followed it was the Sikhs who went down in history as taking advantage of the opportunity to shed blood. Their atrocities were horrific beyond belief. 'It's a scary thought,' she said quietly.

'But worth following up when you see Gopal.'

'Yes, indeed. He's a Brahmin, you know. He's very proud of it.'

'It's a good thing to be. Before the British made laws for Indians, a Brahmin couldn't even be punished for murder.'

'Good lord. Didn't the lower castes demur?'

'They accepted it. Indians are good at accepting their lot. That's why it's up to us to push hard to improve that lot for them.'

'Yes,' she said. 'Yes, I do understand why you feel the way you do. Let's talk after lunch.' She had begun to think about the jewels again.

Clive was not returning to the clinic in the afternoon. They had no sooner settled into the veranda chairs than the glassdoor leading to the landing swung open and Gopal appeared. He came wreathed in smiles. Tall, slender in that bony Indian way that was perhaps an inheritance from generations of starvation, with liquid, gentle, pleading eyes as brown as the trunks of the deodar trees, white teeth against milk chocolate skin, he exuded an air of cleanliness, charm and grace that was as real as the heat, the dust and the flies among which he had been reared. It was no wonder that Jane's cousin had been swept away by his attentions, Clive thought dryly.

Gopal's immaculately clean and pressed white shirt was open three buttons down exposing his smooth chest and a glimpse of the sacred thread he always wore signifying his Brahmin caste.

'Jane! I came yesterday but they told me at the office you had gone out. I thought it was better not to stay here, you will understand.'

Clive rose, nodded to Gopal and went into his bedroom. 'Do sit down.' Jane patted the arm of the roorkhee chair. 'I'm glad you came. It's super to see you, but I'm afraid this isn't just a special occasion.' She smiled at him sweetly, then deliberately hardened her heart. 'Let's be quite open with each other, Gopal. I've had a nasty little adventure and it necessitates my asking you some rather frank questions. I hope you won't mind.'

Gopal looked apprehensive. 'No.'

'You're living with your wife, for starters.'

He sat up straight, defensive, innocent. 'We do not share a bed, Jane. Puniya is at the house of my father because my father brought her there when he saw I was in love with Helen. She is only seventeen and has not finished her education. We were not to be together for another two years.'

'I see. Well, you may think it's none of my business, but bear with me.' She smiled kindly at the Indian boy. 'Tell me, Gopal, why did your father choose a Sikh wife for you?'

Gopal's fabulous lashes flickered down. 'There are many, many Hindu/Sikh marriages. My father considered it a good match and it would have been, if I had not met Helen.'

'Yesterday I had that rather unpleasant experience when I went to your house and—'

'I am sorry, Jane,' he cut in, the colour rising behind his dark skin. 'My father will apologize. He does not understand.'

'You mean,' she asked bleakly, 'your family think I am Helen and you haven't managed to persuade them otherwise?'

'It is unfortunate, Jane, that you do look like Helen. There is ill-feeling in my father's home. My father is upset because I do not wish to abide by his choice of a wife for me. As well, Puniya's family are upset, that I should not want their daughter. And to Puniya herself it is insulting that I do not wish to sleep with her. Her mother and father want the family to go on. While I do not sleep with Puniya they cannot have grandchildren.'

'Why can't you simply get a divorce?'

'This is India,' replied Gopal unanswerably, 'I have to find a way round this problem without offending. I would not wish Puniya's family to take revenge.'

'Revenge? Right!' Jane's fine brows shot high above her startled eyes. 'That's what I am coming to.'

'It is not just that I fear revenge,' Gopal broke in swiftly. 'Puniya is in my karma. You must know that the soul is advanced or retarded according to the way we behave in each incarnation. By ill-treating Puniya and making her relatives and mine unhappy now, I could destroy the possibility of a better future for myself in eternity.'

'Yes, that's all very well, Gopal, but I've a problem that is a little more immediate than your next incarnation,' Jane observed tartly. 'I was chased last night by a Sikh.'

'Oh, I am sorry. I am very sorry, Jane. But that is not to say he was a relative of Puniya.'

'Also, someone tried to climb in at my window in the middle of the night.'

'But this is terrible, Jane.' Gopal was genuinely distressed.

'Why don't you do the rounds of Puniya's relatives and find out which one has a cracked skull?'

'You hit him?'

'I walloped him with a bottle of whisky. He didn't have to wait until his next incarnation to find his soul retarded. His

84

brain may be retarded after what I did to him last night.'

Gopal said gravely, 'His soul is not your affair. Nor mine. Nor anyone's. Why have you come to Kodapur, Jane? Because Helen begged you to?'

'No. I came to look for Ashley. He sent me a card with Kodapur on it. You know he disappeared right after my mother's funeral?' Gopal nodded. 'And there are papers for him to sign. The family want the estate cleared up. No one can get any money until he signs.'

'I see.' Gopal's eyes were grave pools of darkness. 'I do not think he can be in Kodapur. There are only two Englishmen. Dr Retford and a man called Hills.'

'But he was here. He had to be here to send the card. And he's here now. I saw him in the back of a taxi yesterday.'

Gopal shook his head. 'I do not understand. He has not come to see me.'

'You know his father is buried in the English cemetery here?'

'Yes. I found the stone. I started to clean off the inscription. I cleaned it enough to read it. What's the matter, Jane?'

Her jaw had dropped. 'You scraped the tombstone?'

'Yes. I'm sorry if you're displeased. It was only curiosity. I must go now,' Gopal said hastily, embarrassed and somewhat taken aback by the shock his admission had produced. 'It was nice seeing you.'

'Please don't go.'

Gopal looked ostentatiously at his wrist watch. 'I need to go.'

'Why? You're on holiday. Is it that you think those inlaws of yours are watching you? Are you scared of Puniya's Sikhs, too?'

'No, no,' he replied hurriedly. 'You're taking what I said about them too seriously, Jane. I am not afraid of them. They're nice people. But I must deal with this matter slowly. One does not ride rough-shod, as it were, over anyone, if one can avoid it, whether one fears repercussions or not.'

'No, I suppose not.' She rose, mind weary and unhappy. 'If you see Ashley, you'll tell him I'm here, won't you?'

'If Ashley is in Kodapur he will come here, to this hotel, Jane.'

She went down to the foyer to see the Brahmin off. When he had gone she stood in the little courtyard looking up at a small building opposite. Half a dozen brown children gazed down at her, big-eyed. She went to where the rough, overgrown plants clung to the edge of the drop and stood looking up at the veranda side of the hotel. From their quarters the servants could certainly see her going in and out of her bedroom. It would be child's play to locate her window on the other side.

There was the sound of a car and she turned to see a jeep approaching up the drive. She had begun to walk back into the hotel when something familiar about the small Hindu driver swung her back. 'Jane, my dear!' The jeep had scarcely stopped when the Rajah bounced out of the passenger seat, a young-old man with energy to match his charm. 'How glad I am to find you here.'

She went to meet him, holding out her hand. 'You came to see me? How nice. Come to my veranda and I'll see if I can persuade someone to bring us tea.'

'Yes, my dear. But first I must find my friend Barry Hills. He left yesterday, you will remember, when you were with me and he has not returned. The place is without a telephone so I have come to apologize for my rudeness and to make arrangements, for we are to go together to the foothills tomorrow, you know.'

She smiled at him winningly, though her heart beat a little faster, 'Is your offer still on? Will you take me with you?'

'Of course.' He was delighted. 'And you have met up with your brother?'

'I'm afraid not.' His face fell, touchingly. She said, 'I'll see you when you're through with Mr Hills. We'll talk then.'

She went upstairs thinking how strange it was that a man should want his lover's two children to be close to him. Clive was back in the veranda chair. He looked up, grinning. 'Well, did you get anywhere?'

'With Gopal?' She heaved an enormous sigh. 'He's either as slippery as an eel, or, since I don't want to be uncharitable, I'll add, as resilient as a rubber ball. I thought I knew him, but I only know his English side which I suppose is laid on rather thick in London because there's no Indian backdrop. I do get the impression I could be the victim of his in-laws' vengeance. At least he has made me aware they might be trying to chase me out of town. Anyway I'm leaving tomorrow. The Rajah has turned up to see this other Englishman. He's coming to have tea with me so if you hang around I'll introduce you. He's off to the Bhunda tomorrow and he's going to take me. Did I tell you he'd offered?'

'What other Englishman?' asked Clive, his face strangely still.

'Someone called Barry Hills. He was at the palace yesterday when I was announced. The Rajah left him in his study and then got so carried away over meeting me, he forgot about his guest and the guest got tired of waiting and disappeared.'

'Yes,' said Clive quietly. His face had gone ashen.

'Yes what?'

'Sit down,' said Clive. 'Yes, Barry Hills has disappeared. He shot back yesterday afternoon, picked up his gear, and went in a hired car. And now you say he disappeared from the palace when you were announced. Sit down in that chair and describe your brother Ashley to me. Very carefully, Jane. Very exactly, please.'

'What on earth—'

'No, I'm serious. And get a move on, before the Rajah turns up.'

Even as she talked the truth was darting in little poisoned spearheads through Jane's mind. 'He is about five feet

87

eleven, thinnish, with black hair, dark eyes. A broadish nose.'

'Well-cut mouth, widish lips and extremely even, very white teeth?'

She nodded. Her nerves seemed to be on pin points, her eyes dilated. She said in a whisper, 'The servant announced me to the Rajah when Ashley was there with him. Oh God! Hills is Ashley's alias. I knew, I knew, I was absolutely certain that taxi turned into the drive. But it never occurred to me it could have been Ashley in the study. You see, I was concerned with the scraped tombstone, then. I thought he'd made a pilgrimage – even though it didn't make sense, I still believed it.' She went on distractedly, 'But Gopal says it was he who scraped the tombstone. That makes sense. It was a red herring, though. Perhaps, vaguely, when I was at the palace I might have thought, without letting myself think it I mean, that he was skulking in the garden with a gun, only that didn't make sense, either.'

'I see now,' said Clive, 'why you didn't come across Barry Hills. Both nights you've been here you were late for dinner and yesterday you missed lunch.'

'Yes. That's it. I'm flabbergasted. Let me think.'

'There's not much time for thinking, now. The Rajah's going to learn the truth and be here at any moment.'

'Are you suggesting Ashley has gone to get the necklace? How can he get it? It's behind seven doors guarded by – Clive! How could an Englishman possibly get into the cave? And why should he run when I appear?'

'I don't know how he would get in, but clearly he has found a way. And he doesn't want you to know. Naturally, he wouldn't want you to know – or anyone,' Clive added quickly, seeing the sensitive mouth droop. 'He was going along with the Rajah, until you appeared. Knowing you, he'd know you wouldn't approve. Or maybe he even thought he might have to share the treasure with you. You forced him to get off the mark in a hurry.' Clive frowned, puzzling. 'What baffles me is that the cave will be opened on a certain day. Nothing can alter that. He can't get there early and get off with the jew – the necklace.'

'You know all about this Bhunda, don't you?' she asked, her voice suddenly sharp with suspicion. 'You said the cave will be opened on a certain day.'

'A bit. I've heard about it from my patients,' he replied evasively. He rubbed his forehead, intent upon his problem. There was a missing link. There was no point that he could see in Ashley running, and thereby raising the Rajah's suspicions. It would be so easy to avoid Jane. Ashley merely had to leave Savakar's. 'Here, Jane, where are you going?'

She was already running along the veranda. Clive leaped out of his seat and ran after her. She raced him down the stairs. The Indian clerk was at the desk. Prakash was coming back through the revolving doors. They could see out into the courtyard. The jeep was nowhere in sight. Jane turned to the manager, her cheeks bright, her eyes startled. 'Has the Rajah of Kodapur gone?'

'Yes. He has gone. He was looking for a guest who has left.'

'Mr Prakash, please could you get me a taxi,' Jane asked, urgently.

'Certainly. For now?'

'Yes. I'll be ready by the time it arrives.' She swung round and crashed into Clive.

'Steady.'

'Sorry,' she apologized breathlessly, 'Clive, the Rajah is obviously going after Ashley. I've got to get over to the palace.' She fled across the foyer and took the stairs two at a time but Clive was there with her. 'Jane, this is madness!'

'I don't see that it is. Why don't you come too? Why aren't you interested in the necklace?' Perhaps you could get it. You could certainly help stop Ashley getting away with it.' They had reached the veranda. She paused outside her door.

He caught her arms and swung her round. 'Jane! Don't go.'

She tried to pull herself away but he was too strong for her. 'I have to go.'

'Listen to me. There's more to this than you know.'

'Yes,' she flashed, 'you are involved. I felt it. That's why you've got the gun, isn't it?'

'Jane, get out and go home.'

'No. Somehow, I've got to stop Ashley. And stop the Rajah—' a small sob that was part frustration at his staying hands, part terror, broke loose. 'Clive, I don't think I've ever met such a potentially dangerous man as the Rajah. And he believes Ashley's father had a hand in his troubles at Partition. I've got to get between him and Ashley.' Clive's fingers loosened and she broke away, swung through her bedroom door, banged it after her and turned the key in the lock. She picked up a canvas holdall, threw the contents of her handbag into it, then added a pair of walking shoes, an anorak and a jumper.

Chapter Ten

Clive's first reaction was to pull his pack out from beneath the bed. Then he kicked it back, sat down with his head in his hands and groaned. He heard Jane go, heard the soft, swift patter of footsteps across the veranda and then silence. He found his cigarettes, lit one, smoked it through to the end then lit another. He looked at his watch. There was always a chance, of course, that the Rajah would refuse to take Jane with him, now. In that event, she ought to be back in an hour.

The hour passed and his mind began to spin ideas. Would the Rajah listen if Clive told him Jane was after his jewels? Unlikely. If he told the Rajah the truth, that Barry Hills was Ashley Bellamy, he would listen then. Jane would hate him for it, but it might save her life. He strode out to the veranda. Night had descended. His nerves were stretched like tight elastic for the sound of the footsteps that never came.

Clive paid off the taxi and ran up the steps of the old palace. He lifted the ornate leopard-head knocker, crashed it noisily. The door was opened almost immediately by a tall Sikh. A handsome Indian woman whom he recognized as the Begum, wearing a gold sari, stood behind the Sikh in the big, empty hall. 'What is it you want, Sahib?'

'I am Dr Retford from the clinic. I would like to see the Rajah, please.'

The Begum came forward. 'He is busy. He is going away shortly. He is making preparations.'

'Yes, I know, but I'd very much like to speak to him, if it's possible.'

'I would not like to disturb him,' she said. 'He is—'

'Yes, I know,' Clive broke in impatiently. 'But it is important. Really very important. I have some news for him. I know he's going to the Bhunda, and I have some very important information.' The woman exchanged glances with the Sikh. 'Is the girl with him?' Clive asked. 'Is Miss Bellamy here?' He had stepped forward into the hall. Though he could not put a finger on it, he felt there was something strange about his reception. He had to make certain he was not in a position to have the door slammed in his face.

The woman's eyes narrowed as she saw his move. She said, ignoring his question, 'My son is downstairs. In a storeroom. If you are willing to see him there—'

'Yes, yes. Of course.'

She signed to the Sikh to lead the way and Clive followed him across the hall, then round a corner. There was a narrow staircase leading down. 'Please go ahead,' said the Sikh.

It was not that Clive sensed danger, only that flitting across the top of his mind, not quite taking form, was the fact that it seemed odd for the Begum to follow, and at a distance. It seemed odd, too, that the Rajah should have a gorgeously turbanned Sikh servant. Jane had said the men who waited on her here were small Hindus, drably dressed in khaki and with their shirts hanging out.

'Please to go down,' repeated the man. Committed, he began to descend. It was gloomy here. The stairs were uncarpeted. The corridor at the bottom was covered with worn rush matting. A single naked bulb glittered palely in the ceiling. Above them a door shut with a bang and Clive started. The Sikh paused at a white painted door but he did not open it. Clive looked at him sharply. The Sikh nodded. There was something about his waiting posture as he put a predatory brown hand on the door knob, easing it and yet not moving, watching Clive, that put Clive subconsciously at the ready. He sucked in his breath, made a step backwards, then the door opened.

What happened next was so sudden that he did not see it in clear focus. With one hand, the man must have slid the door silently and easily aside. The other hand fell square in the middle of Clive's back. The blow caught him off balance, sent him flying into the room. He careered forward, arms flung out. He saw the Rajah's startled face, then came up against a chair and crashed with a shuddering thump to the floor. The door slammed. The Rajah had leaped up from his seat and was banging on the door, kicking it, hurling furious Hindi abuse. Dizzily, Clive picked himself up. Jane was asking, 'Are you all right? Are you all right?' She seemed to be swinging in circles with the Rajah's rage splintering round her. And then she was on her knees asking, 'For God's sake, Clive, have you broken anything?'

He blinked her into focus. 'No,' he said faintly. 'No, I don't think so.' The room became still except for the Rajah's unbridled, throbbing anger. He had turned from his assault of the door, his face a mask of animal fury. 'What is this?' he shrieked. 'What is this? How did you get here? Who are you? You are the English doctor! Well, I'll be damned!' The Rajah stood back, staring at him.

Clive staggered to his feet. 'What's going on?'

'You ask me what's going on!' The Rajah howled. 'You know as much about it as I do. Tell me this. How do you come to be in a position to be pushed through this door, Doctor.'

'I came to find Jane. She said she was going with you to the Bhunda. I worried about her.'

'Why were you worried about her?' The Rajah thrust an aggressive chin up towards Clive's face. 'Why should you be worried about her if she is with me?'

He thought fast. 'I had told her at Savakar's I considered it unwise for her to go to the Bhunda. I came to try to dissuade her.'

'Why did you think it unwise for her to go with me to the Bhunda, I should like to know?'

93

'It is a Hindu ceremonial, is it not? I felt it was no place for an Englishwoman.'

'And your nosey parkering has landed you in here,' the Rajah stated with satisfaction. 'It serves you right.' He swung round 'Rafiq! Shobha! Mangal!' He repeated the names over and over, over and over again until his voice, rising to a pitch of insane excitement, cracked.

Clive stood with hands on hips regarding the Rajah in bewilderment. 'Did you arrive here the same way, Jane?' he asked without turning his head.

'A little more gently. But, yes.'

'Rafiq! Shobha! Mangal!' the Rajah screamed at the closed door.

'Jesus wept!' Clive put a hand to his head. Jane clapped both hands to her ears. Clive walked to the window.

The Rajah saw him. 'It is no use. There is a guard. Of course there is a guard. Did you think I would be here if there was not? He will slice off your head with his *kirpan* if you try to get through there.'

Clive paced to the other end of the room and back. 'They have obviously removed your servants. There's really no point in yelling like that.' The Rajah grunted. Clive continued pacing. 'What are the chances of our breaking down that door?'

'None. It's as solid as a rock. We could take the furniture to pieces and batter it but we'd never get the door down. Besides, the Sikh would be waiting with his *kirpan*. What weapons have we? None.'

The room was about thirty by twenty feet, with a low ceiling. The window in the one outer wall that stood opposite the door was half above, half below the ground. There was very little furniture. A table, a rush mat like the one in the passageway, a worn sofa, some tattered armchairs. It was obviously some sort of all-purpose room, vaguely lived-in. Clive tried the handle of the door to the left of the entrance. It led into a short passage at the end of which another door stood ajar. There was a lavatory behind it, the paint blistering on the wooden seat. The Rajah, his face flushed and angry, went to one of the old armchairs and sat down. His head was high, the tiny beard thrust out aggressively.

Jane had seated herself on the floor below the window, knees drawn up under her chin. Clive went over to her and stood looking down at her. 'This has to do with Ashley,' he said quietly, bitterly. He saw her stiffen. 'Is he clever? Ruthless?' She put both hands over her face. 'He has gone,' said Clive. 'He wouldn't hire an Ambassadore car then creep back into town. He's working with someone. The Begum, obviously. He has arranged to have the Rajah held prisoner while he gets the jewels.'

Jane's hands fell from her face. 'Sit down. I want to say something—' She glanced across at the Rajah. He seemed absorbed in his own thoughts, head bent now, elbows on the arms of his chair, fingertips touching. She whispered, 'There's something I don't know. When I say "necklace" you say "jewels".'

He smiled, but his smile was strained, without the customary softness. 'A necklace could be referred to as jewels.'

'Yes, that's it. The way you said it. It *could* be referred to as jewels. Clive, you know something I don't. Are there other jewels in the cave?'

'You said our host told you people make offerings to the gods. There may be a lot of necklaces there.'

'You're hedging.' She sighed sharply. 'I can't imagine why you don't tell me. We're here together for the duration of the damned Bhunda. We're not going to get out.'

'I don't know why you should imagine—'

'I'll tell you why. Because of the funny way you said, when I first met you in the cemetery, and I asked you where you were going to get the money for your hospital, you said, "That's the sixty-four dollar question". And also, I'm not a fool, Clive, I know the Maharani of Jaipur was thrown into

95

jail by Indira Ghandi's government for allegedly hiding jewels and gold she was supposed to give up at Partition.'

Clive squatted on his haunches before her. 'When I came here,' he whispered, 'I heard rumours in the town to the effect that the Rajah may have got away with some of his valuables. I mentioned it when I wrote home and my mother came up with this tale of the trek to Tarand immediately before Partition.'

'Did my mother know yours, then?'

He shook his head. 'No. But Carlyon was well known. As British Resident, everyone knew him. And so they had an ear open for gossip about—'

'About Louise. Don't bother about being tactful,' Jane said tightly. 'After what's happened, I can take anything. So you reckon the Rajah's horde of precious stones – was he ankle deep in them, as you said some of the princes were?'

Clive smiled, and this time his eyes were soft. 'He's only a small prince, really. But yes, my mother thought it possible that he and the then Mrs Carlyon, who became your mother, who ostensibly went off to the foothills to see a bit of Indian folklore, took the Rajah's pack of jewels and—'

'I know!' Jane whispered with awe. 'I've got it! They gave the necklace to the god in return for his guarding the jewels until the Rajah felt it was safe to collect them! But it's never going to be safe, Clive. As you said, he's never going to be able to spend money here without drawing attention to himself. And as you also pointed out if he wanted to go abroad – I see! He's using Ashley – Mr Barry Hills! He's made a business arrangement. But—'

Clive nodded grimly. 'But Ashley is double-crossing him, isn't he?' He saw her colour recede, saw the stark pain and anger in her face. Some of her embarrassment flooded over and she whispered accusingly, 'And you? You've got a gun. You were after the jewels too. Why did you say you weren't?'

'I said I was not after the necklace. It's the truth. I didn't

96

know about it. And at the time, I didn't want to tell you.'

'All right. Fair enough,' she agreed. 'How were you going to get into the cave?'

'I couldn't. My plan was necessarily very uncomplicated. I found out the date of the next Bhunda and I established the fact that the Rajah was going. In the meantime I had dug around and established the interesting fact that he had not been to Tarand since Partition. It was a certainty that at some point he was going to retrieve the jewels. He's not getting any younger. It's thirty years now. It seemed reasonable to assume that the heat was off so far as the authorities were concerned. I understand they kept an eye on him in the early days. I had a hunch and I decided to play it.'

She said in a fierce whisper, 'Yes, but you haven't said—'

'I'm coming to that. Keep your voice down. I was relying on robbery, plain and simple. I was going to hold him up as he left the village with the jewels in his possession. I had counted on the fact that he wouldn't wish to have anyone in on the secret, so he ought to be alone. And I had also counted on the fact that he couldn't report me to the authorities because the jewels belong to the government.'

'Then, how could you use them for your hospital?'

He said dryly, 'But for me, the government would never sight the jewels. I've done some ground work with the authorities. They're very sympathetic to my plans but it's a question of funds. I reckoned if I produced the jewels they would be only too happy to allow me a share.'

'Why didn't you simply tell the government of your suspicions?'

'And get bogged down in their taboos and their gods and their caste problems? Not likely. Besides, if this treasure is to be channelled into my hospital, it has to be collected by me.'

'You were pretty sure of yourself.'

'I had only one man to cope with at the time. Yes, I was optimistic, he agreed wryly. 'Over-optimistic, as it turned out.'

'Poor Clive.'

'What are you two whispering about?' The Rajah had left his chair and and was approaching them.

Clive rose to his feet. 'We're wondering how we can escape.'

'You can't escape. There is no way out of here with a guard at the window and another at the door.'

A woman's voice called out in Hindi, and the Rajah swung round. '*Amma*. Let me out!' Jane jumped to her feet. All three went and stood just inside the door. The Begum spoke again.

'What is she saying? Can you understand?'

Clive translated. 'She's saying it's necessary to keep the Rajah here until she has her necklace.'

'*Amma*,' the Rajah wailed, his black eyes moist with self-pity, 'you cannot have the necklace. I would do anything for you, but you cannot have that. The god will punish you. He will punish us all. Besides,' he added, 'while I am in here I cannot get it for you.'

She spoke again, in Hindi. 'She's saying,' Clive muttered, 'that Barry Hills has gone to get it for her.'

'The necklace. He cannot! He cannot take the necklace!' The Rajah looked stricken. 'It was an offering to the god!' He spoke as to himself, half in a whisper. A whisper full of dread. Something that looked remarkably like panic darted behind his eyes. Something fanatical and at the same time, sincere. Then suddenly he was at the door again, hammering with his fists, crying out in Hindi like a tortured soul.

The Begum poured out a flood of Hindi, too, mostly drowned by the barbaric row the Rajah was making. Clive shook his head in confusion. 'My grasp of the language isn't that good.' Then the Rajah ceased his punishment of the door. '*Amma*,' he cried desperately, talking over the top of her words so that she was forced to stop, 'listen to me. You will not get the necklace. This *goondah* you have sent will keep it for himself.'

98

Her laugh was sharp and cruel. She, too, spoke in English now, deliberately it seemed. 'Do you think I have not seen that? Do you take me for a fool, my son? I have made my arrangements. This *goondah*, as you call him, will not have the necklace for long. Do you think I would trust an Englishman?'

Jane turned and made her way to the far corner of the room where she sat down again on the floor. She looked so utterly defenceless, so frightened, that Clive went and sat down beside her putting an arm round her shoulders. She was trembling and her hands were cold.

The Rajah shouted angrily, 'It will not work. You sent a man to collect that necklace twelve years ago, but he failed.'

'He failed because he was a Hindu and afraid of the anger of the gods. Mr Hills is English and not concerned with our superstitions. He will not hesitate to remove a gift meant for the god. I wish you would be quiet, my son. It is unseemly to scream in this manner. And it will not help with your release.' They heard the soft brush of her slippers and then silence.

'She's had twelve years,' Clive muttered. 'It ought to be long enough to work out the perfect, foolproof plan.'

'She does not have to work out a plan,' the Rajah said miserably 'There was something I wanted from the cave. A small thing, I assure you,' he lied outrageously, 'that I had banked there for safe keeping. I told Hills I could arrange for him to change places with one of the goldsmiths. They are not anxious to enter the cave because, though they must go in by tradition, they must also die within the year.'

'Die?' Jane's nerves tensed with shock.

'That is what my mother meant by our superstitions. Hills said he wanted to go into the cave because he is studying Indian folk lore. I believed him.' The Rajah exclaimed harshly, 'A man who has accepted my hospitality, become my friend, could do this to me!' He hunched forward, a little, a very dangerous man. His black eyes were hooded, their gleam condensed to a dagger point of brilliance. Jane shivered and turned away, unable to look at him like that.

Clive rose and went restlessly to the window. Jane turned unhappily to the Rajah. 'Isn't anyone likely to look for you?'

'Where are my servants?' he demanded angrily. 'That's what I want to know.'

'Isn't the Rani coming back tomorrow—'

'Yes. But she will think I have gone to the Bhunda. There is not one chance in a hundred that she will come here. And if she did come, she would not come in time for me to get to Tarand. If I am to stop that intolerable spy from bringing out the necklace, I must be there before the cave is open. I was to leave tomorrow morning.' He groaned. 'Minakshi will not return from Bombay until tomorrow. Already it is too late.'

A faint glimmer of light was showing in Clive's face. He turned to Jane, asking in a whisper, 'What's Ashley like? Arrogant? Fun loving? Is he really interested in Indian folk lore?'

'I don't know about the latter, but yes, he is arrogant,' she admitted. 'He'd have to be, wouldn't he,' she asked, her heart twisting painfully, 'to take on such a thing? And fun loving? Yes. Yes, he is full of nonsense when the mood takes him. Why?'

'I was wondering if he would run off immediately he got his hands on the jewels. Or if he'd be brazen enough to stay and see the fun.'

'You two are whispering again,' stated the Rajah pettishly.

'We were talking about the possibilities if your wife were, by some remote chance, to turn up.'

'What possibilities?' asked the Rajah resentfully. 'This *goondah* will take the jewels and run.'

'Jewels?' Jane picked up the word, pointedly. Her query brought a dark flush to the Rajah's face and momentarily he looked disconcerted. Then regaining his composure he snapped, 'The necklace.' He turned away.

Jane and Clive exchanged faint, humourless smiles. 'Why press it?' Clive heaved an enormous sigh. 'We're in possession of the biggest bit of useless information anyone ever had.'

'We could pray.'

'Do you think I haven't been doing that ever since the key was turned? Now innocence is forced on me, I can. When I was prepared to shoot anyone who got in my way I couldn't very well call on the Almighty to help. Could I?'

Jane caught her breath. 'Ashley? You were prepared to shoot my brother?' Their eyes met. He heard the harsh intake of her breath, saw the incredulity, the disbelief in her eyes. The Rajah broke the silence by going back to the door and beating on it in a frenzy of rage.

Chapter Eleven

They slept little, Jane curled up in a chair, the Rajah on the sofa and Clive on the floor. By morning the cigarette packet was empty. Clive flung it furiously at the wall. The Rajah wakened, sat up and glared at them in the faint light then relaxed again into sleep.

At seven o'clock the Sikh guard descended the slope outside the window and peered in. The Rajah pushed up the sash, speaking to the man in Hindi. The window came down with a bang. The Rajah pushed it up again, yelling at the top of his voice. The Sikh snarled, raising one hand threateningly. The Rajah turned away.

'He says they have expected a lot of noise and are ready to deal with it. I hope you will not shout,' he said as though it had been they, not he, who cried out. 'They mean what they say.'

Jane washed her face and hands in the small lavatory basin. Clive looked up as she re-entered the room saying dryly, 'What a pity I didn't drop my shaving gear into a haversack.'

'I'll lend you my comb, if it's any help. You can always start growing a beard.'

'Thanks. I may have to.'

At nine o'clock there was a sharp rap at the door. They started to their feet. 'You are well, I hope?' It was the Begum's voice. Brisk. Unfeeling.

The Rajah rushed over to the door and stood before it, hands clasped in blind supplication. '*Amma*, how can you do this to your son?'

'I do not want to be unkind to you, but I have told you it is necessary to keep you safely here until I have my necklace. I want my necklace very badly, you know that. I have arranged some food. It is perhaps possible to put it through the window.' The guard descended the steep little slope outside the window bringing chapattis and cheese in a plastic bag. He raised the sash and thrust it through the bars. Clive offered the bag to Jane. She turned away. 'No thanks.' They did not talk any more. The Rajah, after eating two or three chapattis seemed to have retreated into a world of his own. He settled down cross-legged on the floor with eyes closed. Clive paced round the room.

'What day does the Bhunda start?' Jane asked. Her heart was bleeding for Clive. Only in the middle of the night did she think of Ashley's perfidy and even then her mind shied away.

'Thursday.'

'And today is Sunday.'

Clive nodded. He was thinking that if Ashley stayed to view the Bhunda ceremonies and the Begum's henchman waited to rob him on the way back, then they could expect to be imprisoned here until Thursday of the following week. Twelve days from now! Clive groaned aloud. Jane glanced up. He had not the heart to tell her she could be here for twelve days.

It was a long, long wait. Afterwards, Jane often remembered with a shudder and wondered how, once the tension went, and with it the hope, she got through the alternate bouts of dumb misery and angry despair. The Rajah alternated between violent rages when he called abusively on the numerous deities, and silent prayer when he repented, begging for forgiveness and rescue. The Begum did not come again. Outside, the Sikh paced up and down, the soft crunch of his feet on the gravel path a continuous reminder that there was no way out, no point to the never-ending wracking of their brains. The torment and the tension grew, faded into despair, swelled again. The garden was silent, the house like a tomb, the blue sky lifeless with heat. Once Jane said miserably, 'What Ashley is about, whatever the moral issues, he is still my brother.'

Clive put an arm round her and held her close. It was tearing him apart seeing her frightened and distressed like this, knowing he was partially to blame. Then he remembered that one chance in a hundred that they might escape. That he might find himself with a gun in his hand in a situation where it was a million hungry, dirty, needy Indians against Ashley and he moved away. He hadn't many scruples regarding the acquisition of the Bhunda jewels but one of them must be not to make advances to a girl whose brother he might have to kill.

On the second day their guard put some plates through the window bars, following them with a plastic bag containing curried meat and vegetables. The Rajah asked for cutlery but the Sikh did not come again and they had to serve out the food and eat it with their hands. 'It is the way the ordinary people of my country eat,' the Rajah said. He was growing despondent. He was giving up.

The commotion began late on Monday afternoon. Raised voices filtered down from the hall. The Begum protesting. And then another voice, of a woman. The Rajah leaped to his feet with an exultant shout. 'My wife! My wife! Minakshi has come.' Jane and Clive flung themselves in a frenzy of excitement at the door. The Rajah rushed across the room, screeching at the top of his voice. 'Minakshi! Minakshi!'

'Help! Help!' They battered on the door. Battered until their fists were numb.

'Minakshi! Minakshi!' shrieked the Rajah. There was a violent rattling of the door handle followed by a torrent of Hindi, then an appalled silence. The Rajah cried in despair, 'She has taken the key. Of course she has taken the key.' He beat the door again with his fists, babbling incoherently, like a madman.

Clive exclaimed, 'The window!' He was there in a flash. The Sikh who had been on duty day and night had fled. Clive threw up the sash, then leaping on to the sill began kicking at the iron bars. 'The table!' He leaped back into the room, upended the solid table on which they had taken their meals and began to bash it on the floor. 'Here, help me. Jane, stand on the top. You—' that was the Rajah, '—help me pull.' With an agonizing scream of metal against wood, one of the legs came away. Clive rushed it to the window and fitted it between two of the bars. They all lent their weight. It bent a little, and then a little more. They tried again.

The Rani was now standing in the courtyard looking down at them, her round, plain face, with its magenta *bindi* mark on the forehead, puffed with indignation and distress. She was chattering like a magpie with angry, highly pitched bewilderment; a little round woman in a magnificent green and gold silk sari.

Suddenly the bar snapped. It must have been weakened a little by the rust that was powdering away as they pushed. Clive dragged it aside. The Rajah crawled through. They would have helped him but he did not need them. Agile as a monkey, he scrambled up the bank. Jane followed, and then Clive. By the time they reached the courtyard the Rajah and his Rani had gone, her bird-like ejaculations dancing and spitting in the air as she ran in pursuit of her husband.

Jane dashed after them. Clive swooped on her and wrenched her round. 'Where do you think you're off to?' he asked brusquely.

'He's going after Ashley. I have to stay with him.'

Clive took her firmly by the wrist and ran her forcibly towards the drive. 'You're not going anywhere,' he told her grimly. She tried to jerk away but it was useless. He kept running and, short of falling in the rough gravel, she had to run with him. Still holding her wrist, he reached the road with her and hailed a passing taxi.

'What are you going to do? Let me go. What are you going to do?' She tried to jerk away but his grip scorched her skin.

'Savakar's,' he said to the driver, and to her, 'Get in.' He gave her a little push. He knew what he was going to do but the release had come so suddenly he had not worked out what to do with her. It was only important, for the moment, to get her away from the Rajah. He did not answer.

Prakash was in the foyer. He came forward to meet them, noted their dishevelled appearance, the fact that Clive had not shaved and said, 'By jingo, Doctor, there has been something happening to you.'

'Yes. We got into a bit of bother.'

Prakash said, 'Mr Behera has been often calling. You do not say you leave hotel, Doctor. Miss Bellamy.' He was patently hurt. 'I have to wonder about meals.'

'I'm very sorry,' Clive apologized. 'We should have told you.'

'And there is a matter of an Ambassadore car which came for you yesterday. Early. Four o'clock it was, and they want me to pay. You are not here.' Jane swung round. Four o'clock Sunday morning! He had been going to slip off without telling her!

'Where is the car now?' Clive carefully avoided Jane's eyes.

'Gone. You are not here.'

'And you paid?'

'Yes. Is on your bill.'

'Now, will you please ring through and ask them to send it back.'

'Tomorrow?'

'No, now. Tonight. I want to set out immediately it arrives. I'll leave my stuff, if you would be good enough to look after it. I'll pay my bill, of course.'

'I do that.' Prakash was somewhat mollified.

When they had gone upstairs Jane said, 'You'll let me come with you?' Clive did not answer. He was sliding his key in the lock, rattling it as though to drown her words. His face was partially averted but she could see where the skin

106

was drawn tight over the jaw line. She said angrily, 'I want to share your Ambassadore car.' He disappeared into the room, banging the door in her face. Jane stood still, crucified by her own fear of what he was going to do. It was not only Clive who was after Ashley, but the Begum's henchman and the Rajah. Three tough, very tough men. The Rajah as Nemesis, she knew, now that she had seen the best and worst of him, could be brutal. As brutal, she was certain, as any Sikh with a knife. She had to go with Clive. She flung his door open, stood in the doorway, hair dishevelled, blouse creased, and the blue of her eyes drowned darkly in anguish. 'You've got to let me go with you. You've got to!'

He had taken off his shirt. It lay crumpled on the floor and he was staring into space, one hand clamped to either side of his head as though he really had paused in mid-stream to examine with horror what he intended to do. Then his hands dropped to his sides. He heaved a sharp sigh. 'I can't.' His eyes met hers with bitterness and something else. Something more powerful, more painful, and outside of their control.

'Of course you can. You can if you want to.'

'How are you on heights? The Old Jalori pass is ten thousand eight hundred feet. It's necessary to acclimatize oneself gradually to that sort of height. I shall be crossing within twenty-four hours of starting.'

Only by the faintest flicker of her eyes did he sense her shock and initial withdrawal and then she said quietly, 'Tarand is in the foothills.'

'The foothills go up pretty high. It's all foothills until you get into the Himalayas proper which is what the experts climb.'

'How do you know you can take the height?'

'Because I've done some climbing. I shall be walking for days with a pack on my back and sleeping out.' He saw the anxiety give way to something tougher, saw her chin come up. 'Look, it's no good your even entertaining the idea. I'm all organized. I've got pack ponies waiting at a little village where the road runs out away up beyond the Kulu valley. It's two days' drive from here. It's all properly planned. I can't add on an unacclimatized, inexperienced person. It could be fatal all round.'

She felt herself enveloped by a rush of decision. 'I can't let you go after Ashley with that gun. We'll work out something together. We'll get the jewels. But I can't let you — Clive! He's my brother!'

His eyes rested on her beautiful, tossed hair, those blue eyes that could turn a knife in his heart when he thought of her brother's villainy. He hardened his heart. 'Ashley is bigger than I am and ten times as ruthless,' Clive said quietly. 'Let's say it aloud, Jane, and then we'll both be able to face up to it. He's a common thief and an unprincipled scoundrel. I'm going to get those jewels from him and if I have to use the gun I shall. This is no place for you.'

'You can't! You can't do this, Clive.' She grasped his arm, looked up into his face with anguish.

'Listen,' he said, 'this is my dream. I've got a last ditch chance of still getting it and I'm going to take it. I'm prepared to risk my life to get those jewels.'

She drew in a long, slow breath, squared her shoulders and faced him levelly. 'Okay,' she said, 'I am prepared to risk my life to go along with you.'

He laughed harshly, but he was shaken, all the same. 'Yes, and knock the gun out of my hand just at the crucial moment. That's the sort of thing you're thinking of, isn't it?'

'I'll talk him round. I'll make him see—'

'All Ashley's kind sees is the beach at Copacabana, or a penthouse in New York, or the Marbella Club. If he gets away with this, remember he's not a criminal, Jane. No one will be after him because only the Rajah knows what's in the cave, and he has no right to it. For the sort of lush life Ashley envisages, he's going to fight, believe me, and you're not going to like this but I've got to say it, I'd guess his sister wouldn't count for much if she got in the way.'

As Jane went dejectedly back along the veranda a little breeze butted in from the outside bringing with it the smells of the lowering night, jasmine, the tarriness of pines and a distillation of the unacceptable smells of the town below. She went into her own room and sat down on the bed to think. There had to be a way. Somehow, she was going to find a way.

Chapter Twelve

Darkness dropped over the town in that meteoric way to which Jane had scarcely had time to accustom herself. She said to the desk clerk, 'It's important the driver speaks English.'

He nodded. 'I arrange.' He looked curiously at the bulging haversack she carried but he made no comment. Jane went into the courtyard to wait. When the taxi came up the drive she was in almost before it had stopped. 'Take me across the bridge, please, then up the road past the market. I'll direct you from there.'

The road where the Behera family lived was in total darkness. She said, 'Stop here. The house is just ahead with a babul tree in the garden. No, please,' as the car moved forward, 'don't go any further. I'd like you to turn the car round, then go in and ask for Gopal.'

'Gopal?'

'Yes. If he is there, bring him out. And don't tell him, or anyone else, who it is wants him.' She sat back in the seat where she would be hidden. The driver turned the car round and climbed out. She waited anxiously after he was swallowed up by the darkness, straining her ears for returning footsteps. At last they came, and Gopal's voice asking querulously, 'But who is it, man?'

She put her face up to the window. 'Gopal.'

'Oh, it is you, Jane.'

'Ssh. Jump in. I want to talk to you.'

He climbed in beside her, anxious, concerned. 'Where have you been? I have asked at Savakar's but you were not there.'

Without answering him she addressed the driver. 'Take us

back to — well, just to the bottom of this road,' she said. They climbed out, paid the man and the taxi bumped off into the darkness. 'I want your help, Gopal. Do you own a car?'

'No.'

'Could you borrow one?'

'Perhaps. What is this all about?' he asked, patently mystified.

'It's about Ashley. Listen.' She took his arm and they walked forward together towards some trees faintly lit by a street lamp. 'I'll make it as brief as possible.'

He heard her out in astonished silence. 'But if this is true, how would Ashley get the jewels out of the country?'

'He's audacious enough to march blandly through the Nothing to Declare exit at Heathrow carrying them in a plastic bag with his duty free liquor. You know that, Gopal. He must have come to an arrangement with the Rajah to get them out of India for him. Now it seems he is going to get them out for himself. He'll know how.'

'He's double-crossing the Rajah!' In the darkness, Gopal's eyes were enormous.

'I suppose,' said Jane in a tight little voice, 'the Begum, when she heard Ashley was going to the Bhunda with the Rajah, told him how to get the necklace out and offered him some sort of bribe to do it. We're assuming she didn't know the Rajah had already told him how to get into the cave to get the jewels for him.'

'And all the time Ashley intended to get them for himself!'

Jane bit back the sharp, loyal reproof that rose to her lips. There was no point in being sensitive about this. 'Evidently the Begum isn't interested in the jewels,' she said, 'or doesn't know about them.'

'And the doctor is ready to tackle all these people?' Gopal commented with awe. 'Really? Ashley, the Rajah and the Begum's henchman?'

'He's desperate enough. Gopal, Ashley doesn't know about the henchman. Or Clive. We can't sit here and see my brother murdered.'

'No, we can't,' Gopal agreed solemnly. He had an Indian's inbred concern for the family. 'But how could we—'

She broke in. 'Anyone can do anything if they're desperate enough. We've got to move fast. We've got to catch Clive before he gets to a village up beyond the Kulu Valley where he has pack ponies waiting. He's ordered a car and he's going tonight. We've got to follow him.'

'We can't do that. Not unless he is held up. But anyway, it's not important. I know the village he's leaving from and can easily find my way there. I've been trekking in that area. The only track leading directly to Tarand from the top of the Kulu Valley goes from a village called Taksit. I believe it meets up eventually with the Hindustan-Tibet road. I couldn't find my way, but if we could catch Clive there, we could use his guides. Jane, do you realize how far this is to drive? Two days at least, and then two or three days' climb—'

She stopped him peremptorily. She did not want to think about the difficulties. 'Right. Where can we get some sleeping-bags and a tent?'

Gopal shook his head. 'Nobody in Kodapur sells those things.'

'Could we borrow them? What about those hippies down at the Ashram? They must have some gear they're not using at the moment.'

Gopal sucked in his lower lip. His eyes were uncertain. 'The Swami is not very friendly towards me. I took Helen away, you know.'

'It can't be helped, if he's our only chance. Come on. We've got to find another taxi now.'

The Ashram was on the edge of the town. 'Let's pay off the taxi here.'

'But it can go right to the entrance, Jane. It is another quarter mile.'

'I want to walk.' She clutched Gopal's hand nervously. 'Please, I want to walk.' Too much had happened to her during the past few days. She did not want anyone, especially a Sikh taxi driver, to know where she was going. They were set down in a twisting lane bordered by tin roofed shanties, sacking lean-tos, cloth shops, a stinking, badly lit little lane with the fetid smell of garbage and urine, rotting vegetables, curry and garlic. Jane, glad indeed of Gopal's presence, instinctively cupped a hand round her nose. Under a lamp half-way down was a brightly painted shrine that housed a stone image of an obscene, fat bellied god with a necklace of marigolds, and in front an enormous, grotesque phallus, symbol of India. Old men squatting in doorways smoking their acrid smelling bidi tobacco looked at Jane with curiosity and distrust, the beggars held out their hands, the half-naked children followed with a mixture of shyness and avarice. They turned another corner and the lane was creepily empty, hemming them in with closed doors. Somewhere among the jumbled, tumbling buildings a sitar strummed. A solitary buffalo tethered on a corner looked at them with interest. Jane and Gopal made their way gingerly across the deeply pitted dried mud that lay around the entrance to the Ashram, through the patch of impenetrable darkness shed by a pipal tree, and there, lit by a single lamp, was a large mud hut with a corrugated iron roof and the notice PRAYER HALL. There were more huts, smaller than the prayer hall, but equally primitive, and between them dust, with a few starved tufts of grass. The door to the hall was closed. From behind it came chanting that rose and fell, the thin clash of cymbals, the windy echo of a conch shell. Suddenly the door opened and out came a wave of humanity, white, coffee coloured and dark, all with a sameness of grubbiness and untidiness in their long cotton skirts, torn-legged jeans, and with unkempt hair on their shoulders, boys and girls alike. Propelled forward in their midst was a weird figure in long saffron robes and a flowing beard. Some of the disciples looked curiously at Jane and Gopal standing beneath the light of the lamp. Others sailed by with exultant expressions on their faces, as though their feet trod on air.

Gopal stepped forward and those round the guru stopped as though he had pressed some invisible button, moving away, leaving a space between them so that Gopal might approach. 'Is it possible to have a word with you, Swami?' Gopal asked. 'I am sorry to butt in like this, but it is urgent, and important.'

The Swami was looking hard at Jane, so hard that she wanted to shrink from his strange eyes. 'It is always possible to talk to those who go out of their way to find me,' the holy man said gently, still not taking his pale eyes from Jane's face. He indicated by a smooth pushing movement of his hands that those followers who still waited round him should go on their way. 'What is it I should do for you, please, Gopal Behera?' His eyes seemed to swim hazily when he looked at Gopal so that he had a look which seemed at the same time both saintly and evil.

Gopal said brusquely, 'I'm about to ask a favour of you, Swami. I imagine there are some young people here in your ashram who have come a long way.' The swami nodded. 'Perhaps they have gear they're not using for the moment. I was wondering if we might borrow a couple of sleeping-bags and a tent for a week or two. We want to go on a trek and there's no one in this town, as far as I know who could provide us with gear. We would pay, of course.'

'Ah! You wish to go to mountains?' Those piercing eyes seemed to look right through them, looking for their souls. When Gopal shifted uncomfortably under his gaze the swami chuckled as though he understood their reticence, though he felt it was clear they were running away together. 'Of course you go to mountains. Who would walk and sleep in desert or flat fields of Punjab?' The swami clasped his hands together and smiled on them benevolently. 'Is beautiful time of year to walk in hills. At best you find it spiritually uplifting. At worst, good exercise. And yes, I like to help. My pupils, too, full of kindness. Come.'

They followed the strange, robed figure into a primitive little mud hut lit only by a smoking oil lamp. There on the dirt floor, kneeling before an acrid-smelling dung fire in a shapeless, dirty cotton gown was a fair haired girl. She was stirring something that looked like white porridge. There were two metal platters on the ground. She looked up as they entered gazing into the swami's face, her eyes glowing with something approaching fanatical devotion.

'I have brought friends of mine,' the swami said, leaning down and helping the girl gently to her feet. 'They want to ask favour. This is Dolly,' he said. 'She comes from Surbiton, I think in Surrey, is it not?'

Jane was silent as they made their way back up the stinking little street carrying their sleeping bags and tent.

She looked up into Gopal's face. 'Was it like that for Helen?'

Gopal did not answer at once. A pariah dog came down the lane, circled them, sniffing, then went on his way. At last Gopal said quietly. 'It is not funny. As the Rajah said, the guru hypnotizes them, so that they don't know what they are doing. A young girl is very vulnerable in such hands.'

'Are they all like that?'

'No. Some of them are very wonderful people.' A little flock of goats came down the valley shepherded by a small boy wearing only a waist length shirt and purple velvet pill-box hat embroidered in gold, passing them in the malodorous gloom.

The swami threaded his way through the primitive little cantonment and knocked on a door. A high, thin, nervous voice called, 'Who is that?' in Hindi and he replied, 'It is I, your guru, your father.'

'Come in.'

The Begum had been reclining on a string cot. She heaved herself to her feet. There was nothing more in this hut than in any of the others. On the dirt floor a brass lota brightly polished with ashes; an oil lamp and a small table on which lay a copy of the Bhagavad Gita. On each of the walls were large garish prints of Vishnu the supreme being and Shiva, the deity associated with destruction and therefore also with renewal. Shiva, who glowered down on the Begum, reminding her of what she must do. The swami would have liked something better for the Begum than this humble mud hut but she understood it was lack of funds, not lack of good will that put her here. One day – but that was in the Begum's hands to deliver up the necklace for the good of them all.

He said, speaking in Hindi, 'The boy Behera has been here with the English girl to borrow some sleeping bags. They are going also to the Bhunda, it might seem. It was as well you locked her in. But now that things have gone wrong, you will advise Kumar Singh?'

She lifted her head high, smoothing the crumpled line of her beautiful silk sari. She did not like the guru telling her what to do. He was her spiritual adviser, and for the moment the spiritual side of her life had to give place to more urgent matters. But he was right. That fierce fellow Kumar Singh who was also the brother of Gopal Behera's wife whom she had thought would deflect suspicion from herself because he had an axe to grind on behalf of the family, and who had made an unholy mess of dealing with the girl so far, could be given another chance. Where better for Louise's daughter to have an accident than in a noisy Hindu religious festival where the fanatics could go wild? 'Yes,' she said, 'I will go now and talk to Singh.' With that splendid cut-throat rascal, whose family had served hers for generations, effecting Hills' introductions to the goldsmiths then holding himself ready to relieve Hills of the booty as he left the village, with Kumar Singh dealing with Louise's daughter, she would sleep peacefully in the knowledge that the necklace would undoubtedly be returned. The problem of whether she would later give it up to the guru in order to secure her spiritual redemption was something she would deal with in due course. First, get the necklace. She took the beautiful pashmina shawl from the low table by her cot and draped it over her head.

Chapter Thirteen

The car was an old one. Though Gopal's friend had bought it only three years ago it had been old then, with the mileage turned back to a ludicrous five thousand. Jane and Gopal were silent as he manoeuvred it out of the quiet road and turned into the deserted main thoroughfare, rattling across its rutted surface in the shaft of its own golden headlights, pursuing the star silvered blackness ahead. Gopal relaxed in the driving seat. Jane rolled up the window against the cool night air and the dust. 'You're sure you know the way?'

'We're going south for a while. The quickest route is across the Punjab which is flat. We'll drive east for a hundred miles or so then turn directly north into the mountains on the Mandi road. Why don't you try to get some sleep? We have about three hours before daylight.'

Jane nodded, certain there was no way she would lose consciousness. And yet she did. The strain and excitement of the past days were now catching up on her.

She opened her eyes to a lifting of the darkness and a paling of the hazy moon. A pearled strip on some level horizon in the east widened as she watched. She opened the window to let in a breath of the chill morning. The dust curled in with it bringing that strange earth smell that was a compound of India. She yawned and stretched. 'How are you doing, Gopal?'

'I'm fine.'

They ground noisily uphill, dragging round bends sharp and steep with the rocky bank hanging precariously above, and parched scrubland falling away below. Gopal changed gear and they lurched over a rise to pelt downhill again.

She watched the pinks and reds in the sky flame slowly into a kaleidoscope of unearthly beauty. A huddle of shacks, ghostly in the early light, reeled by and Jane said nervously, 'I know we're in a panic, but do let's be sure we get there.'

He changed down with a harsh grating of metal and the engine took control. 'Sorry.'

'If you would let me take a share of the driving, perhaps we could keep going non-stop. Clive won't be able to do that unless he has two drivers, or unless he persuades his driver to let him take a turn.'

'You are a good driver, Jane? This is not an easy car for a woman to handle and you have seen the roads. They will get worse later when we get into the mountains.'

'But we must be nearly in the Punjab now. You said Punjabi roads are straight and flat. I'll take over there and you can see for yourself.'

All round them in the early light the land was taking shape. On the banks, solemn government signs. AVOID RUMOURS AND LOOSE TALK. And further on, YOU HAVE TWO THAT WILL DO. Ahead lay the plains. Bobbing noisily across a rickety wooden bridge that straddled a stony river bed, they came on to a grey stick of a road narrowing until the distance ate it up. The sun had cleared the flat horizon, a startling orange ball in a pale sky. Over in the west the moon grew opalescent.

Crops came up on either side, maize tall and strong, young barley, some wheat and sugar cane. A white fuzz of cotton on the ground. 'The road surface,' said Jane wryly. 'like the country, is startling in its inconsistencies.' Gopal agreed. The car was lurching and reeling over stones and indentations. 'Look! There's near perfect tar seal!' At eight o'clock they turned aside to drive into a bus station for breakfast, Gopal blasting his horn at buffaloes and donkeys that wandered haphazardly among the vehicles. 'Thank heaven for a stretch,' said Jane slapping the dust from her clothes, stretching cramped limbs. 'That's a very respectable looking café.' It was serving hard-boiled eggs, chapattis and coffee.

'Even yoghourt,' said Gopal, looking in at the window

with interest and pleasure, 'but I wouldn't recommend it to an English stomach.'

'I'm going to walk while I eat,' Jane said when she had made her few purchases. She toured the yard, glad of the exercise. She threw a piece of chapatti to a crow perched on the cab of a Tata Diesel truck and another piece to another crow hopping round energetically on the rump of a buffalo. 'Look, Gopal,' she exclaimed delightedly as he came up beside her, 'there's an old man in striped pyjamas milking a cow wedged between that taxi and the camel! Can you see him?'

But to Gopal it was not a novel sight. 'Come on. Let's go.'

She hurried back to the café calling, 'I want to buy some fruit for later on.'

By the time she ran back to the car the Brahmin already had the engine going but he moved without demur to the passenger seat, sitting ramrod straight, his shoulders tense.

'Relax,' Jane said cheerfully. 'There are some things women can do even better than men.'

'Yes, it may be,' he replied hunching his shoulders worriedly. 'Like cooking and sewing and having babies. But I do not think driving is in the same category.'

'What a chauvinistic pig you are.'

'You cannot call a Hindu a pig. It is not nice,' but he smiled all the same, airing his cosmopolitan side. Gradually, as he assessed her ability to handle the car he relaxed, leaned back against the seat and actually fell asleep.

For most of the morning they dashed through the plains along a dusty road, like velvet ribbon frilled at the edges. One straggling village followed another. They jostled for priority with Public Carrier trucks flaunting their floral tailboards and their painted goddesses; galumphing camels; meandering cyclists; dreamy buffaloes in shafts driven by gorgeously turbanned and immaculately dressed Sikhs. Soon the mountains began to show through the heat haze ahead and they turned north into the foothills. They stopped to eat their fruit lunch beneath the shade of mahua trees where flocks of mynahs gathered among the blossoms and the sweet fragrance of the neem and acacia lay lightly on the air. Beside them stood a hoarding supporting a picture of Indira Ghandi heavily defaced with flung paint. Opposite, the late Mahatma smiled down on them, his poster decorated with a necklace of marigolds. Gopal had brought a canvas bag, a *chagal* he called it, full of boiled water. They drank thirstily at every stop for the rushing air was dry as the dust in it. All afternoon they followed a rising road that wound in and out of low, scrub covered hills.

'We're coming into a small town now,' Gopal said. 'Do we stop here for the night? There's bound to be an hotel of sorts, if you don't mind roughing it.'

'I don't want to stop. Please, Gopal, let's keep going. I know you haven't had much sleep, but I can drive in the dark.'

Gopal was doubtful. 'The roads can be excessively bad. And there are often landslides.'

'All right, if we come to a landslide we'll be stuck. I accept that.'

He said with genuine and touching respect. 'You are a very courageous lady, Jane.'

'That's nice of you. I'm really rather a desperate one.'

They stopped at a *chaikhana*, a ramshackle lean-to on the outskirts of the town and ate a goat pilau at a small wooden table by the roadside. The light was fading, the air growing cool. The Indians in their loose garments of grey homespun sat in a circle of light made by a petromax while black kettles simmered over charcoal braziers and huge iron pots bubbled with curry stews. Panniered donkeys tripped daintily by, ushered by small ragged boys. Heavily burdened camels waited disdainfully near by and the air was full of the smell of burning cow dung.

'D'you think I'll survive this?' she asked, forking

doubtfully through the pilau. 'Always boil water', they said, but there was more to India than boiled water. Jane's cousin Helen had gone down with dysentery. 'Heaven alone knows what I'll get from this,' she said, grimacing. But there were inner demands to eat.

They left the town with the sun sinking towards the western horizon, flaring among those strange earthy purples, pinks and golds. Ahead lay the mountains where a peak could grasp it early and flood the valleys in a startling moment with night. The road rose, slowly at first, then more and more steeply until they were brought to a snail's pace, grinding round hairpin bends with the headlights gilding high, tree-browed banks and a black cavern of nothingness below. Hour after hour they climbed, leaving the heat with civilization far below, talking only desultorily, their minds numbed by the engine's clamorous trumpeting and the sameness of the turns.

At midnight they stopped on a strip of near-level road and walked up and down, stretching their legs and arms and backs, breathing deeply of the pine scented air.

Somewhere in the distance far below they could hear the rowdy fracas of water over rocks. 'I wish I could see.' The moon was high but it was not bright enough to show more than the road.

'You'll see it all in the morning.' Gopal stifled a yawn. 'Jane, I think we must have a rest,' he said wearily. 'We've been driving for nearly a whole day and night and we're now on a really dangerous road. It is not good to tackle this very steep road when we are so jaded.'

Jane bit back a protest. Living on her nerves, holding the tiredness on another plane, she knew in her heart that her reactions were no longer good. Even arguing with Gopal back at the last town she had known she was not being reasonable, but her commonsense was suffocated by the overwhelming weight of Ashley's danger. 'All right.' They moved the car in to the bank. The temperature had dropped alarmingly. They took their packs out of the boot and slid into sleeping bags, then locked the doors. Gopal stretched out, as far as his long frame would allow, on the back seat. Jane on the front. The night was silent except for the sound of the torrent far below.

They wakened to a bombardment of bird song, a shrill fanfare that rose to a startling crescendo falling on the ear like a wild, open air orchestra. The hillside faced north and though the sun was not yet up there was light in the sky. Above them the bushes quivered and jumped with the morning ecstasy of a hundred tiny birds.

Gopal said, 'One doesn't need an alarm clock. You see, we were both very, very tired. It was wise to stop,' and Jane, yawning and stretching out of her cramped sleeping position, had to agree. It was sharply cold here in the trees. A faint mist hovered at tree top height giving the pines an unearthly, silver-marbled look. They had climbed a long way in the hours before giving up and now they looked out on ridge after ridge of forested hilltops striped whitely by the cloud-filled valleys between.

Jane said, awe-struck, 'I never knew there was so much space in the world. Louise said India made her feel small and humble. I know what she means, now.' And it was frightening, too, all this space. A man and his enemies could move a long way from the law. 'Let's get moving, I'll feed you some fruit, if you want to drive.' They climbed higher. As the sun rose, their car was crawling like a noisy ant in a vast perpendicular world, round interminable bends that multiplied as carelessly as the Indians themselves, through forests of stately pines red-patched with Virginia creeper and split in the valleys by turquoise streams flying over boulders in a white mist.

Towards midday they came up on a ridge that seemed like the roof of the world. There were flattish grassy patches, tiny bungalows, occasionally little villages, their grey slab roofs silvering in the sun's rays and every now and then, startlingly, unacceptably, a roof or two of corrugated iron. 'It is very one-up to have a corrugated iron roof,' Gopal told Jane solemnly. 'You English introduced them. As you know, what is English is good.'

Jane was enjoying Gopal's company. There had not been much to laugh about during the past few days. And now that he was away from his family the English side had emerged. He was once again the Gopal she had known in London, the pale faced Brahmin with the English degree who taught school and strummed a guitar cross-legged on the floor of Helen's flat in Earl's Court. Sometimes the land would level out and there would be surprising patches of rice, barley and maize. Gopal explained everything. 'Rice grows to seven thousand feet if there's water.'

It was at the beginning of their descent that they encountered their first landslide. Two men stopped them with flags. Gopal heaved an impatient sigh. 'We must get out and shelter under that rock. They are blasting. Always blasting,' he said.

'Damn.' Jane climbed out, stretched, jogged up and down for a moment then went to crouch with Gopal beneath an enormous overhanging rock.

'Cross your fingers,' Gopal said. 'These hills crumble so easily, the explosion is quite likely to block the road.' And it did. After the echoing boom of the dynamite, there was a fall of earth and stones. Indians were erupting from everywhere. Spindle shanked old men in their dhotis, young women in bright nylon saris with small children in their arms, young men carrying shovels. They all stood gazing in big-eyed silence at the spectacle of an English girl in tight blue jeans.

'Get back into the car, please,' Gopal implored her. 'They'll never clear it while you stand there.' They were away in half an hour, for what the roadgang lacked in speed and strength they made up in numbers. The women held a rope attached to a shovel. Men dug it into the dry crumbled earth and stones. 'Are they so weak they can't use a shovel alone?' Jane asked, appalled.

Gopal said sadly, 'You will understand, then, Clive's attitude. Many of my people have never had a square meal.'

They stopped for lunch at a little village where they bought curried potatoes with sliced onion and green chillies, served direct from black bubbling pots. They ate it standing because they had been sitting too long. 'Don't eat the chillies. They'll turn your English tongue into a flame.'

'Whew! Just in time. My mind was miles away.' She had been thinking of Clive and what he wanted to do to help India's plight, thinking of it despairingly because even a hospital seemed like a mere drop now in the bucket of India's need. Around the little *chaikhana*, lovely, soft-eyed women squatted in the dust spinning wool, flicking away the flies as they watched Gopal and Jane. Around them again were small children, dressed in rags, patiently accepting the flies that clung to their beautiful little brown faces. It was hard to believe that the Rajah of Kodapur could want to take a fortune in jewels out of this sad country so that he might live like a king.

After lunch the land grew wilder and more steep. Jane found herself clinging to her seat, eyes closed in cowardly resignation as they crept along narrow ledges where landslides had been only partially cleared and where a raging torrent spun through the rocks a thousand feet below. 'My God!' she exclaimed once, but only once. India showed one clearly how humans could survive.

They came into the valley on a junction of snow fed rivers and turned north. It was a relief to be on flat ground again. The road wound along by the side of the water with green-grey mountains towering on either side. The sky was cloudless, the air cool. Apple orchards bordered the wide, evenly surfaced road. 'Some of them,' said Gopal mischievously, 'are owned by your old Colonels who married their cowgirls.'

'Cowgirls?' Jane gazed around her at the tranquil beauty of the green pastures that came as a shock after the wild mountains. Buffaloes meandered dreamily along the roadside pursued effortlessly by men in embroidered velveteen caps.

'Some wives took the children home to be educated and couldn't face returning,' Gopal said.

The men always liked India more than the women, Jane knew.

They stopped at a busy little town where they bought more fruit and drank nimbu pani ice cold. There was an Ambassadore car in the single street. Jane grasped Gopal's arm. 'Look! Look, Gopal! Outside that stall selling sweat-meats. There's the driver. The one eating something that looks like fudge.' But Clive was not in evidence and the car was facing the wrong way.

'I'll go and see what I can find out.' Adopting a nonchalant pose, Gopal strolled towards the vehicle. Jane went back to their car. Five minutes later the Brahmin returned, his fingers sticky with fudge. He was wearing an exultant expression. The air around him was dancing with flies.

'Clive is at the headman's house in Taksit. He's waiting for his ponyman.' Gopal added solemnly, 'It seems an Englishman called Hills gave a message that Clive did not require him, after all, and the ponyman left. Clive's bad luck is our good luck.'

He jumped in, started the car and they sped along the valley.

Now that they were actually catching up with Clive Jane grew silently apprehensive. 'He'll be furious,' she said once.

'It's true, he will be furious,' Gopal conceded, 'but you knew that before you started out.'

The little village of Taksit lay at the head of the valley. Gopal parked the car in the stony street that any self-respecting vehicle would hesitate to enter. The day had been calm, the sky clear but now a dark cloud had begun to move across and the wind made vicious swipes at the loose surface of the road, filling the air with dusty grit that tasted unpleasantly of goats. Shielding his eyes with one hand from the flying particles, Gopal spoke in Hindi to a man leaning against the corner of a building. He was wearing a homespun wool jerkin with a goat hair rope belt, pantaloons and one of those flat, round caps she had seen before trimmed with green velveteen. Their arrival had already been broadcast. Indians were coming from everywhere. The man led them off into a rutted stony lane, a retinue of half the village following behind.

The headman lived in a large, square house in the centre. They found him sitting cross-legged on a sheltered veranda with a small set of scales before him, meticulously weighing out some lentils against a quantity of rice one of his people had brought for barter. The usual crowd of men, women and children lounged against veranda posts, squatted in the street, or merely stood serenely looking on, swatting flies. A sweeper was indolently and uselessly using a whisk broom among the feet of the uncaring crowd. The headman saw them and rose. Their guide introduced them and he shook hands with great courtesy. 'Your friend is here,' he said in reply to their query. 'Please come into my house.'

Jane cast an apprehensive look at Gopal who smiled reassuringly. 'Play it by ear,' he said with that bright-eyed air of confidence he always adopted when producing an English colloquialism. 'Take off your shoes, now.'

'My shoes? Why?' Anything to hold him up, to put off the moment of meeting Clive.

'It's the custom where the streets are also public lavatories.'

'Ugh.'

They slipped their shoes off on the veranda and followed the headman into the house.

Chapter Fourteen

The sweet serenity of the kohl-eyed girl, barefooted in her silver trimmed, sky blue sari did nothing to quell the nervy impatience in Clive. Damn and blast that ponyman for disappearing. He'd give him half an hour and then he'd go and hire another porter and see if they could carry the food and utensils between them. They would do without a tent. If they didn't find resthouses at appropriate stopping places they'd sleep by a campfire. So long as they could cross the pass about midday, they ought to be able to spend the two nights no higher than seven thousand feet. At that height, at this time of year, they would not encounter snow and ice. And food was not so very important, he told himself firmly. The packaged soups were light, as was the dried mince. With that, and the chocolate sent from London they should be all right. He knew he could not rely on replenishing rations at Tirand. By the time the village had fed all the visitors their storerooms were likely to be bare, but he would worry about that later. For the moment, it was only important to get away.

'You are worried,' said the girl. Her Indian voice was soft and soothing. She put the teapot down and smiled shyly at him.

'Yes,' he admitted. 'I am worried. Who's to say the pony-man will be willing to return here? Or he may even have been re-hired by someone else. Time's running out, and it's not as though I can't manage this walk without horses. It's only a matter of paring everything down to a bare minimum.' He leaned back on the blanketed couch, staring round the bare little room with its board floor, its wooden chairs and tiny iron grate, not seeing anything, only feeding his premonition of alarm about Jane; his conscience.

'If the weather stays fine, you could manage,' the girl was saying, 'and at this time of year it ought to, but you cannot count on it. The mountains are always treacherous. Always.'

Clive looked at his watch. It was half past three. He was determined to get in three hours of walking before dark, or rather three hours of walking tonight, regardless of light. He had to. He'd just finish his tea, then go and see the porter.

The door opened. 'Your friends have arrived,' said Mela Ram. 'Siliya, please to get our guests some more tea.' The girl looked at the new arrivals with carefully concealed surprise and made *namaste* with a demure little bow. The doctor had not said he expected friends.

In that first moment of confrontation Clive simply did not believe what he saw. He blinked, but the apparition with the wind blown, dusty hair refused to go away.

'We thought we'd surprise you,' Jane said nervously, looking at the small rush mat that was the only floor covering. Not looking at Clive.

Mela Ram was no fool. He said, 'I have something I wish to do. Excuse please.' Siliya's soft glance stole away from the English girl's tightly fitting, boyish clothes that she found faintly obscene. 'Come, daughter,' her father said.

Clive got his breath. But it was not just his breath he needed. He needed to overcome his ridiculous emotional relief that this idiotic girl was not, after all, exposed to God-knew-what in Kodapur. He needed to gather up his anger at her being here. The warring uncertainties fused, giving him the front he needed. 'For sheer audacity, you take first prize.'

Gopal said earnestly, 'Of course Jane does not want Ashley to have the jewels.'

'Of course,' agreed Clive. He made a vicious swipe at the flies that hovered around his forehead. 'Totally apart from the unacceptability of the main issue, I don't propose to lumber myself with a girl.' And this girl in particular, with her candy coloured hair falling over her shoulders, her golden skin, her feminine-boy's way of standing with one curved hip stuck out and chin high. She was the most determined looking, the most courageous looking girl he had ever seen. He quelled the near-panic that was rising in him, told himself to be pitiless, obdurate, unyielding; to at all costs keep his head. 'I gave myself a deadline,' he said brusquely. He looked at his watch. 'It's arrived. I've two days' walk ahead of me and there's no time to waste. My porter is ready. I'm going on. You're welcome to my pack train, if it turns up.'

Gopal said, 'It is foolish, Clive. To walk all that way, without help, I mean.'

'Foolish for Jane, and perhaps even for you,' he retorted, his voice tight, cold. He turned, tight lipped, and started for the door. His going released something beyond Jane's control. 'Are you crazy? Have you lost all commonsense? You can't walk over those mountains – call them foothills if you like but they're mountains to you and me – with an inadequate supply of food and cover. You're not a hillman. You're a – a – You're a—'

'What?' asked Clive, turning round slowly. They stared at each other, two hostile faces with eyes blazing. 'All right. Finish it. Get it off your chest.'

'You're a blind, uncompromising, stiff-necked, bloody-minded—'

There was a long, shuddering silence. Then Clive heaved a great sigh. 'Perhaps you're right,' he said, his voice quiet, reasonable, calm. 'Okay. So long as you understand I am prepared to do anything, anything at all,' he repeated, 'to get my hands on those jewels – so long as you understand that – you can come along with me. But don't expect any help. I have a job to do, and if you get in the way, that's going to be just your bad luck.'

'Well!' said Gopal amiably, 'that seems to have brought everything out into the open, in a nutshell, so to speak. Shall we compare notes and make certain we've got enough food between us? I assumed you had the campfire utensils so I brought only one small pot. But for cooking, some rice, and dahl, and a bit of flour for chapattis.'

It was then, and with horrifying suddenness that the rain began to fall. It came down in torrents and it lasted for a full half hour. The streets, that were undrained except for meandering channels criss-crossing from house to house, became within minutes a raging, fetid flood. Children stood out in the downpour, delightedly rubbing the water through their hair. The adults stood in doorways or on covered verandas to watch, laughing and shouting as tins and plastic bottles hurtled by on the crazy brown stream. Then, as suddenly as it had begun, it stopped.

'It will not rain again today,' Mela Ram told them. 'The air is clear. It will be a good start.' And indeed the air had been washed and smelled good. Lama Chand, the ponyman, came trudging up the village street with his little string of ponies. He was thin as a rake, his clothes hanging raggedly on his narrow frame. On his head he wore a bright red wool cap but that was the only brightness of him. If he was, in the Hindu tradition, expiating heinous crimes of the soul, then he was doing it tiredly, with resentment and ill will. Tsring, the tough, nuggety little porter had been squatting on his haunches in front of the headman's veranda fingering his prayer beads and chanting mantras under his breath. He jumped up, his flat face split into a broad smile; a piratical teddy bear of a man with blackcurrant eyes, short legs and the strength of an ape. Within ten minutes the packs were loaded into sacks, as protection against the trees and rocks on steep inclines, the porter said. Then they were pushed down into panniers and hooked to the pack saddles. Too late, Jane realized her waterproof had gone, but it was obvious there was no getting it back before they reached the first camp.

'Tsring is a good man,' Mela Ram told them. 'Half Tibetan and very tough. He speaks good English too. He has trekked and climbed with many, many English people. You are all right now?' He spoke to Clive with smiling concern. 'You are in agreement?'

Clive shrugged. He was not ready yet to admit to the mixed sensations within. At least while this idiotic girl was with him she was not doing anything behind his back. And she was going to get one almighty shock when she saw what she was in for. He turned, involuntarily, and met her apprehensive eyes as blue as a mountain flower, saw the hope flaring with his brief attention. He said gruffly, 'Thank you very much for fixing things up, Mela Ram. I'm more than grateful. Yes, everything's going to be all right.'

'It was nothing. You were wise to wait for the ponies.' An old man squatting on the edge of the headman's veranda smoking a hubble-bubble took a moment's respite to spit. Mela Ram moved smartly to avoid it and the spittle swung away on the gutter water to disappear from sight.

They set off at a fast pace up the winding track above the village, the pony bells tinkling prettily. The ground was slippery after the rain but you could not have everything. The fine dust that puffed up unpleasantly into English noses, was more of a hazard. Tsring, still chanting his mantras, a heavy rucksack on his back, ice-axe in hand, led them up a steep incline that cut through the zigzag track the horses had to follow.

Clive had seen Jane's startled eyes as they lit on the ice-axe. He said, resolutely keeping up the uncompromising attitude he was determined to hold, 'It's not a stroll down Bond Street, you know.'

Tsring heard and turned to her with a broad smile. 'Axe break fences, Memsahib. Not ice. Not ice, now, Memsahib.'

Within an hour the sun was moving a little too close to the mountain-tops, the valley, already filling up with the neutral gloom that serves the hills as a sort of early twilight. Pausing for a rest they could see the village clinging like brown fungus to the base of the hill below.

'We're not going to make the forest resthouse,' said Clive,

'but there's a stream, Tsring says, where the animals can be watered and where we'll have to get to, so don't let's waste any time.'

'What's a resthouse?'

'Two or three rooms, sometimes with a bathroom of sorts, and a veranda. Travellers can stay there as they pass through. They were initially built for foresters.'

'And do we get food there?' She had not thought much about food. Now, with the great empty mountains looming ahead, their first goal achieved, she felt a little tremor of apprehension as new priorities took over.

'No. There's a chap called a *chowkidah* who looks after the building but he provides only blankets. Travellers in India carry their own food and utensils. Don't let me raise your hopes,' he said. 'I'd have made it if Lama Chand hadn't gone off, but we're not going to make it now.'

'I expected to sleep out,' she assured him hurriedly. 'I wasn't expecting any sort of comfort.' The food they had brought seemed to her bare minimum but Gopal had insisted it would suffice. The ponies were coming up the zigzag behind them. Jane's legs were already aching, her breath coming short. She turned back to take the zigzag. Hurrying along the narrow track, she realized with surprise that Clive had fallen in behind her.

'We're getting high,' he said, excusing her, it seemed, and she flashed him a surprised, grateful little smile. The great hills westward were already squeezing sunset colours from the sun and the air was growing cold. Jane's woollen jumper was tied round her waist. She undid it and put it on. Considering what a comparatively short distance they had come from the village, the country was surprisingly wild, with an air of remote emptiness. The mountains swept in great desolate arcs, peak upon peak with ridges sliding away boldly until they drowned themselves in the half light of the valleys. Behind the walkers now the desiccated Lama Chand trudged without hope, by the look of him, for even the relief of death. 'He's ill,' Jane said compassionately, speaking half to herself and Clive replied, 'His kind have probably always been fractionally ill. Bred from a half starved mother, given too little care with never enough food, and since earning his living this way, never having enough shelter.' Tsring, the tough little Tibetan was an obvious asset. So wiry. So cheerful.

A ragged, freezing wind caught them as they came round corners, then crept away to gather its strength for the next ridge. Nobody talked for the following hour, except when Clive said, 'The village was three thousand feet high. The stream, if we can make it, is at six thousand. It's a big jump from sea level.' Jane already knew. The air seemed too thin to fill up her lungs and her feet were dragging, oddly weightless as though her muscles were not co-ordinating properly. She thrust into the back of her mind the frightening knowledge that the pass was another five thousand feet higher. There were primroses here and viburnum, the pink Himalayan rose, and then grey coated monkeys chattering and quarrelling in acacia trees. The track was running into woodland now, a forest of deodars, the Himalayan cedar. They caught up with the porter squatting on thin grass waiting for them, fiddling with his beads, smiling. 'Dark,' he said, holding up a torch.

They followed him through the enveloping cedars, walking in single file. It was creepy, coming like that into sudden darkness, sliding on smooth round stones they could not see, losing balance, scraping their hands on the prickly plants that grew beside the track. For twenty minutes that seemed like an hour they followed the eerie, golden pool of light ahead and then the trees thinned out and there was a sort of daylight in front. Tsring switched off the torch. The track ran straight here with grass on either side. There was no longer anything to be seen, for night was coming down on the mountain. Sensing their apprehension, Tsring announced cheerfully with a flash of his small, white teeth, 'Is not far. One hour.' The pack ponies and the sad ponyman had long since fallen behind but once or twice when they stopped for a rest they could hear the faint tinkle of bells.

By the time they came to the little stream Jane was lurching, at the limit of her endurance, exhausted by the shock of the vast mountain, the load of darkness weighing down on them, and the long, hard climb. The men began collecting wood and pine cones for a fire. She dropped down on to the cold grass in a coma of fatigue, stretched her limbs, and the next moment, it seemed, there was a touch on her shoulder.

'It's not a good place to sleep,' said Clive. 'Tsring has the meal almost cooked and here's some soup.' He held out a metal tumbler.

Jane sat up stiffly, shivering. Someone had spread a sleeping bag over her but the cold from the ground had crept into her back. 'Help! I must have gone out like a light.' There were three or four flies on her face, light, gutless little creatures sleepy with cold. She brushed them aside and they rolled indolently down her chest.

'It was not a very good idea in the circumstances to fall asleep, but we hadn't the heart to wake you. This will thaw you out,' said Clive kindly.

Twenty feet away a fire crackled and blazed. She gulped the soup down. The metal container burned her hands and the soup burned her throat but with senses numbed by exhaustion she only half cared. 'That's marvellous. Thank you so much. Have you had some?'

'I'm about to get it.' He went back to the fire. Tsring had put up the two tiny tents and in the firelight Jane could see her pack in the entrance to one of them. Clive came back. 'Gopal's going to share my tent,' he said.

She smiled. 'How nice of you. Though my honour is already besmirched. We slept in the car last night.'

'Let's not besmirch it further,' he returned casually. 'And by the way, there are bears round here. I've just sent one away. Shall I tell you how to catch and kill a bear?'

'You're not serious.' She couldn't see his face, shadowed as it was against the firelight. She wished she had not said that. She had declared herself ready for anything.

'Killing a bear is a very serious matter.'

'Then tell me. The knowledge may bolster up my courage since I am to sleep in that tent alone.'

'Come in with us if you'd like to,' Clive offered with a kindly leer. 'Three's a crowd, but it's warm in a crowd.'

She laughed, and he laughed too. Involuntarily, she reached out and gripped his fingers. It was a peace pact, of sorts.

'You were going to tell me how to catch and kill a bear.'

'Oh yes,' he said. 'Here's the recipe. Take a stout bamboo stick. Sharpen the end. Every bear has a white patch over his heart. When he runs at you, pierce the white patch with the sharp point of your bamboo stick, while holding on tightly to your end. The bear is a fool. He thinks he has you on the end of his stick, so he pulls the stick into his heart in order to bring you nearer. By the time he reaches you, he's dead.'

Jane laughed weakly, delightedly. So long as they didn't talk about Ashley, she thought, it might be all right. There was no way they could talk about Ashley and remain friends. Tsring had the meal ready. The rice and dahl was basic Indian survival diet. The dried mince was extra. They were hungry enough to eat anything and too tired to notice how it tasted. Tsring, whistling cheerfully between his teeth, washed the tin plates in the stream, built up the fire into a wonderful, aromatic blaze and rolling himself into a grubby grey blanket, settled down to sleep just out of reach of the flames. Lama Chand, having hobbled the ponies, did likewise.

The two men and the girl disappeared into their tents. Nobody saw the lone Sikh two hundred yards down wind, nor heard him as, tucking his short, curved sword carefully beneath him, he wrapped himself from turbanned head to booted foot in his homespun cloak and settled under the enveloping umbrella of a rhododendron tree.

Chapter Fifteen

The sun came up at five. Tsring beat it by ten minutes with his cheery call of 'Bed tea, Sahibs. Bed tea, Memsahib.' Jane wakened to a view of the little, flat featured porter's profile in the tent doorway as he waited with polished decorum, eyes averted, for her to collect his unsolicited, good natured offering. Clive and Gopal, snug in quilted anoraks, took the tents down while Tsring, crouching over the fire, by turns chanting his mantras and whistling tunelessly between his teeth, cooked them a thick grainy porridge in a pot that did not bear close scrutiny. 'It's good clean mountain dirt,' Clive told them with a grin as he distributed chocolate flaked with a pocket knife in place of sugar. There was no milk. Later, Tsring told them, when they came to the leopard country over the other side of the pass, there would be high altitude shepherds called *gujjars* who kept buffaloes, and they would be able to buy some milk.

Leopard country! Jane glanced up sharply but Clive and Gopal ostentatiously avoided her eyes. A little way off two black crows jigged on the ground, watching balefully. Jane remembering the aggressive, threatening creatures that had accompanied her to the Behera house, shivered and hugged the fleecy lined anorak Dolly from Surbiton had so kindly loaned her at the Ashram.

Gopal saw. 'Someone walking over your grave?'

'Perhaps.'

They made an extraordinarily fast get-away. Lama Chand, held up by paroxysms of coughing, and hawking loudly, managed to pack the gear on the horses in double quick time. Travelling North east with the sun coming up behind the mountain, the sunrise was hidden from them but there was light enough to see. The track wriggled on and up, sometimes achingly steep, sometimes in flattish zigzags. They glimpsed a brown bear but he saw them first and scuttled drunkenly away on short legs. There were harsh screams from peacocks, and a little later as the sun gradually spread the mountain out to view they saw the elegant, strutting creatures with the light glinting on their blue feathers. One or two golden orioles scampered into the weeping pines. They had left the stately deodars far behind, indeed left much of the ragged undergrowth and before long all the insects, and that, thankfully, meant the flies. It was a relief to be without flies. The forest was strangely, eerily silent.

This morning Jane found the climbing increasingly difficult and by ten o'clock she knew, with rising panic, that she could not go on. She had removed her jacket for the sun burned fiercely through the thin air. Tsring had said they were at eight thousand feet and they were still climbing. No matter how deeply she breathed, the air seemed to stop short at her throat, as though refusing to enter her lungs. And her legs had gone curiously, inexplicably light, so light they seemed to have detached themselves from communication with her suddenly weighty body. Clive and Gopal had noticed. It was in their anxious expressions as they cast surreptitious glances behind. To Clive, the implications of Jane's being affected by the altitude were unacceptable. It was a new challenge to harden his heart. Tsring came up with the answer. He ran ahead calling out to Lama Chand and caught the one pony that was not supporting a pack. He had a rough saddle of sorts. The ponyman arrested the leader. 'You will ride horse,' Tsring said to Jane, his dark face creased up with consideration and an eagerness to please. 'Too high for Memsahib.'

Jane nodded. She was too giddy, exhausted and apprehensive, to talk. She placed a foot on a convenient mounting stone then waited, idiotically disorientated because she had lost the ability to lever her body after it.

Tsring, with admirable lack of restraint, gave her bottom an energetic push and she swung up on to the tiny pony's back.

'Oh, what a relief!' And it was a relief to the others. They smiled at her. The pony had no bridle. The porter told her it did not need one. No one could make a pack pony obey. The leader went in front, the others followed nose-to-tail and there was nothing a rider could do to change it.

'Pony down *khud*, jump off quick, Memsahib.'

'*Khud?*'

'Down there,' said Clive, pointing. 'If he takes fright, he's liable to head down the *khud*, into the valley.'

'Oh thanks!' Now, with the weight off her impossible, traitorous legs, Jane could laugh again. It was not easy to readjust to these little flashes of kindness when something inside that hard crust Clive wore made warm little forays towards her. Then it would retreat to keep faith with the main part of him that did not want her here.

Now, the track was scarcely more than a footprint wide. The *khud* fell away, not sheer but very steep for hundreds of feet. Jane gazed with renewed wonder back into the valley they had left the afternoon before, then over the alternate bars of rolling ridges and matted patches of forest that ran interminably in every direction, a vast, silent emptiness, awe inspiring in its limitless expanse. She had never felt tiny like this. Pinhead sized. Vulnerable. A vulnerability that was something between fear and exaltation, as though their ant-like party lay outside the normal range of self protection, in the very womb of destiny.

Tsring said, 'Is going steep zigzag, Memsahib. Hold tight mane. Moment now.'

She looked up. Fifty yards ahead the track turned back on itself. 'Heavens! This poor horse will be on its hind legs like a begging dog and I'll need glue on my bottom to stay aboard.' She laughed about it, wanting Clive to think she was at ease, making a lighthearted adventure of that which was becoming hourly more and more a frightening ordeal. The beast turned into the foot of the zigzag and the mountainside presented itself once again to view. Out of the corner of her eye she thought she saw a movement several yards below. It was more as though she sensed, rather than saw, someone enter the outcrop of forest. 'Clive!' But he did not hear her and then the make-shift saddle began to slip as the pony dug his small feet into the hillside and hauled his muscular, vigorous little body up, battling stolidly with the steep rise. She had to cling to the mane in order to keep her seat. When she could look behind again there was no one there, but the disquiet remained. The men climbed in silence, their slow movements indicating the imperative demands they made on bodies not truly fit enough to climb up to nearly eleven thousand feet. When the track levelled out again and Jane was able to turn once more she caught her breath in shock. A tall figure in a pink turban moved between the trees. She swung back in fear.

'Gopal! There's someone following.'

Out of breath and without the strength to be dismayed, he replied mildly, 'There are always travellers in these hills. The Indian is a great traveller.'

'This man is alone.'

'That is usual.'

'He's wearing a turban. A pink turban.'

'That, too, is usual.'

'Gopal you can't have forgotten it was a Sikh in a pink coloured turban who chased me.'

'Back in Kodapur. Yes. The height is giving you flights of fancy, Jane.' He undid his haversack and, dropping it wearily beside the track, sat down looking at her quizzically while the pony snatched at tufts of grass. 'You are a beautiful girl, Jane. He has driven for two days, then climbed up to this pass for you.' Gopal's knowledge, that lay closely under the skin, of a woman's inability to fit satisfactorily into a man's world, had risen in the thin ether. Jane glared at him.

'You'll see,' Gopal told her good-naturedly. 'He'll catch us up soon. An innocent traveller going to visit his relatives.'

But the turbanned stranger did not catch up with them. They crossed a small ridge and stopped about midday at a tiny lake in a bowl of the mountain where the sun beat down on one shore and the other, in the shadow, was white with snow. It was a beautiful lake, glistening green and silver in the sun. Jane slid off her pony and walked to the rim. Clive had thrown himself down on the grass. 'Are you going to have a swim?' he asked, teasing her.

'I might if it was not full of green slime and tiny water beetles all going mad. Come and see them. They're leaping and dashing and diving at tremendous speed.'

Clive closed his eyes. 'It's all right for you. You've been riding.' Tsring waded in from the bank, filled his metal water bottle and drank deeply from it. At the sound of splashing Clive opened his eyes, meeting Jane's. 'It's all a matter of anti-bodies, isn't it? If one acquires them early, one survives.'

Jane sat down on a rock, gazing round her. 'Isn't this idyllic? Tsring says we're at ten thousand feet, now.' Under a sky of the purest blue, surrounded by brown oak, holly oak and frail bamboo, with a lone lammergeier circling overhead, Jane said, 'I think we're on top of the world.' Her eyes kept shifting to the track that came over the ridge behind them. If the man she had seen was innocent, she told herself, he should have put in an appearance by now. She knew it was no use bringing up the subject again. They would think she was being neurotic.

Gopal, having removed his shirt, stretched out on the ground, the sacred thread of his Brahmin caste lying across his chest. The sharp winged, lone lammergeier's black shadow sped across the water, circled over the snow, then came back again. 'Let's have lunch. Smoked salmon, fresh lettuce, a bottle of Chablis, say Montmeins '69,' said Clive extravagantly without opening his eyes. They all laughed.

Tsring produced some tins of fish from the depths of one of the panniers and some chapattis he had cooked that morning. They ate hungrily, Lama Chand sitting apart with his horses, coughing.

When the lone walker still made no appearance Jane's apprehension grew until she was scarcely able to take her eyes off the track. Clive saw and said, diverting her attention, 'That's a splendid horse you have there. By Dead Beat out of Follow-up.'

'I'd like to like him,' she replied, gazing broodingly at the pony, 'but there's nothing there. Nothing at all between the ears. Pack ponies, it seems, move when their owner shouts and stop when told to stop. Well, sometimes they do.'

'Mm.'

They banged unconcernedly up against trees, too, when trees grew in the way, and they trotted down slopes out of sheer inertia, as Gopal said, because they were too bone idle to put on the brakes. 'I hope I don't find myself in a situation where I need some extra speed.' Her eyes crept back again towards the approach track. Suddenly, she was rigid. Was that a movement in the bamboo? A smudge of colour in this landscape that provided only greens and browns? She said, her voice high with fright. 'There's someone over there! There *is* someone following us. *Gopal!*'

Her intense fear got through to him. His face changed. The easy smile went. The two men stood up, their eyes following hers, then in silence they walked to the little rise that overlooked the lake. They stood there for a long time, talking. Tsring gave her a puzzled look. 'There's someone following us, Tsring.'

He nodded, chewing a grass stalk, conspicuously casual. 'Oh yes. Plenty walker.'

The men came back. 'There's no one there,' said Clive.

'All right.' She was convinced in her own mind, but walking as she was a tightrope of acceptability, she dared not press the point. Someone was there, stalking her in his Judascoloured turban, with his long, curved Sikh's knife called a *kirpan* at his hip.

Gopal said, 'Come on. Let's go,' and began to step out towards the track.

'Heights do funny things to people.' Clive told her sympathetically.

'As a doctor, you would know.' With nerves snapping, Jane thrust her foot into the improvised stirrup and propelled by the force of her anger, swung herself up, flew across the pony's back and landed flat on the grass on her back.

Clive and Gopal came running. 'Are you all right?'

She lay there part winded and feeling slightly foolish. 'Lack of gravity,' Clive said grinning, then added hurriedly, 'as a climber, I know.'

'Is altitude,' Tsring explained sympathetically. 'Jump too high, Memsahib.'

The pent-up fear, the thin air, was taking its toll. Jane burst out laughing. Knowing she was being idiotic, knowing there was nothing funny about her fall, she laughed until her ribs ached. In the end, Gopal slapped her face. She was glad it was Gopal.

'Sorry,' she apologized soberly. 'I couldn't help it.'

'Is altitude,' Tsring explained once more in his kindly way. He led the pony to a low boulder from which she was able to slide one leg over his back. They walked for an hour. There was still no sign of the Sikh. 'Short-cutty,' the porter announced. 'Next rest at pass. Meet ponies at pass.'

Clive turned to Jane. 'You'll stick with the animals.'

The fear came swinging back. She knew she could not join them. They were now fifteen hundred feet higher than the level where her legs had given up.

'Sorry,' said Clive. 'We can't take the ponies because there's scarcely any track at all and the trees are too close. We'd lose the packs. But according to Tsring we can save a couple of miles between here and the pass.'

The porter shot off into the trees and with a cheery wave Clive and Gopal hurried in pursuit. Jane was alone with the sad ponyman and his plodding little string of animals. Their going brought irrational panic. Jane had never been a coward but her defences were weakened by the lack of oxygen. Cold sweat came on her forehead and the palms of her hands. The track narrowed here, running between high, delicate bamboo that brushed her arms and face like soft, thin knives. It met overhead, the thin leaves slapping at her eyes and folding themselves lingeringly across her face, parting with reluctance.

And then there came another sound. A foreign sound that had nothing to do with the scraping and crunching of the ponies' shoes on the stones. She swung round in instinctive alarm. And then the sound came again, unidentifiable, but real. A footpad, light and stealthy. And then the teasing, noisy leaves blanketed out the sound. This time she was shudderingly certain there was a man moving in on her in her little enclosure within the shifting sea of frail bamboo. She kicked into her horse's flanks but the pony, staring stonily ahead, plodded on at the same slow, even pace.

She jerked up in the saddle, screaming. 'Lama Chand! Lama Chand!'

And then that strange, quiet sound came closer. A footpad, firm, clear and recognizable now, accompanied by the knock of stone against stone. 'Lama Chand! Lama Chand!' She made to leap off, panic outweighing commonsense. Then suddenly, like a benison from heaven, the tall plants opened out and she saw Lama Chand not thirty yards in front and for one giddy, relieved moment, before the brown hand came down on her pony's rump, she was not alone any more.

Chapter Sixteen

Clive, Gopal and the little porter made the pass in less than an hour. The ponies were not there. 'Slower by path,' Tsring said reassuringly. 'Slow.' He could see now that the doctor was distinctly worried about the girl. He had sensed it earlier, at the lake. The wind was blasting round the rocks, coming off hundreds of square miles of mountain ridges covered in snow, cutting into their damp bodies, freezing the sweat. The view was magnificent but it was suicide to sit here. 'Is *chaikhana*,' said the porter, pointing. Half-hidden under a rock bank topped by some gale-bitten scrub oak stood an open fronted booth, its sagging roof of corrugated iron and dead vegetation propped up by six foot poles. Grouped in the smoky interior, squatting on small boulders and on the earth floor itself were half a dozen thin-shanked Indians wrapped in shapeless grey homespun. A fire danced merrily up through round holes in a stove-like contraption of baked clay. One of the men took a blackened pot and rubbed it conscientiously inside and out with an equally filthy rag that was lying on the dirt floor. He filled it with brown water from a bucket, threw in some buffalo milk, sugar and tea leaves. Clive, who had been watching musingly, said, 'There's plenty of body in that.' Boiled, it tasted surprisingly good.

From the shelter, looking towards Tibet, they could see Deo Tibba, Manali Peak and Indra Sen standing in a line, frosted mountains of unearthly beauty glistening against the clear blue of the empty sky. Clive put his tin mug down on the earth floor and glanced at his watch. 'Shouldn't Lama Chand be here by now?' he asked again. Tsring nodded.

Gopal had found himself a boulder that provided a certain

amount of shelter and from which he could look out over the view. As Clive came up he said dreamily, 'So wonderful. As Jane said, like the top of the world. I must bring Helen here. One day, Helen and I must come here together.'

Clive looked down at him, arms folded, his face closed. 'Your family are not very pleased about Jane being here. They don't want you to go to England.'

Gopal nodded. 'But my people are very good. Very sensible.' He added, looking cloudily through the facts, 'They want only my happiness.'

'You're sure about that?'

'Yes, I am sure.'

'She told me she got a poor reception when she went to call on you.'

'It was a shock, of course, when Jane arrived on the doorstep without warning. That was the trouble. If I had been able to tell my family that Helen's cousin was coming it would not have happened. They would have been expecting a resemblance. It was very unfortunate,' said Gopal, his black eyes large and innocent.

'Hmm!' Clive looked at his watch again, then out over the vast sunlit mountains that rolled away interminably. He was feeling increasingly strung-up, increasingly impotent.

'And perhaps it's unfortunate that your wife's a Sikh. As I understand it, they're quick fingered with their *kirpans* as well as hot on revenge.' Gopal shifted uncomfortably on the hard ground but did not reply.

Clive wished he could get out of his mind the memory of that fellow Kumar Singh who was Gopal's brother-in-law. The man who had worn a pink turban when Clive saw him at the gunsmith's. He turned back to Gopal. 'What about the Sikh chasing Jane through Kodapur? What did you make of that?'

Gopal's spirits slumped. He did not like being asked such direct and disagreeable questions. 'Jane is a very pretty girl,' he said evasively. 'Men follow.'

'I doubt very much anybody's ability to see her pretty face in an overgrown garden at that hour of night without a torch.'

'No.'

'Did Helen ever have an experience like that?'

'She had the protection of the guru, and then I took her away and looked after her.' Gopal looked up, his nice face bright, a little surprised. 'Perhaps it is not safe to walk in Kodapur at night any more. You never asked me these questions before. Why do you ask now we are not in Kodapur?'

'I thought she was in cahoots with Ashley. If she was after the jewels, and spying on me, she had to expect something like that.' He looked at his watch again, then across to where the trail broke through the trees. 'We won't hear the pony bells in this wind.' He moved from one foot to the other. Tsring glanced up, broke a twig from a bush and began to brush his teeth with it. Clive walked out to the edge of the precipice. It fell away here over a thousand feet before the hillside jutted out a little and the shale and earth became green with pale mountain grass. He came back quickly, his nerves snapping. 'Listen, Behera. Would you be prepared to say, unequivocally, there isn't a single one of your Sikh in-laws who would be mad enough to follow Jane up here, having mistaken her for her cousin Helen? After all,' his mouth moved into a stiff and humourless smile, 'Chinese are inclined to look alike to an Englishman. It's possible blonde girls all look alike to Indians.'

Gopal said miserably, 'I would not have Jane hurt for the world.'

Clive went back to the precipice. The wind cut into him like sharpened blades. Ice cold. To the left, above the pass, the cliff soared hundreds of feet towards the empty sky. A lone eagle circled, then dived, white against the rock face. Why had he left his gun in his pack? 'I'm getting my priorities muddled,' he said to himself. Nothing mattered, except that he should get the jewels. Nothing at all. Nothing.

Tsring's voice, behind him, broke into his thoughts. 'Indra Sen is holy mountain. No one climb. Is for gods.'

'You mean, the gods are pacified about people climbing the other two if you keep off Indra Sen?' Clive wished his own life could be driven into black and white compartments like that. He looked at his watch again, then swore violently under his breath as his resolution snapped. 'I'm going to meet the ponies. We'll never get there if we don't chivvy them along.'

He had fierce eyebrows, strange, blazing black eyes and a cruel mouth. He was very tall and he walked very straight, head high, proudly, and with cold arrogance like a man who knew what he was about. He wore a hillman's outfit of grey homespun blouse and dirty white pantaloons that looked incongruous with his beautiful pink turban and climbing boots. He carried a thick, knotted walking stock and his *kirpan*, the long, sheathed knife, shuddered from his waist as he walked. He was close beside Jane now, his body touching the flank of the horse. He kept looking into her face, or rather her profile, as she stared directly ahead, stiff with horror, like a cat being tormented by a mouse. She had called out to the ponyman a dozen times but he had taken no notice. And her useless imbecile of a pony would not step out of line.

Lama Chand was tired and weakened by his continual cough. He knew what the man was about but it was not his responsibility to interfere. Even if it were, what could he do against one of those murdering Sikhs? He knew Sikhs. His cousin Boota had married one. They used their *kirpans* first and asked questions afterwards, if they asked them at all. Poor Boota never dared treat his wife as a Moslem wife should be treated. She ran his cousin's household, actually ran it herself, scolding and screeching and telling Boota what to do instead of getting on with the work herself. She rode the family donkey and made him walk carrying the load so that all the neighbours laughed at him. And Boota, scared half to death of his wife's brothers who would strike off the head of a chicken without even a mutter of prayer, had to put up with it in case they struck his head off with their sharp swords. That one back there now, so the ponyman had heard in the village of Taksit, had followed the Brahmin and the girl all the way from Kodapur. He was not going to be put off by a consumptive Moslem half his size.

'Lama Chand! Lama Chand!' The girl was terrified, he could hear it in her voice and he felt sorry for her but he kept doggedly on, eyes front. He'd have blood all over his packs, that was certain. They prided themselves on taking the head off in one slice.

'Lama Chand! Lama Chand!' Jane's voice was indeed shrill with terror. The Sikh was enjoying himself, looking up pitilessly into her face, walking so closely beside her now that her long leg rubbed against his body. He was the man who had chased her under the bridge in Kodapur, she was convinced, and no doubt pursued her through the Rajah's garden. She tried to question him, but he only muttered something in Hindi that she could not understand.

The track moved on and up the bare slope, on and up. Out in front now there was another patch of bamboo and oak, not more than two hundred yards ahead. Oh God! It was going to happen there! That was what he was waiting for. For the sheltering leaves. She could hear his fast, shallow, excited breathing, see the flash of his brilliant eyes.

'Lama Chand!' The name was a scream on the air, but still the ponyman ignored her. Without looking, Jane saw the brown hand move to the man's waist, slide to the hilt of his sword. Black terror caught her in its grip. She was going to die. She was going to die the moment they entered the treacherous cover of that greenery in front. And they were coming inexorably nearer. Mesmerized, she watched them come, in slow motion, while the Sikh, without taking his black eyes from her face, drew his weapon slowly, slowly from its sheath.

In a mindless frenzy of terror, knowing there was nowhere to run, Jane sprang off the pony's back and this time she was not screaming for uncaring Lama Chand. 'Clive! Clive! Clive!' Knocked faintly off balance by her wild leap, the pony tripped on a branch of withered scrub and a little avalanche of dirt and stones broke away from the track, spinning down the *khud* with her as she slithered helplessly, gathering speed, hurtling towards the valley thousands of feet below.

Perhaps because the chill wind blew that way carrying the sound, perhaps because the gods were watching, Jane's last frantic scream penetrated the thin forest. Clive was already running. He raced down the track bouncing off tree-trunks, sliding off stones, regaining his balance and hurling himself forward again; leaping down banks to cut off an S bend, lurching, scraping his hands on rough branches, tearing his clothes. Sunlight, and the open hillside. The ponies, and the thin, ragged ponyman standing bleakly in the track.

'Where's the girl?' he shouted but the words had scarcely been caught from his lips by the wind when he saw the Indian in the pink turban moving with light, animal leaps down the hillside. And the ponyman, wrenched from his torpor, was pointing. Clive was off the track in a flash, hurtling after the man, sliding, running, somehow keeping upright. He fell, rolled over twice and flung himself erect by the sheer force of his desperation. On he went, bouncing and leaping, too fast to stop. He'd hit the bottom! Break a leg. The knowledge was in his mind along with the fury, but fury was uppermost.

The Sikh heard him and swung round but it was too late to get out of his way. The two men collided with a force that should have knocked them both senseless. They sprawled separately head first down a bank where the grass had fallen away in one of the many miniature landslides.

Clive hit something soft, and then something hard and came to an abrupt stop. He pulled himself upright, head reeling. He was caught in a track that had been shelled out by some sweeping winter torrent cutting deep into the light earth. It had left a curious little raised ledge wide enough to catch a falling body and strong enough to support it. He pulled himself dazedly to his feet. Jane was just above him, the Sikh a little to the left. The Sikh stood erect. Jane saw him, only him, and fainted. Clive rushed to her, lifting her tenderly, pushing her head down between her knees.

'What the bloody hell are you up to?' he raged at the Sikh. The beautiful turban had fallen apart. It swung snake-like from Kumar Singh's shoulders. His thick black hair and long beard, twisted together and emerging in a topknot on his head, gave him a strange, womanish look that went ill with his fierce, masculine and surprisingly young face.

'She fell off the horse,' the Indian whined. 'I help. I help, Sahib.'

'Like hell you helped!' There was a rattle of stones, a scitter of earth and they both looked up to see the little Tibetan porter sliding down the *khud* towards them with Clive's gun in his hand. The Sikh was busily rewinding his long scarf into a turban. Clive grabbed the gun and cocked it. 'Now get the hell out of here before I'm tempted to blast your brains out.' Beside himself with rage and the aftermath of fright, he loosed the safety catch. Tsring rattled out something in Hindi and the Sikh, galvanized into anger, hurled an insult in return.

Jane was coming round. Clive handed the gun to the porter, lifted Jane gently, supporting her against his body. He heard the Sikh slinking away and changed his mind. 'Stop him,' Clive rapped out. 'I want a word with him.' Tsring pointed the gun, snarling some words in Hindi. The man hesitated. Tsring spat another order and the Sikh turned.

'Who sent you?' Clive demanded.

'No one. I go to join my uncle at Tarand. I go to Bhunda, Sahib.'

'Who told you to follow us?'

'I don't know track, Sahib. I never go Tarand. I follow Sahib for track. Just for track. Girl fall off horse. I save her.'

Jane sat up slowly. Clive looked down at her with pity and anguish. 'What happened?'

She said faintly, 'He was going to kill me. I jumped off because he was going to kill me.'

The Sikh, who was listening with wide, shocked eyes shook his head vehemently. 'No! I use horse to help me walk, Sahib. Very steep hill. Useful tail of pony, is it not?'

'I screamed and screamed. Lama Chand wouldn't take any notice. He knew what was going on.' Clive put an arm round her to still the violence of her trembling. She was cold with shock.

The Sikh flung out his hands in supplication, a picture of injured innocence in his pretty pink turban that was now rewound but covered in dust. 'Why should ponyman stop? I do no harm.'

'Your sister is Gopal Behera's wife,' returned Clive. He pronounced the words slowly and very, very distinctly.

Jane gazed numbly up at Clive. He in turn glanced up towards the track. Where the devil was Behera, anyway?

Singh was patting his turban, tightening it against his head. He seemed concerned now only that he should cut a good figure.

Tsring asked something in Hindi, then turned back to Clive. 'He says, going Tarand. But *Badmash*, Sahib. *Badmash*.'

Clive nodded. He turned with a heavy sigh to Jane. 'Can you stand? There's nothing broken, is there?'

She shook her head. He pulled her gently upright. 'Ouch!' She was bruised from head to foot. Tsring took one of her arms, Clive put an arm round her waist and they started the slow ascent. The Sikh was hurrying on ahead, sending down little rivulets of soil and stones as they broke away beneath his feet. 'Gopal—'

'Don't talk. You're going to need all your breath for this. And so am I.' It was ten minutes before they managed to struggle on to the track. Clive lifted Jane gently back on the pony. He gave a curt signal to Lama Chand and they moved off. Walking, he looked up into Jane's face. She was dirty, there was a great lump over one eye, and tears in her eyes. Rising up in him was that inexplicable emotion that always came when he saw her looking a mess. He tried to shrug it away. 'Do you think you could have been mistaken?'

She said shakily, indignantly, 'You know when someone's going to kill you, Clive, believe me, you know. Thank you for saving me. Thank you for coming back. Whatever happens,' she swallowed. 'Whatever happens, I'll never forget that.'

'Any time.' He gave her a reassuring smile of sorts and squeezed her hand. Her hair was hanging round her face in a tangled mess, full of dried grass, bits of twig and soil. For the first time she looked really defeated. Clive was thinking that Kumar Singh had a fairly watertight case. Walkers did use a pony to help them along. He had often enough held on to a pony's tail himself on the steeper inclines. And why should a lone walker not use the party as a guide to the Bhunda? Except, of course, that if the man was serious about attending the festivities he should already be there, for Clive and his party were running two days late. Jane's nerves were, understandably, on edge. Lama Chand could not have thought she was in danger, or surely he would have reacted? Again, and irritably, where had Gopal got to?

He was there as they emerged from the patch of forest that had nearly been the scene of Jane's demise. Kumar Singh was walking in front. Clive saw them meet with affection and pleasure. Jane saw too and felt sick to the heart of her. Clive asked grimly, 'What do you make of that?' She could only shake her head dazedly.

Chapter Seventeen

It was quite a different matter going downhill. The hot, sweet tea had restored Jane to something like normality. She had not witnessed the brewing of it, Clive had seen to that. He had tucked her up in a grey blanket borrowed from one of the Indians in the *Chaikhana* and made her a shelter by a boulder with the aid of a piece of corrugated iron. Here, she could look out on the wondrous trio of dazzling peaks that lay between them and Tibet. Indra Sen for the gods. Manali and Deo Tibba to climb. There was a lifting of the spirit when one looked at them, an apogee of brimming wonder. Clive had made her chew glucose tablets and then eat an unpalatable looking mixture of lentils and rice. 'Protein and sugar,' he said cheerily. 'That should fix you up.' They had not told Gopal about her near-escape. He knew only that she had jumped off the pony and had consequently lost her balance and rolled down the *khud*.

'Surely, if he's in this,' Jane said, 'he would pretend he didn't know the man.'

'He can't. Singh would tell him I'm aware of his relationship to Puniya.'

'I can't accept it.'

'You'd better,' Clive told her grimly. 'Start thinking of Gopal as an Indian instead of as a chum. Just because he speaks English well that doesn't mean you know what goes on in his mind. Our families spent two hundred years trying to anglicize the Indian, Jane. And failed.'

She knew she ought to listen to him for what he said made sense. Gopal was a product of his ancestors with their signs, their portents, their soothsaying. Of course the mantle he adopted in English circles could be thrown off at will. She had seen that in Kodapur. But to stand idle while a relative killed her, Helen's cousin? She said, 'It doesn't make sense.'

And it did not, Clive privately agreed, but he knew it would be foolish, not to say stupid, of either of them to relax their guard.

'I'm the only one with a gun,' said Clive. 'I got Tsring to look in Gopal's pack. He hasn't got one. How are you feeling now? Well enough to go on?'

'Yes. I'm all right.'

Clive had said it was straight downhill for a couple of hours, then through open country. The little porter, chanting his mantras, fingering his beads, had gone ahead. 'He says there's a sacred lake with a temple and a *pujari* in charge. A *pujari* is a priest. These men are actually hill farmers who adopt the temporary mantle of a *pujari* when they take their turn at looking after the temple. I'd feel happier if I could have you under his care for the night, inside four walls, preferably without a window,' Clive said. 'And also, I'm not very keen on camping out in leopard country. They say horses can defend themselves but it's my view it'd take more than a leopard to get these chaps on their mettle. If we keep up a good pace, Tsring says, we'll make it before dark.' Gopal had wanted his brother-in-law to walk with them. 'No,' said Clive unconditionally.

'But why not?' Gopal was incredulous at their lack of hospitality. 'He does not know the way.'

'He should have brought a guide.'

'He cannot afford a guide. He is a poor man. He heard we were going and he followed. Why not? It's lonely for a man on his own,' said Gopal with proper innocence. And in the end Clive had decided regretfully that the lesser of two evils was to allow Singh to join the party. At least, if he made the two Indians walk in front, he knew where both of them were. He wore his revolver now, openly, on his hip.

Gopal had laughed. 'You do not really expect to see a leopard? They are shy animals and hide in the forest by day.'

'I sincerely hope so.' Clive gave him a level look. 'I feel confident carrying a gun, just as your brother-in-law feels confident carrying a knife.'

Gopal shook his head. 'All Sikhs carry a knife.'

As they came down the winding track through the thin trees a new, grim thought struck Clive. He took the revolver out of its holster and slipped the safety catch. Jane looked up at him nervously. 'What are you doing?'

'Just checking.' He restrained her with the touch of a hand on her arm. His fingers were gentle and they lingered. When the little string of ponies had disappeared round the next corner he lifted the revolver, aiming at a tree forty feet or so away. He pressed the trigger. There was a loud report. Some bark broke away and fell. Clive looked into Jane's eyes, bemused.

'What's the matter?'

'I'm wondering what it means. Why should that gunsmith give me a good revolver if his cousin was coming along with the idea of slitting the throat of one of the party?'

There was a shout in front and Gopal came running back. 'What's the matter? We heard a shot.'

Clive called laconically, 'Just trying out my revolver.'

Gopal waited for them to catch up. His face was a study. He looked from Jane to Clive then back to Jane. 'Come on,' said Clive. 'We're wasting time,' and Gopal did not ask any more questions. They fell into step again. Within an hour they had left the bamboo and stunted scrub oak behind. Now, open downland stretched out before them, patched with forest. The great peaks had disappeared behind the pass. Before them lay ridge after ridge of brown mountains filled prettily with a soft grey mist going on into infinity. Tsring had told them that by this evening they should not be too far as the crow flies from Tarand, but they were not crows. There was still a long way to go. The forest here, about two thousand feet below the pass was more dense. Chil pines had taken the place of the poor mountain oaks of the higher levels and trees grew so closely together that there were times when the pack ponies were unable to pass between them. Occasionally the animals fell, losing the loads, for the narrow track was treacherous with small boulders. They collected the pots and pans, the metal plates and cups that scattered among the trees, the packages of food, and put them back, hurrying for it was cold here where the sun did not penetrate.

Then civilization, of a kind, returned. They passed the flat roofed, dried earth, windowless huts of the *gujjars*. The path had ceased now to go directly downhill. Jane was flagging on the upward slopes. 'Hadn't you better ride?' Clive asked. He was attentive now, kind. And he smiled more often. Neither of them spoke, or even thought, of Ashley. The problem of Ashley had moved to a different level.

'Perhaps I should. I'm sorry about this,' she apologized wearily. She was not only sorry, she was embarrassed. He had said she would not be able to cope with the heights. She took one of the glucose tablets out of her pocket and put it into her mouth.

The sun was sinking towards the mountain tops, the air growing cold, as cold in the open now as it had been in the forest. The porter pointed to one of the mud huts in the hillside and they turned their heads more directly uphill. 'We get buffalo milk. Maybe curds.'

They paused outside. A black buffalo came out of the single door with a child clinging round its neck. Two more children, ragged, filthy and strangely beautiful emerged shyly and lined up to stare. The *gujjar* brought curds and Clive paid.

Jane found herself smiling delightedly. 'He's pure musical comedy, isn't he?' The man wore bunched trousers, jerkin and studded leather shoes, the curled back toes giving him an unexpectedly elegant look. His wife, a tall, handsome woman in the long homespun robe of the hill people wore an incongruous pink and silver nylon scarf draped round her head. It was a welcome moment of peace, of normality, the first of the strained afternoon. Then memory struck and Jane, on guard once more, glanced apprehensively towards the Sikh who was sitting on the grass a hundred yards away. He had not come near her since the incident on the other side of the pass.

Gopal put a hand on her knee and she jumped. 'You are nervous,' he commented, smiling in his gentle way. 'Don't worry, Jane. Kumar says the sacred lake is just over the next hill.'

'He doesn't know the route,' she flashed accusingly. Gopal looked momentarily taken aback. 'I suppose the porter told him. You have had a bad day,' he said sympathetically.

'Yes,' she agreed bleakly, 'I have had a bad day.'

'Are you worried about the leopards?' Gopal was solicitous. 'They don't come out much in daylight and there are really very few left.'

'No.' The sun was too near the horizon. The hillside was already steeped in gloom. The brown ridges that had been full of soft mist were merging darkly together. They were once again caught on the mountain at dusk, but this time there was menace, and it did not come from the leopards.

They arrived at the rim of the crater as night fell around them. It was just possible to see the strange, pagoda-like temple with an open fronted, two storeyed building alongside, and beyond, in the middle of the grassy hollow, an oval lake with a bare circular island in the middle. A shallow, stepped track led down. Clive walked protectively with one arm lying across the pony's rump; incongruously, as the Sikh had walked earlier.

'It's a fourteenth century temple built by a rajah for a sage who used it as his Himalayan retreat,' Clive told Jane. 'Now *pujaris* guard it. I understand they're hill farmers taking a rota.'

'What do they do with their time?'

'Tsring says they sit on a stone reading the Bhagavad Gita in Sanskrit.'

'What's that?'

'India's favourite religious book.'

'And they perform the rites of the *puja* night and morning,' Gopal, who had been listening, put in. 'It's a religious ceremony.'

Gopal went to interview the priest. 'Where's Singh?' asked Jane nervously a few moments later.

'Very sensibly keeping out of the way. Maybe he went with Gopal.' Jane was jumpy as a cricket, watching the dark with unseeing eyes.

Gopal returned alone. 'The *pujari* will allow us to stay,' he said, 'but he'd like us to attend his nightly service. I think it would be a courtesy.'

'Okay,' Clive agreed. 'When does it start?'

'He will blow a conch shell. That's the signal.'

Clive turned to Jane, his eyes amused. 'There's an experience for you.'

'I think I've had enough of new experiences for one day, but if we must do it as a courtesy, we must.' At least they would be together a little longer. She did not want to burden Clive with her mistrust of the night. The thought of going to sleep with Kumar Singh in their midst had been a continuous torment.

As they journeyed up the final slope to the basin's rim Tsring had gathered dried branches and small logs, loading them on top of the panniers. Now he set about starting a fire. Jane helped him. He gave her one of his white toothed, infectious, warm hearted smiles. Lama Chand went off to attend to the ponies. Clive and the two Indians put up the tents then Clive came over and stood looking pensively at the fire. Jane rubbed her cold hands together.

Clive said, 'You'd be safe in the *pujari*'s house. Shall I get Tsring to ask? A priest, even a temporary one, ought to be a good enough guardian.'

'I suppose so.' She cast a strained look towards the temple, a menacing shape now in the darkness. It had been a torment worrying about Ashley's safety. Now that it had been compounded with her own and the possibility that she might never get to her brother to warn him, she seemed to be caught impotently in a web of frustration and fear. Even as she heard Clive speak to the porter, she knew she did not want to enter those mysterious looking buildings.

'Ask the *pujari* if he will allow Memsahib to sleep in his house tonight. I don't want the others to overhear.'

The Tibetan nodded. 'Sikh *badmash*.'

'You're sure?' Tsring nodded once more, his round face pinched with unaccustomed gravity. 'What do you think about the Brahmin, then?'

Tsring fingered his prayer beads. 'Okay. I think okay.'

'But he's a relative of the Sikh.' The porter shrugged. 'Go and ask the *pujari* if he has a spare room.' Clive and Jane stood together at the fire once more, looking down in silence into the leaping flames. There was little to be said. They were together in an impossible situation. When Tsring returned he was carrying an armful of coarse material. 'What on earth's that you've brought?' Clive asked.

'Is all right for room,' he said quietly, then added, 'Longys.'

'What?'

'For wearing *puja*. Always wear *longys* for *puja*,' the porter said gravely. He held out a bundle to Clive.

Clive unwrapped the stuff. It was a straight strip of grey homespun. Tsring showed him how to fold it round his waist and tuck the end in rather as women wear saris. 'Very warm. No trousers, please, Sahib. The goddess don't like.'

'Do we really have to attend?' Jane began to laugh. The material did not reach to Clive's ankles. His climbing boots emerged ludicrously from beneath.

'Yes, Sahib,' Tsring assured him gravely. The Sikh had returned. He stood just outside the ring of firelight. 'Oh hell!

And no shoes. That's always *de rigueur* in a temple. And there's going to be a heavy frost tonight.'

Jane said, 'When in Rome . . .' Clive grimaced.

'Not women clothes,' Tsring insisted, concerned about Clive's embarrassment. '*Longys* not women clothes.' He added comfortingly, 'I not go *puja*. I cook supper. Supper very good today.'

'Great. It will be appreciated.'

The two Indians accepted their *longys* without protest. Respect for the gods was an integral part of their heritage, and anyway they were accustomed to seeing a wide variety of clothes on their countrymen.

'Memsahib?' Jane took her skirt from the porter and wrapped it round her hips. They were a weird foursome standing there in the flickering firelight. Jane deftly removed her jeans and left them on the ground by the fire.

The porter said, smiling up into Jane's face, '*Pujari* say you second Memsahib here.'

'Me? You mean, white people have been to the sacred lake?' A little tremor ran through her, escalating the strangeness.

'One Memsahib, *Pujari* say, come with Rajah Kodapur long ago. Thirty year.'

Clive and she exchanged glances. 'Louise!' So Louise had come this way with the jewels! Jane asked in a whisper, 'Clive, do you believe the dead know?' The ghost of Louise, watching the burgeoning of the mischief she had begun. Waiting, perhaps in torment, for its tragic end.

'Perhaps,' Clive replied queerly, 'it's their punishment.' He took her arm and the unseen, cold wraith of Louise slipped away.

They crossed to the precincts of the temple and leaving their shoes outside, went through a gap in a low wall into the temple yard. The conch shell was crying thinly, echoing round the hollow. The stones were cold on their bare feet, the courtyard dark and creepy. Kumar Singh paused.

'Go in front, Singh,' snapped Clive. The Sikh seemed to hesitate. 'Go on,' said Clive. He flashed a small torch on the stones. The *pujari* and his wife came out of the building behind them, nodded courteously, then led the party through. The Sikh walked in front with Gopal behind. Clive and Jane brought up the rear. Beyond the inner courtyard there was an archway leading to a chapel or room. They came into darkness. A darkness weighted with something more than mere night. Jane inched nearer to Clive's side. Those in front parted and there was a little row of candles flickering ghoulishly on the stones. Beyond that, a chimney-like embrasure with a goddess inside. She wore a gold crown, a dress of gold, and the inevitable necklace of marigolds round her neck. As they came nearer the candles flickered on a black, savage face marked in red. Jane flinched and moved closer to Clive. The air in here was stale, the atmosphere sinister.

The Sikh had moved in his stealthy way up to the embrasure. Behind him on the wall a candle burned in a little holder etching his profile weirdly. A straight nose, a mouth that was at the same time cruel and sensuous, large black-pupilled eyes narrowed to slits beneath fierce brows. The flickering candle light came and went like tree shadows on water in the wind. A tremor of disquiet went through Jane and she glanced away towards the stones that were laid before the goddess. Stunned, she saw now that they were stained with dried blood. The Sikh's eyes followed hers. Compulsively, breath caught, she felt her own eyes drawn back to him. He was looking concentratedly at the red stains.

And then his black, strange eyes came back to her. Petrified, she stood in a cold sweat, waiting. She did not see the priest taking up a tiny saucepan, did not hear his muttered prayers. Her mind was a spasm of dread. This Sikh was a savage! A cut-throat. And Clive made arrangements for her to sleep in the lodgings of a hillman who must also be a savage at heart! Sacrifices had been made on this altar and who was to say they were not still made here, two days' walk from civilization where no white people ever came? Except Louise, all those years ago on her mission that was now to culminate in evil. Perhaps in bloodshed. Panic rose up in Jane out of a shuddering fear that was beyond and outside of her control.

The *pujari* was holding his small vessel over a candle flame. He rose, solemnly handing the pan round the little group, indicating that they all take a small portion of some granularly mixture it held. Clive nudged Jane. She started, took a tiny ball and put it in her mouth. It tasted like unsweetened corn. The *pujari* was again down on his knees, muttering prayers.

Jane's eyes went back compulsively to the stains on the floor. The Sikh wore his *kirpan*, Clive his revolver. The Sikh looked up, looked directly at Jane. She began to back away, silent in her bare feet.

Once out of range of the candles she swung round, tiptoed to the arched entrance, then picking up the folds of her *longyi* fled bare foot across the inner courtyard that was filled with suffocating darkness, across the outer and then over the low wall. She could see the blazing fire and little Tsring crouched over it. She flung a terrified glance behind her, then ran like a hare.

Tsring looked up in surprise from his cooking. He was mixing chapattis in his little black pan. 'Finish quick, Memsahib?'

'No.' She held her trembling hands to the blaze. 'No. I couldn't stay. It frightened me.'

He nodded as though he understood. 'Nice dinner,' he said soothingly. There was no sound from the outer darkness.

'What are we having?'

'Mince. Dahl. Very good chapattis. Lychees. Curds. You like lychees, Memsahib?' He turned his bright face towards her, eager to please.

'Yes, I do. I'm sure the meal will be lovely.' She pulled on her jeans and folded the *longyi* carefully, then she sat down beside the little Tibetan porter and stared numbly into the flames. 'You're so kind, Tsring. So frightfully kind.' His bright eyes shone in his flat, dark face. He was a haven, a refuge. She wanted to tell him that India scared her. That death seemed to hover round every corner, in every patch of darkness. But he would not understand.

Chapter Eighteen

Clive brought her shoes. He threw them down, looking at her queerly. 'Thanks.' She pulled them on. 'I'd rather sleep out under the trees with the leopards than in that building,' she said.

'You may have to. The *Pujari* was looking for you to show you the room.' Clive was bleak again but she knew he was worried, for her sake. Annoyed with himself, too, for giving in to worry. Reminding himself she had no right to be here. That she was Trouble, and it was going to be worse even, at the end of the journey, than it was now.

They ate the meal in silence. They were all very tired. At the end Clive said, 'Let's go over and have a look. We've asked a favour. We had better see what they're offering.'

Jane rose. She could not, anyway, talk in front of Singh and Gopal. It was very cold, now. She hugged her jacket tightly round her as they went the length of the long, open fronted block that Gopal had said was used for putting pilgrims up during religious festivals. The *pujari*'s lodgings were at the end of a narrow dirt lane, a sort of annexe to both the temple and the big building. Clive shone his torch on a closed door. It opened with such abruptness that Jane jumped. The *pujari*'s wife beckoned them in. She opened a door near by. There was no light. Clive shone his torch. It was a bare cell not more than eight feet long and six feet wide. There was a window covered with sacking and a string bed.

Jane said, 'There's no way of blocking either the window or the door.'

'You could wedge the door shut with a bit of wood.'

'That still leaves the window.'

'I'm afraid so.'

The woman was standing behind them, watching. She did not want Jane. The girl could feel it in her bones. She said desperately, 'I can't sleep here. If that bloodthirsty brute wanted to get at me why should these people interfere and get their own throats cut? Lama Chand turned a blind eye up on the mountain.'

Clive sighed sharply. 'Your imagination's running away with you again.'

'All right, if it's my imagination, why are you suggesting I sleep here?' she flashed angrily. 'You clearly don't think I'll be safe in a tent.'

'Because you're worried. I'm doing my best to put your mind at ease.'

'I'm not sleeping here.' She added miserably, 'If for no other reason, it's just a stone's throw from that barbaric god. You saw the blood all over the stones.' Clive did not answer. The woman said something in Urdu, then taking hold of the rough wooden catch on the door, she indicated with a negative gesture that they leave. 'She knows I don't want to stay,' said Jane. 'Come on. That settles it.' She made an awkward attempt at the gesture of *namaste* and added for good measure, 'Thank you very much.'

As they went back across the grass Clive asked, 'So what am I going to do with you?'

Stung by his tone, she flared, 'I'm a nuisance.'

'I didn't say that.'

'I'll sleep in the tent. Why don't you share it with me? Put Gopal and his beastly relative in the other one.' He did not answer. Somehow, he had known all along it was going to come to this. That he was going to lose. He had tried to hate her, and failed. If she got him into her tent tonight that would be the end. She knew how to keep him away from Ashley. He'd been a fool. He'd been soft. He could not think straight and he knew only too well why, but he would not face up to it. A doctor ought to be able to control his emotions. Adopt a clinical line.

He swung away from her and walked swiftly towards the lake. The moon had risen now, the stars were out, diamond bright. Over where the rocky land rose towards the rim he could hear the ponies dragging at the tough grass with their teeth, hear their small hooves knocking against stones. The lake glittered, unbearably beautiful in the moonlight. If it were not for the cold he would dive in. Tsring's little bowl of hot water in the morning was luxury, but by the time he had shaved there was not much left for washing. A little breeze nudged the tents playfully as he walked past. He paused at the edge of the lake.

Jane stood unhappily by the fire. Gopal and Singh had disappeared. She looked across the lake, blinked, then looked again. The island was floating across the water towards Clive. She gave a little gasp of amazement and delight. Tsring looked up from where he was squatting nearby washing his pans in a bucket of lake water. 'Is float island.'

'A floating island?'

The Tibetan nodded vigorously. 'Sacred floating island.'

'But how fantastic!' She saw Clive bend down as the island came slowly towards him on the breeze to nudge at the swampy edge where he stood. He pushed it away, watched it settle, then return on the breeze to his feet. Jane began to run towards him. He heard her and looked round.

'Would you believe it?' His face was soft with wonder and awe. Spontaneously he reached out and drew her within the circle of his arm. 'We're at Shangri-la.' It was a magic moment.

Suddenly, there was a terrible scream from the direction of the temple and the *pujari*'s wife came running, shouting at the top of her voice, brandishing a stick. Tsring jumped up and wrested the stick from the woman. She was jabbering incoherently, pointing to Clive's booted feet, then Jane's shoes. Tsring called, 'Lake sacred like temple, Sahib.'

'Oh damn. Sorry. Tell her we're very sorry.' They hurried back towards the tents, the magic smashed like frail china, the moment gone. Clive swung away from her and she went back to the fire.

He climbed to the top of the rise, to the basin's rim. The lake was a monster looking-glass with a fuzzy patch where the island lay. Outside, in the distance, the snowy white triangles that were mountain peaks shone like ghostly sentinels in the moonlight. He leaned on an outcrop of rock gazing at them, thinking of Jane and of the ludicrous situation fate had arranged for him. He stayed there for a long time, cold without feeling it, trying to sort out his values and coming up with confusions one upon the other.

There was a rattling of loose stones behind him. He turned round. Her face was soft in the moonlight. The long, bouncy hair that had looked such a mess in the afternoon had been combed back from her face and tied in a loose knot. She was smiling very faintly as though she had turned in every direction and, having to come back to him, had done it with a shy sort of confidence. And of course there was no one to help her except himself and a half-Tibetan porter with a shaky command of trekking English. Telling himself he was a stupid, suicidal fool, he put an arm round her and drew her close against him. She felt warm and pliant, but he could sense the apprehension in her. He drew her closer and kissed her hard, lingeringly. He had seen her catch her breath and now he felt the hard pumping of her heart.

She said, 'Please share the tent with me,' selling herself for a life.

He had told himself he did not believe, any more, that Kumar Singh had tried to kill her. He thought the entire episode was a figment of an imagination heightened by what was called altitude sickness. He had told himself this because if he accepted her fear it meant he had to have her at his side when they reached Tarand, protecting her at the same time as he needed all his strength, his wits and his concentration. While she was protecting Ashley from him. He hardened his heart. 'What are you up to?' he demanded to know, his words harsher even than he intended, because of the traitorous longing in him.

'I'm scared.'

He was lost if he believed her. He looked at her for a long moment, at her pale face that, in spite of its bruises, was beautiful in the moonlight, then he took her arm, turned her round briskly and they walked down the hill in silence. His pack lay beside the fire. Tsring had rolled himself up in his blanket and was preparing to lie down in the open beside the blaze. Gopal and the Sikh were sitting cross legged on the other side of the flames. He went to the flap of the tent and picked up his pack. 'You two can share that one,' he said curtly. 'I'm going in with Jane.' He did not look at them.

It was dark inside the tent. Jane had spread out her sleeping bag and he could just make out the form of her, sitting with knees hunched under her chin. He unrolled his own bag and put it on the ground. In doing so he brushed up against her. She took his hand convulsively in her own and held it against her cheek. When she let go the back of it was wet with tears. In that moment, just for one moment, he hated himself, and then he knew what he had not allowed himself to know before. He was not a man to commit rape, however gently. And it would have been gentle, but it would also have been unforgivable because whatever the mode of the execution, there was rape in his heart put there by fear and by the memory of the courtyard packed with patient, sick Indians cross-legged in the dust, drowned in their humility, their resignation, tormented by flies as they waited for attention from the pathetically small staff which was all the clinic could afford.

'Sleep well. I'll have my hand on the gun, but I hardly think Mr Kumar Singh will break in.' He unzipped his sleeping bag and slid inside. 'Sleep well,' he said again. When he closed his eyes it was with a curious sensation of not actually having lost, after all.

In the morning their refuge was white with mist like a

giant saucer full to the brim with smoke. The tents were stiff, and white with frost. By the time daylight came creeping over the rim of the crater they were already packed up. The *pujari* and his wife were not there to see them go. At least they were spared the ordeal of the morning *puja*.

They climbed to the rim of the crater then went off down the hill in single file, the ponies and the Sikh, according to Clive's orders, in front, then Gopal, Jane and Clive behind. Why Gopal wanted to walk with them he did not say. He had given Jane a queer look when she emerged from the tent, a queer, sad look and Jane remembered with a little bubble of laughter that in his ill-reasoned fashion, he thought of women as goddesses. He said nothing, though, except to remark cryptically that Kumar snored.

They walked downhill all morning. Again, thankfully, the day was cloudless, the sun burning with fierce intensity through the cool, clear air. There were lammergeiers flying high with grass snakes in their beaks. 'Look!' exclaimed Jane. One of them hovered high above, waiting to execute the murderous drop to death. The snake landed on a great outcrop of rock near the track and slithered helplessly, its back broken, until with a whoosh of wings the great bird swooped and carried it away.

They left the open downland and came into a wild and desolate rocky gorge where crazy pines grew precariously on gouged out cliff faces, where raging torrents lashed their way down starkly beautiful ravines. From time to time a piece of rock dislodged itself and went clattering and thundering down into the abyss. It was not a place to dawdle. They hurried through. Inevitably, they were held up where deodars had fallen across their track. Lama Chand led his ponies down the *khud* and back in large half circles, shouting at them, encouraging them to break through the trackless forest while little Tsring, agile as a monkey, dashed from one to the other, balancing-up their packs, tightening the ropes, pushing, a tiny figure with immense strength, shoving at the rump of a pony when its back legs were sliding, its front legs losing their grip.

There were bear droppings all the way that morning but thankfully, no bears.

And then, out in the open below a wild chaos of trees and granite cliffs there were signs of civilization once more. Women wearing bright scarves round their heads, cutting ferns and grass for fodder and throwing it, tied up in bundles, down on the track. They screamed shrilly when the ponies snatched at their bundles, brandishing their fierce looking scythes. Further down there were wild strawberries, their berries gone, a blue campanula, kotoniasta with big red berries and glades of iris that must be heavenly in spring. They met pack trains, too. The ponies jostled discourteously for position, the losers climbing frenziedly up the steep hillside or tipping head first down the *khud* to the imminent danger of their packs. They were all kept busy flying from one animal to the other, pushing the packs back into position. Only Kumar Singh stalked out in front as though the excitement was none of his concern. They met flocks of goats here, too, and lovely, elegant white sheep with black faces and curled horns. They dived among the ponies, bouncing on sharp, dainty hooves, then scurrying away.

Just before midday they came round a corner and there, too late, was a resthouse, a tiny bungalow with a veranda and some craggy apple trees. It stood on a hillside looking out on the great mountains of Spiti towards Tibet. Tsring produced his *chapattis* and some bananas. They ate them sitting on the veranda and drank deeply from a spring nearby.

In the afternoon the birds began to appear again. The long-tailed Himalayan magpie, and grey kingfisher. There were black crows, noisy and discordant as a cracking branch, with a pretty green sheen to their feathers. And then, dropping down swiftly they came upon paddy fields and huddled brown villages with piles of fodder and golden maize drying on the roofs. Young mothers with their silver rings in their ears sat placidly on stones holding naked babies to the breast while small children dashed suicidally round high, unrailed verandas. And again, those black flies.

Gopal said, pointing, 'There's an old Bhunda rope,' and they looked up with tired curiosity. It was hanging in loops from the eaves of a storehouse, a tightly twisted cord about three inches thick. 'And there,' added Gopal pointing to a white post three hundred yards across the valley, 'is the post they attached it to for their ceremonies.'

Jane stared at it, thinking bleakly of Louise. And then a new chilling fear swept through her. What lay in store for them all at Tarand?

Hours later they came round another corner and there was Tarand across the valley, a large brown village that sprawled prettily down the hillside, its grey slate roofs gleaming in the sun. They were too tired to be more than relieved. They had accomplished in forty-eight hours what no trekking party in their right senses would attempt in less than three days. They were not there yet, but their goal was in sight. They wound down the mountain in a silence broken only by the scrape and clatter of the ponies' shoes on the stones, their own softer footfalls and the tinkling of the bells.

From here they zigzagged across terraced ridges where clear mountain water sparkled through irrigation ditches. Further down there were more of those monkeys chattering and quarrelling in acacia trees. It was hot now, and the ponies were sending up little puffs of fine powdery dust with each footfall. Down near the stream by the little board bridge they met a *gujjar* from a nomadic tribe with a copper pot on his head, taking buffalo milk up to the village to sell. They climbed slowly and wearily through the stone walled fields until they came to the edge of the village. The light was failing. Lama Chand, the ponyman, paused waiting until they came up with him.

'Where's Kumar?' Gopal asked, looking round in the gloom. 'He's not here.' Jane caught her breath. Gopal spoke to the ponyman in Hindi and he replied tiredly. He had begun to cough again.

'What's the matter?' asked Clive.

'He says Kumar disappeared suddenly.' Gopal looked upset.

Jane was watching Lama Chand. His eyes met hers and surreptitiously he drew a finger across his throat. Her heart turned over with fright. 'He says Kumar Singh is going to kill me,' she said, her voice rising, a spasm of that too familiar panic catching her once more in its grip.

'Who says?' Gopal swung on her.

'Lama Chand.'

'How can he? He doesn't know English.' Gopal spoke angrily to the man. He did not answer. He was doubled up in a paroxysm of coughing that may or may not have been assumed.

Darkness was falling round them. Clive said with assumed calm, 'Let's find a spot to pitch the tents. Lama Chand, follow me.' Taking Jane by the hand he led off up the hill, floundering through a maze of irrigation ditches that smelt surprisingly sweet, skirting the village until he found a track that seemed to lead into a field. The ground was rough as though it had been ploughed and the crops recently gathered, but near the top there was a smooth patch. He said, 'This will do. There's some grass for the ponies. I'm going to the village to see what I can find out.'

Jane wanted to go with him but she hadn't an ounce of strength to call on. She collapsed on to the hard earth. The shock of the Sikh's disappearance and the ponyman's eloquent hint had left her limp and stunned. Clive was going to look for Ashley, and she could do nothing to help either one. She dropped back on to the rough, dry, broken ground. It hurt her back but she did not care. She closed her eyes.

Tsring was shaking her shoulder. 'No, Memsahib. Not sleep there, I put tent up fast. Hot soup and sleep.'

She scarcely remembered anything after that. She had climbed into her sleeping bag in a haze of exhaustion. Clive said in the morning that when he eventually returned Tsring was sitting cross-legged outside the tent flap fingering his beads, smiling and muttering his Tibetan prayers. He reached for his travel worn, travel stained blanket and began to wrap himself in it. 'I sleep here. Guard Memsahib,' he said. 'No need fire, tonight.' They were down to nearly seven thousand feet now.

'He knew,' said Clive sardonically later, 'Jane and I weren't such good friends.'

Chapter Nineteen

Tarand, the village blessed with the presence of the patron god and semi-divine hero Situ-Rama was throbbing to the excitement of the Bhunda. People who had been pouring in by foot, by donkey, by mule and buffalo cart had turned routes that were sprawling fingers leading down from the mountain tops to the palm of the village, into wobbling ant tracks. It was a pity a landslide had blocked the road that came down from the Hindustan-Tibet highway, but there were few dignitaries using it. A message had come saying the Rajah of Kodapur had had some difficulty in getting away and that now he was stuck on the other side of the obstruction. One of his relatives, one of the goldsmiths, had been about to set out to meet him when a foreigner arrived saying the message was false, the Rajah was unwell and had sent him in his place.

The crowd that jammed in to the courtyard between the big temple buildings with the elegant fringe of wooden tassels under the eaves, was jocular to a man. It had been a lively and exciting run-up to the festival. There had been the procession of the temple *pujaris*; then the procession of the guru and nine Brahmin girls each carrying on her head a temple vase marked with a large swastika and containing sweet smelling leaves. The girls, who were supposed to be demure with eyes cast down had caught the spirit of the fair that hung like incandescent light over the serious business of the religious festival. They were deliberately exciting the young men with their flirty eyes and swaying hips as they moved along in the wake of the drummers, trumpeters and the musicians with their thin reed pipes. Some of the elders were already afraid that things could get out of hand. One irreligious young person had taken a pot shot with a stone at the god's Egyptian-like, figured umbrella. The rest of the village women who followed the procession clad in long one-piece red dresses girt with white waistbands seemed, to the highly critical elders, to be flaunting themselves rather like bitch pi-dogs on heat. Great were the speculations of the young men of the village as to which girl was, or was not, ripe enough to be thrown down in the long grass beyond the temple buildings at the height of the religious fervour when the sacrifice came on the rope. But if the crowd was excitable, it had not lost its native sensitivity. When one of the important gods, being a snake of large proportions evidently requiring a good deal of space for his gyrations, came by in a huge copper *degcha* of great beauty, there had been a silence so profound a priest had been moved to state categorically that one might hear the blink of an eyelid.

In the field above the temple the little party were wakened by the quarrelsome chatter of the mynahs in the trees. Tsring brought them bed tea.

Jane's feet were sore, her ankles ached and though she had had a good sleep she was tired still. Clive put his head in at the tent flap. 'All right?'

'Fine. Well, fairly fine,' Jane corrected herself wryly. 'Remind me not to look into the mirror for a week or so. My feet feel raw and I'm stiff as a board. Apart from that, as I said, I'm fine.' She reached into her haversack for the comb.

Clive settled himself down on the groundsheet, smiling. 'Your pukka sahib ancestors would have been proud of that stiff upper lip.' He looked at it. It was short, and it curved outwards over her pretty white teeth. She was lucky not to have lost some of those when she spun down the *khud* yesterday. The bruises would go. He shook himself because he was once again ploughing the wrong furrow. 'I haven't shaved.' And his hair was tousled. He brushed it back with his hands.

'Where did Gopal go last night?'

'To look for Singh. He's upset about Singh disappearing.'

It seemed to prove the Brahmin boy's innocence. The Sikh's guilt. Jane's tensed nerves relaxed fractionally. 'Did you find out if Ashley's here?'

'No. Nothing about Ashley.' Jane watched his face. She was certain he was telling the truth. 'But the Rajah's here,' Clive added. 'He's staying with the headman and I've located his house. I saw some hippies, but they were talking German. Apparently there's a lot of cannabis growing wild in the valley so it's something of a hippy paradise. There are people sleeping all over the place, in the streets, on verandas, with friends and relatives. Hundreds of them are jammed in two big open-fronted buildings built specially for the purpose like the one we saw at the sacred lake. And by the way, I've made a friend. We're going to be given a guided tour. It's the best way, I think, to find out what we want to know.'

Jullunder Cariappa dashed through the town, threading his way between the sleeping bodies that lay around the streets, avoiding the little cooking fires. He was small, slender and very agile, dark skinned with bright black eyes. One day, he hoped to join his brother in Bradford, England, where Chaman worked in the woollen mills, and so it was important that his grasp of English should be as good as he could make it before arrival. This was a bit of luck, a real bit of luck, finding the Englishman who was so interested to know details of the Bhunda. He, in his turn, hoped that by proving useful he might persuade the Englishman to talk about England. He knew already that the people of Bradford never slept in the streets or indeed under the sky at all, and neither did they cook out of doors except in the high summer when they – but only the richer ones – had something called a bar-bee-q. There was a lot more to learn, though. He didn't want to embarrass Chaman by his lack of sophistication when he arrived in Bradford.

Clive waved as Jullunder came running across the rough

field towards them. 'Good morning, Doctor. You are ready to come to the temple? It is early, but important to go before processions and crowds.'

Jane came out of the tent. Jullunder thought he had never seen anyone so goddess-like and at the same time so confusedly like a boy. But he was not certain he liked to see the shape of her below the waist like that. It was exciting for a man. He turned away, swallowing, because he couldn't keep his eyes off her crotch. Chaman hadn't warned him that girls in Bradford dressed like this. Chee! It was going to take some getting used to. The English equivalent of the mother goddesses hadn't given this Jane much to feed the baby with. Scarcely more than a sharp little point, and carefully covered up at that. Chee! If he could only hang on to these people for a few days he would certainly improve his education and arrive in Bradford, England a sophisticated man.

Clive, Jane and the Hindu walked up through a labyrinth of alleys choked with Indians cooking their food over tiny fires, breast feeding their babies, sleeping, smoking their smelly bidi tobacco and came out eventually in the village square which was also packed with visitors who had very evidently spent the night there and were now hawking and spitting in chorus as a prelude to the day. Jullunder pointed. 'Entrance arch to temple.' Jane and Clive paused, gazing in fascination and wonder. It was made of stone strongly bonded together with a framework of deodar beams.

'That,' said Clive, 'is an elephant god. The one sitting rather unsuitably on a lotus flower.'

Their guide chuckled. 'Unsuitable, yes.' Above, surprisingly, for Tarand was a very long way indeed from great rivers, there was a carving of a crocodile, its teeth fearsomely bared. 'Come.' They took off their shoes and went through a low stone doorway guarded by a group of friendly looking Indians. The guards, nodding to the guide, ushered the little party into a square room. There was a cobbled floor. With a distinct shock, Jane saw it was covered in cow pats. 'The cow is sacred, you know,' Jullunder told them, 'and may walk through the temple.'

'Of course,' Jane agreed politely, solemnly removing what might in the circumstances be a discourteous expression from her face as they picked their way delicately on bare feet on the cleanest stones they could find.

Another door led into the temple courtyard past a monumental statue of the god Vishnu. Before them then, in a grass-grown square was an open, chalet-type shrine panelled with carved wood. 'There it is!' Clive sucked in his breath. On a wide ledge some six feet off the ground stood a bronze bust with an inscription round the bottom. It wore a necklace of marigolds and there were candles set around it. More marigolds were scattered before and behind, and small spring flowers.

'I don't know what I expected,' said Jane, 'but not that.' The bronze bust looked too ordinary in these barbaric surroundings. The sort of object one might see in a museum anywhere. 'And where did they get jonquils, at this time of year?' Clive did not reply. Her gaze shifted to a magnificent jewelled object that might have been a headdress and beside that a pearl necklace on a plinth. Further along a bracelet glowing with red stones. Jane, grasping Clive's hand in excitement now, felt his fingers tighten. 'Rubies! Clive, real rubies!'

Jullunder heard and his eyes shone. 'First three pieces of jewel goldsmiths touch in cave,' he explained. Half a dozen guards in long draped robes lounged at either end of the platform supporting the god and the jewels. They eyed the visitors with friendly curiosity.

The Hindu indicated the bronze bust with pride. 'Is god. Sit here entertaining divine visitors. Here,' he pointed to a heavy door fastened by enormous chains which were taken up to the floor above, 'where god lives and treasure kept. Is cave.'

The cave! Jane and Clive exchanged involuntary glances, then looked away. Here was the sacred precinct Ashley had to enter if he was to steal the jewels!

The Indian was pointing to the south eastern corner of the yard where a curious, shed-like building stood. 'Is where preparation for death ceremony of Situ-Rama's human victim made.'

'Human?' Jane's mind flew back to the bloodstains on the stones at the sacred lake.

Jullunder smiled engagingly. 'Not human, now. Is not allow. But still carry out ceremony as always has. Man weave rope. Tomorrow, he taken into shed.' Just inside the door stood a huge, painted head. Jane stepped forward but one of the guards vigilantly barred her way. 'Is Kali Mai,' their guide explained, adding apologetically, 'Is not good to go close.'

'But the man who plaited the rope goes in? Right in?' she asked the Indian.

'Yes. Must go through preparations for death ceremony. Rites of dying Hindu. Is necessary to look on dread face of Kali. For him. Not for you.' Cariappa waved an admonitory finger before Jane's eyes.

'But he is not sacrificed?' She had to make the Indians confirm what the Rajah had said. A goat went on the rope. Her mind flashed back as it did all the time now to the blood on the stones in the temple at the sacred lake. It haunted her.

'Not man now,' and again Jane heard with a chilling sense of the macabre the same regret in Jullunder Cariappa's voice as she had heard in the voice of the Rajah back in Kodapur. She moved nearer to Clive. And then, out of the ether, there came once again a disquieting sense of Louise that was not part of memory. An unacceptable, even creepy, sensation that Louise was here. She shook the feeling away. Louise, after all, had been here. And she, too, had been dismayed. Perhaps she had left something of herself in the strangeness of Tarand. The shocked spirit of an Englishwoman.

Clive was looking down at her with concern. 'What's the matter?'

She shrugged off the feeling, laughing a little, but her voice when she spoke allowed the apprehension to show through, 'My imagination is running riot. It's all so – so Indian. So strange.' So far outside of everything she had been brought up to accept. Clive was looking at the jewels lying beside the god on the platform, his grey eyes narrowed, his mouth grim. 'Is there any more treasure in the cave?' he asked.

'Yes. Much for god.'

He turned, frustration beating up in him as it always did over the blind waste of India. Cariappa, he knew, was not referring to the Rajah's jewels for the ordinary villager would not know the Rajah had used this cave as his safe deposit. The Begum's priceless necklace with, as Jane had said, rubies the size of pigeon's eggs had lain here for thirty years. What other valuables were there, given to the god for one reason or another at different Bhundas over the centuries? Clive's rising anger reached out uselessly to the princes long dead who had deprived their countrymen in order to gratify their own wishes. His mind flew to the consumptive ponyman trekking over the wild foothills, sleeping rough when he ought to be in hospital receiving treatment. To the blind beggars in the streets who only needed cataracts removing from their eyes but for whom there were not enough doctors; and after that not enough hospitals. To travelling medicos, performing operations not casually, but inevitably roughly, in open fronted barns with the dust of India blowing through. And all the while heaven alone knew how much of a fortune lay in that damn cave!

'God knows what the pearl necklace over there is worth,' he muttered. Tantalizingly out of reach, it glowed on its plinth. 'And after this barbaric ceremony, it goes back where it can do no good for anyone!'

Jane said, 'Ssh. Don't be angry.'

'I have to be angry,' he burst out.

The Hindu was asking, 'Is something wrong?'

'No, no,' Jane told him hurriedly. 'We were just talking.'

He nodded. 'Today, god's brass drinking vessel be taken, in procession, to Chandi spring and fill up. "Worship of Spring" ceremony. When vessel filled, ready to go back in cave tomorrow with god.'

'To provide the god with drinking water for the next twelve years?' Jane asked, trying to smile, trying hard to enter into the spirit of the thing.

'Oh yes. But do you know,' the Indian boy confided, his black eyes glowing with a kind of religious fervour, 'when vessel came out with god, water at same level put in last ceremony. Same level.'

'There has to be a scientific explanation,' Clive muttered, pushing away what was unacceptable to him, rejecting the gods as they closed in. Jane felt the same sensation of strangeness creeping over her again. The feeling of sinking beneath the weight of the gods; the weight of fear, and a thousand omens as old as the voice of India, its mountains and its taboos. They could climb Manali Peak and Deo Tibba so long as they left Indra Sen for the gods. The Rajah could hide his jewels in the cave so long as he left the ruby necklace for Situ-Rama. But Ashley had come to take the necklace. Her mind was scudding, out of control. Louise had cried out to the Rajah when the goat went on the Bhunda saddle, 'This seems to be happening to me.' And Louise seemed to be here, in the air around her, warning her. Jane wanted to get out of the courtyard, away from the painted image of the god staring coldly at them through the open door. They must search for Ashley. They were wasting time.

'All women with husbands alive worship at spring in turn,' their guide was saying. 'Take long time. Then victim esc— er – escar—'

'Escorted,' said Clive.

'Yes, escorted in there—' he pointed to the open door, to

the menacing face of Kali and went on in his sing-song Indian voice, '—for the final rite of ceremony. Mantras recited. White shroud taken to victim and formally devote to death.'

Jane turned away. She had had enough of Kali. And she wished the man would not insist on calling the rope weaver a victim. She wished she could get those bloodstains out of her mind. She wished she had not come here. It was all too primitive, too savage. She went back through the smelly outer courtyard where the cow pats lay, replaced her shoes and stood in the street. A little band of hippies wandered past, the girls in flowing velvet skirts, their feet bare, their long hair bedraggled, their eyes staring, dull. The men bearded in tattered jeans. They eyed her briefly as they passed, without interest.

There was a murmur of voices and the two men emerged behind her. Clive was saying, 'It's very good of you. Yes, we'll look you up later when you're free again.'

'Come house. You know where.'

'Thanks. Thank you very much.'

The little Hindu went hurrying off across the square, smiling happily. Jane said, 'Ashley's hair is very dark. If he didn't wear a hat on the trek and got sunburned he might be hard to identify, wearing Indian clothes.' She pointed to an old man sitting cross-legged on the dusty, stony road. He wore a loosely wound turban that sagged down to cover the back of his neck and drooped over his ears, the voluminous dhoti, and on his torso an ancient, perhaps Oxfam, jacket and thick scarf. 'Dressed like that, one would not know Ashley. And he's had time to learn some Hindu, or Urdu.'

Clive did not reply.

They walked off through the streets. In the interval during which they had been in the temple precinct, the village had come alive. Cloth shops had opened and saris were spreading their sunset colours over wire display stands. Stalls had sprung up. Great samovars stood over small fires. *Chapattis* were being produced for the passing trade. Brass cooking pots with concoctions of vegetable curry filled the air with rich odours. Everywhere idlers chewed betel nut and spat it out in bloody patches on the ground. Wrinkled brown men with startlingly white beards patiently waited for custom on the floors of open stalls, knees tucked beneath their chins.

'I've got to get a lead from somewhere,' Clive said. 'I am going to visit the Rajah.'

Chapter Twenty

The headman's house was a beautiful building, of stone and carved woodwork in the local style with balconies high up under the eaves. It was set at the corner of two of the rough, stony, dirty little streets that intersected the village and were now packed with sightseers sitting cross-legged, waiting for the next procession, smoking their bidi tobacco, chewing the betel nut, sucking contentedly at their hubble-bubbles. The heat was stifling now. Dust lay in the air everywhere. Some of the women lifted the ends of their saris to shield their faces, some seemed not to care. The flies, too, had come in with the sun and clung blackly round the eyes of children; of those too maimed and ill to do more than sit with patience in their faces and in their big dark eyes. An old man, frail as a branch, lifted his stump arms piteously. They hurried by, both thinking obsessively now of the jewels. There was not enough compassion to go round, but the jewels would help if Clive could only get his hands on them.

The Indians on the headman's veranda, their black eyes big with curiosity, moved politely aside to make a pathway to the door. An old man standing in the doorway spoke to them in Hindi and Clive asked if the Rajah was available. He nodded. They removed their shoes and followed him. The passage opened into a small bare room with a rush mat on the floor, some hard sofas, wooden chairs and a small table. It was almost a replica of the headman's sitting room in the village of Taksit where they had waited for the ponyman.

The Rajah, who was seated on one of the sofas, came rapturously to his feet.

'Jane! It's Jane.' He hurried forward holding out both

hands. 'You have come to the Bhunda! Good gracious me! But what has happened to you, my dear? What is that on your face? You have bruises, and your forehead is grazed. My dear!' For all the notice he took of Clive, she might have come into the room alone.

Touched by his solicitousness, she told him they had had a rough journey. 'It is nothing. I fell.' She tried to extricate her hands but his fingers clung. 'What brings you here?'

'I wanted to see the Bhunda. And Clive was interested, too.'

The Rajah released her reluctantly in order to shake hands, then turned swiftly back. 'You walked over the hills?' She nodded. His face lit up. 'And your brother came with you? I am to meet Ashley?'

'No. I haven't seen him.'

'You will bring him to see me when you find him?' He gazed into her eyes and it was all she could do to meet his. She nodded, numbly.

The Rajah said with touching simplicity, 'You have followed in the footsteps of your mother. I would have liked to bring you, if I had known.' He paused. 'If things had been different,' he added.

'Did you catch up with your friend Mr Hills?'

The Rajah's face darkened. 'Sit down. Please sit down and my host's daughter will bring you some tea.'

'No, please. Don't put anyone to any bother. We don't want to stay.' Clive, ignored, had seated himself on one of the hard chairs.

The Rajah had taken Jane's hands again, smoothing them between his own. 'Things are not going well with me,' he said, unhappily. 'I am worried. Very worried. The Begum, my mother, tried you know to get the necklace at the time of the last Bhunda. This time, I fear, she has laid her plans better. The goldsmiths, who are relatives of mine, will not talk to me. Of course they are relatives of my mother, too,' he conceded.

'I'm sorry.'

'There are rumours, but they are very vague.' He glanced towards the door, then leaning close to Jane told her in an aggrieved whisper, 'I suspect my host is keeping those I want to see away from me. I have bribed several of the headman's people, but—' he shrugged expressively, 'I have found out nothing.' He crushed her hands feverishly against his breast. 'I am in great distress, Jane. I am afraid there is a conspiracy among all the influential people who are connected with the Bhunda. I am not to be told anything.'

'But why would they do that to you? You who are such an important man?'

The Rajah shook his head miserably. 'I do not know, except that if something has gone wrong, they would want to cover up. If the necklace has gone already, then they would not want me to know. The ceremonies and the guests are important. I understand that. The festival must go on. But—' he broke off, clinging unhappily to the hand Jane had not managed to extricate.

'Perhaps, if you could tell us the names of the goldsmiths who went into the cave, we could interview them. Perhaps they would talk to us.'

'I doubt it. There are many, many goldsmiths. They would suspect, if they have already dealt with an Englishman. They would not tell you which members of the family went into the cave. And the village people would not know.'

Clive rose and went agitatedly to the window. Trying to sound casual, he asked, 'What's the name of the victim? Perhaps we might be able to find out something for you from people who know him.'

The Rajah turned towards Clive. His eyes were dark with suspicion. It was clear he did not wish to trust another Englishman immediately upon being tricked by Barry Hills, but he was desperate. 'The man's name is Rafiq Tankha,' he said reluctantly. 'I don't know anything about him. I've tried to speak with his family, but they will not allow me to enter

187

their house. I know one thing. His sister is to marry into the goldsmiths' family.' His fingers tightened on Jane's hands and he gazed entreatingly into her eyes. 'Would you do this for me? Would you try to find out what is going on? For Louise's sake, my dear. For the sake of my dear, dead love.'

'Is no use your trying to see Rafiq Tankha,' Jullunder Cariappa told them as they jostled along with the hurrying crowds in the narrow, malodorous lanes between his house and the square. Jane and Clive had called at the wrong moment. He was about to leave in order to watch the next procession. 'Rafiq in temple below tents. Is guard.'

'Guarded?'

'Ah yes. Guarded, you say. My English, you know, is not good.'

'Why is the victim guarded?'

He shook his dark head, his eyes uncertain. 'This evening dedication to Kali. Rafiq guarded,' he repeated, turning the new word over with interest. 'Goldsmiths now say is right to guarded.'

Clive stepped round a shell of a man with tiny stumps for legs who was propelling himself along at a great pace on the palms of his hands. 'You mean, the victim is not normally guarded?'

Jullunder looked at Clive blankly, stuck on this other new word. 'My English is, you say, rusty. Need practice.'

'No, you're doing very well. Are you trying to say that last time the Bhunda was held, the victim was not guarded?'

'Yes. Not guarded. Goldsmiths say is right this time for guarded.'

'And this temple, where Rafiq Tankha is held under guard, is it the one with the tower? The one below our field.'

'Yes. But cannot visit. No visit.' Jullunder shook his head eloquently. They came round the corner into the dusty square. The crowd was building up, pouring in from the lanes and the noise level was rising as the Indians shouted

excitedly to each other, the young men pushing good naturedly, the children running, squealing, clamouring. Somewhere, not far away, there was a drumming and trumpeting,
coming nearer.

'Do you know the victim? Do you know Rafiq Tankha?'
Clive shouted over the din.

Jullunder was jostling for a good position in the crowd.
'Oh yes. I grow up in village. I know everyone,' he shouted
back boastfully. 'Memsahib, stand here, with me, so to see.'

'You know the goldsmiths, too?' Clive persevered.

'Yes. Yes. Will you be able to see procession, now? You
very tall, Doctoor Sahib. You see over heads?'

'Yes, thanks. Listen, Jullunder.' Clive put his mouth close
to the Indian boy's ear. 'Perhaps you have heard a rumour
that something has gone wrong with the preparations for
the Bhunda?'

'Wrong?' Jullunder turned a puzzled face to him. 'What
has go wrong?'

Clive took a leap in the dark. 'There are rumours flying
round that a stranger has got involved.'

'Involved, please? This man in front, his turban get in
way, for Memsahib?'

She shook her head. 'It's all right.'

'A stranger,' explained Clive patiently, 'not one of the
goldsmiths. There's a rumour that a stranger went with the
goldsmiths into the Bhunda cave.'

Jullunder's black eyes widened. 'Is true?'

'Perhaps you could find out. Ask among your friends.'

'Oh yes. I ask.' He frowned. 'No one tell me this. Is true?'
he asked again, intrigued.

Clive shrugged. 'Well, I don't know. I think it's true.'

'I ask. Look, Memsahib. Look! Doctoor, look!' Some gorgeously arrayed musicians came swinging into view blowing
reed pipes. Behind them a group carrying long poles with
leopard's head at the top and something draped in peacock
blue silk.

'Is god!' exclaimed their guide pointing eagerly. 'Is god, Memsahib.' Jane would have liked to know some details but Clive needed all the man's flickering, dancing attention.

Clive said, 'We'd like to go down and look at the temple, but we'll never get through the streets now. Is there a short cut where we can avoid the crowd?' The drums were approaching, the Indians' clamour growing to a roar.

'You don't want to see procession?' Jullunder's face fell.

'We'd love to see the procession but time is short and we want to see the temple, if you don't mind.'

Jullunder was torn between his English lessons and his very real and natural desire to see every aspect of the festival. 'Come,' he said reluctantly. He did not want to offend the Englishman, and perhaps if he was quick, he would anyway catch the procession up before it reached the spring. His eyes slid again to Jane's jeans, then slid guiltily away. Shaped like that, she ought to be able to run. 'Follow.' He pushed through the oncoming crowd and slipped under a low arch that led down an alley between two buildings. It was breathlessly hot here. They climbed over a low wall and crossed a yard. Two goats raised their spiky heads to look at them with interest. They climbed over another wall and came out on a rocky track edged with spindly castor oil plants. 'Down,' said their guide, pointing, already balanced on one leg for the urgent rush back. 'Follow track. Lead to temple.'

'You're sure he's in that temple?'

'Fasting and guarding Bhunda rope. Yes. In temple.'

They thanked him and he went bounding cheerfully off to his procession. Jane and Clive picked their way down a narrow, stony track between low walls and came out on a wider one that led directly to the building.

It was a considerably smaller temple than the one in the square but fashioned of the same dry stone and deodar beams. There was a heavy wooden door tightly shut and padlocked. At the side, partially hidden beneath a miniature pagoda, stood a giant phallus carved in stone and ringed obscenely with marigold blossoms. An Indian in a dirty, loosely tied turban, pyjamas and a shawl had been perching on his haunches beneath the holy peepul tree. He rose and came towards them. With vigorous arm movements he waved them away. Clive spoke to him in Hindi. The man turned, shouted something and in immediate response, four Hindus with trimmed beards and wearing Western clothes came round the corner of the building. One of them shouted rudely, pointing back up the hill. 'Oh heck, I wish I knew more of the language,' Clive muttered. 'I don't even know the word for goldsmiths.' He addressed the man. 'Do any of you speak English?'

They advanced, walking close together, hands on their knives. One of them replied curtly. 'Is Hindu sacred religious matter.'

'Yes, I know. Are you goldsmiths?'

'Is religious matter. Not to come here.' The man's eyes were menacing.

Jane plucked at Clive's arm. 'Come away. There's nothing we can do. They mean businesss. Don't let's invite trouble.' They retreated in silence up the hill. Clive drew her into the fitful shade of one of the castor oil trees that lined the track.

'Let's stop here and talk about it.' The drums and pipes were banging out their noisome rhythms up above. The sun, outside of the drooping leaves, beat down like a furnace.

Jane said, 'If Ashley did get into the cave, if he did manage to persuade one of the goldsmiths to change places with him, he would not go alone. One of the goldsmiths who went with him could have seen him take the jewels. I mean, he'd be frightfully lucky if he got clean away with anything like that.' Fear was building up in her. Fear for what may have happened to Ashley.

'It would be dark.'

'Possibly. But they'd surely have to have a light in order to see the god. Behind seven doors . . . It has to be dark, Clive.

And if they have a light, they must see what one another is doing.' She removed her hat, pushing the soft hair away from her head, fanning her face with the brim.

'You're suggesting they caught him red handed, and they're holding him prisoner in that temple?'

'It makes sense. Look, Clive. Five men, and Jullunder says the victim isn't normally guarded.' She shivered, thinking of Ashley in there, held by five savages with knives at their hips. Ashley, hoist with his own petard.

Clive chewed the matter over in silence. This was rotten for Jane. He wished to heaven he had not had to bring her. He tried to harden his heart, to look away. It was becoming more and more difficult to ignore her state of mind that showed in the pathetic droop of her body, the occasional rush of tears to her eyes. But there was too much at stake. Some traitorous automatic reflex action kept moving him in her direction. He put an arm round her, held her close for as long as he dared, then gave her a little push and said in a clinical, businesslike voice, 'But this is where the victim is supposed to be held. If Ashley is here, where's the victim?'

Jullunder Cariappa, having witnessed the excitement of the procession taking the god's brass drinking vessel to the spring for re-filling, had returned happily to the Englishman's tents. Clive saw him coming and hurried to meet him. Tsring had cooked them chapattis for lunch but they had remained uneaten. Jane was sitting on the ground crumbling one of them in her hands. Clive asked, 'Did you find out anything?'

'Find out? Oh!' The Hindu's face fell. 'No. I forget find out. No use talking,' he added airily. 'Everyone at procession.'

Clive hid his disappointment. 'Could you possibly take us to the home of the victim?'

Jullunder, too, was disappointed. He had hoped to sit in the field with them and talk English until the final procession this evening. 'Rafiq Tankha house? Okay, yes, I take you,' he agreed resignedly.

'Now?'

'Okay.'

The Tankhas lived in a ramshackle building joined by a rickety upstairs bridge to another ramshackle building that housed some of their relatives. Jullunder knocked at the door. It was opened by a young woman in a pretty red sari. She started when she saw Clive and Jane, her kohl-marked eyes round as saucers and faintly scared. Jullunder spoke to her in Hindi and she replied with resentment, at the same time retreating and pushing the door partially closed.

Clive said, 'I can't understand. They talk too fast. There's something wrong, isn't there?' He turned to Jane, a strained look on his face. 'How's your woman's intuition?'

The Indian boy spoke to Clive, apologetic, regretful. 'She not wish talk about brother.'

'Is he here?'

'She says no.'

'What about his parents? Are they here?' The door banged shut.

'His mother gone religious retreat. Father holy man now. In cave in valley.' At Jane's look of surprise Jullunder explained, 'Is usual. Family grow up take business. Young ideas best in Hindu way. Parents old fashioned ideas.'

'I see.' They seemed to have arrived at an impasse. 'You come to my home tonight?' Jullunder invited them, bright-eyed. 'Is feasting and music after procession.'

'That's kind of you.' Clive spoke detachedly, his mind elsewhere. The woman who answered the door had had a guilty look. It bothered him. Since she could not possibly know who he and Jane were, she must have been suspicious of the colour of their skins. That could mean she knew something about an Englishman. Something she would rather they did not know. 'Where would Rafiq go if he wanted to hide? Could he go to either of his parents?'

'Perhaps.'

'Where is the religious retreat where his mother stays.'

'Bombay.'

'Where is the father's cave?'

The Indian boy pointed. 'Down valley. One hour. Maybe one hour half.

'Would you be prepared to take me there?'

Jane heard and her breath caught in shock. She could manage an hour, even an hour and a half's walk downhill but after the unaccustomed exertion of the past days she knew she would be incapable of keeping up with the men on the return journey. She hid her very real fear at the thought of being left in the village where Kumar Singh was still at large.

The young man hesitated. It would mean missing the procession of the victim from the little temple to Situ-Rama's courtyard. Not that there was any chance of seeing anything more than his actual entrance to the sacred precincts. Only the temple *pujaris* would be there when he came before the dread face of Kali to be formally devoted to death. The door would be closed before the rites as performed over a dying Hindu could take place. Those outside would not even hear the appropriate mantras being recited much less see the washing of the body and the donning of the white shroud. But the band would be wonderful and it would be very exciting.

'I'll pay you well,' said Clive diffidently.

Jullunder struggled with temptation. 'English lessons?' he suggested, hopefully. That seemed a fairer exchange for what he was going to miss.

Chapter Twenty-one

As the sun began to fall towards the horizon, the air to grow cool, the band in the village struck up again. It sounded as though another procession had begun.

Jane said, 'Let's go and have a look, Tsring.'

'No one to watch camp, Memsahib.'

'I don't think that matters much, really. No one has come since we've been here. Everybody is too busy with the festival. And I can't go if you don't come with me.' Gopal had not been seen since morning and besides, until or unless he was cleared of complicity with the Sikh who had made that attempt on her life, Jane was not willing to think of him as a possible bodyguard. They crossed the field together, the tall blonde girl and the short-legged, tough little Tibetan in his climbing boots and woolly red cap, no doubt a donation from some grateful foreign trekker. The noisy band was coming closer and so were the cries of the crowd. 'Let's hurry. This way. I can see the flags.' Tsring's currant bun eyes shone in his flat, round, good-natured face. 'Stay with me, Memsahib.'

'Don't worry. I will.' They ran up one little lane and down another, then paused. 'The band's not more than a hundred yards away now, by the sound of it,' she told the porter. 'It would be fatal to get blocked off behind it. If we're to see, we must be out in front watching the pageant's approach.'

Tsring pointed to a track that ran between two buildings standing close together. 'Short cutty?'

'Maybe.' She turned left, slipped between the buildings with Tsring close on her heels and to her surprise found herself within a stone's throw of the square. 'Quickly, Tsring.' They burst out of the little lane at an ideal vantage point where they could see both the gates of the big temple of Situ-Rama and the approaching procession.

The musicians came first blowing their flutes and banging their drums, then the gaudy fan bearers, and behind them the swaying banner men. The crowd, already pent up with feverish excitement, surged back and forth. The young ones leaped in the air, beat each other round the head in a frenzy of energy, leaped up on willing shoulders, shouted advice, encouragement, abuse. Then, as the musicians went through the square and parted at the gates of the temple, the crowd seemed to go wild. The noise was deafening. Jane pressed her hands to her ears. Indians were rushing into the square from all sides and those already in were going crazy.

Jane's view was blocked by an enormous scarlet banner that had come to rest not more than thirty feet away, its human support hidden by a swaying, rocking mob. Then the banner men moved ahead and she saw a man riding in a cart which was being hauled by several men. He was perched on an immense coil of rope. The handwoven Bhunda rope? And the procession was making for the temple gates. Time seemed to stand still. All life, in that moment of horrified realization, stood still. Even back on, even dressed in that strange long white garment, Jane knew the man in the cart beneath the scarlet banner was Ashley. And then he stood up, took one end of the rope and waved it jubilantly in the air. The crowd swarmed forward in great swelling waves, yelling, screaming; they fell back, swarmed forward once again. Using the rope as a whip or a baton, as though ludicrously, he conducted a crazy band, Ashley, his dark eyes flashing in his handsome face, deliberately stirred the crowd up into a frenzy. He turned this way and that, tall in his long gown, taller than a Hindu but scarcely less dark for the sun, or even some carefully applied colour, had stained his skin so that Jane thought with a sense of shock: He does look like a Hindu! They won't suspect he isn't one. The cart moved on towards the temple gates, then stopped at the entrance and

Ashley swung round, head high, arms raised, like a king saying farewell. An extrovert king, laughing at having thrown aside his decorum, thoroughly enjoying his role.

Suddenly Jane was screaming. Had perhaps been frenziedly screaming all the time, her voice a part of the deafening uproar. The crowd had got out of control.

As they tossed and pushed, elbowed and kicked her, Jane fought her way frantically, desperately forward, trying to get to Ashley. She was making headway of sorts when the cart shot through the gateway into the temple courtyard and the doors swung shut behind it. The crowd, too, fell away, still laughing, though the shouting had ceased. Freed at last, Jane dashed between the retreating figures, rushed up to the great door and began to hammer at it with her fists. Some young Hindus called to her derisively and several women in saris shook their heads, rebuking her for her assault on sacred precincts. Her hands fell to her sides and she slumped against the wood. Somebody spoke to her sharply, reprovingly. She turned away, sick at heart, looking round for the porter. He was nowhere in sight. In present context, with Ashley going in there to God-knew-what it did not seem very important. She went with dragging feet across the dusty square.

It was emptying fast. Tsring was nowhere to be seen. She realized she must not stand here drawing attention to herself. She knew her way back to the camp and it was not far.

She headed for the alley by which she had entered the square. The receding sun had left it gloomy. She walked down it, unheeding for the first time of the smells. The alley was longer than she remembered. And darker. She stopped, looked round uneasily. The light was going fast, the walls shrinking in on her. It narrowed here and the gloom increased. It was then she heard footsteps, light but close.

He had followed her in from the square, stealthily, quietly, walking like an animal. She took to her heels, heading down the only route open to her, a black tunnel. She could hear his feet pounding behind her, gaining on her. She could not see. And then, suddenly there was faint daylight ahead. She put on a tremendous spurt, running like a mad thing, running without hope and without proper breath because she was at seven thousand feet and there was not enough oxygen for lungs accustomed to functioning at lower altitudes. He was gaining on her with his long strides. She could hear his footfalls growing louder, his panting breath. The patch of light in front was growing brighter. With every ounce of strength in her she thrust forward, lungs bursting, the cold sweat like bristles down her back.

And she might have made it except that a small, round stone lay right in her path. She brought one foot down on it, lost her balance and sprawled headlong, her senses anyway numbed by terror and the inrush of black despair. By the certain, unassailable knowledge that this was the end.

Except when he was in the headman's house, the Rajah had not been out of Gopal's sight all day, and from what Gopal had seen it was palpably clear he did not have the jewels. If he had, he would not be moving through the festivities with such a long face and irritable mien, ignoring beggars who were there to offer him redemption and snapping at the headman's family who were designated to look after him and who were clearly doing their best to please. It seemed Puniya's brother, Kumar Singh, had really disappeared, as a ghost, into thin air, Gopal decided gloomily. The next best thing he could do to get back into Jane's good books was to help find the jewels, or Ashley, or preferably, both. Now that Jane had in this extraordinary fashion taken up with Clive, actually sleeping with him and not wanting Gopal near (out of embarrassment no doubt) he was very much on his own. But, more urgently, he needed Jane's esteem for private reasons that had nothing to do with anyone here. That had to do with England and the good life.

The sun had gone down. The last procession was over.

Gopal saw his quarry safely into the headman's house then went back to the field to tell Jane, in case she had not seen Ashley, what had happened. Gopal had watched in shocked disbelief while Ashley went into the temple in the victim's place. Ashley, who was a Christian! A Christian, going into the sanctified heart of Hindu culture, exposing his unbelief to the dread Kali! All the way through the little lanes Gopal dwelt worriedly on the facts, bringing the intelligence and sophistry of his westernization to bear. Of course when they were in London together Helen had taken him to services in the Church of England. He tried to make that a parallel for what Ashley was doing, and failed.

There was no one at the camp. Only the ponies standing idly in one corner. Gopal looked in the tents. They were empty. He sat down to wait. It was cool and quiet here after the razzmataz of the day. He leaned back to rest his head on Clive's pack. There was a hard, very hard object sticking into his ear. He sat up and tried to push it into another part of the pack. It was chunky and hard and cold. What was it? Clive's gun? How careless, Gopal thought critically, to leave a revolver in an unguarded tent. He removed the weapon very carefully, put it down on the ground, then lay back once more and closed his eyes. Half an hour later, when the others had still not come, he decided reluctantly if he was to eat at all he must eat now. Soon it would be time to go back to his vantage point outside the headman's house to await the Rajah's evening movements. He eyed the revolver, considering. It really ought not to be left here. He picked it up and tucked it into his belt.

He took the short cut from the field that led directly to the square. There were several little *chaikhanas* en route set up temporarily for the festival, ramshackle half-buildings made of sacking and stones but none the less emitting delicious odours of steaming curry. He paused tentatively outside of one of them, considering the pertinent fact that those in the centre would be crowded with the evening's revellers. And then, just as he was about to order, his attention was taken by a tall Indian in a pink turban standing all alone by a wall that ran at right angles to the lane. Gopal blinked. Wasn't that his brother-in-law Kumar Singh? He who had left them so rudely and so precipitously as the party approached Tarand yesterday?

The man, who had appeared to be loitering, shot off suddenly in the direction of the square. Gopal, on impulse, ran after him. Kumar, he decided fiercely, was going to have to apologize to Clive if Gopal had to drag him down to the camp by force. He did not want his English friends to have this bad impression of Puniya's family which was his family, too.

Although there were idling Indians everywhere, Gopal could still see the pink turban going on up the lane. He skipped round little groups of loiterers in order to keep his quarry in view. The lane finished here by some low acacia trees, but the man hurried on across the grass. Gopal was pretty sure now that it was Kumar. Then, just as he was going to call out his quarry cut back and disappeared between two ramshackle buildings. Gopal sprinted after him. Behind the buildings was a strip of rough grass and as he ran up a shadowy figure crossed stealthily then paused within the shadow of a low hung tree. Gopal hesitated, frowning. There was another ramshackle building in front. The Sikh, for it was Puniya's brother, he could see now, went almost to the other building, stopped then retreated into the shadow of a bush directly in front. There were two goats tethered to a stake at a corner of the building and a one-eyed man in dhoti and turban huddled against the door.

Kumar Singh walked towards the hut again, and once again turned away. Even resting one hand on the hilt of his *kirpan*, he could not stop trembling. The one-eyed man stared sleepily ahead, not looking at him, just staring. A one-eyed man! It was the worst omen of all in a land of omens, prophecies and forewarnings. Bad luck was certainly stalking him on this mission. First, he had made the tactical error of allowing the girl to see him before the pony entered the forest. That was his own fault, he knew. He had wanted to enjoy himself, to watch her cringe and cry for help before the exciting, final act. Now, by sheer luck he had got her and even found this excellent building to hide her in until darkness fell, because of course, he could not just leave the body lying around in town. He was prepared to walk a long way with her so that she would never be found. The Begum, the swami and his own father who was also Puniya's father, all inadvertently working together for their separate ends, would not thank him, perhaps would not pay him, if word trickled back to Kodapur that the insolent lover of Gopal's had been murdered, as they would hear if the body was found. But what could he do if that man did not move until daylight? Nothing, and no one, would persuade Kumar Singh to enter a building when a one-eyed man squatted outside.

Suddenly a hearty, derisive laugh rang out from somewhere close at hand and Kumar jumped like a rabbit. Gopal crossed the grass with lazy, indolent strides. 'Ha!' he exclaimed loftily. 'You are still the superstitious barbarian, my brother! I will remove the one-eyed man for you.'

As Gopal emerged from the shadows Kumar rushed up to meet him. 'It is all right, brother. I am not afraid. And besides, I do not want to go near.'

Gopal said teasingly, 'But you do, Kumar. I have been watching you. You want to go into that building. What have you there?'

'Nothing. Really, nothing.'

Gopal's dark eyes sharpened with suspicion. He walked forward, spoke to the one-eyed man in Hindi, helped him to his feet and sent him on his way. Then he tried the door. It was not locked. Kumar waited, breath held, tensed like an animal waiting to spring, only half confident that in the darkness Gopal would see nothing. At least there was the advantage that neither of them carried a torch.

Gopal, still chuckling, pushed the door aside. The interior was very dark. There was a scuffling sound as of a small creature. 'You have got something very interesting and very suspicious here, Kumar,' he said, 'and I am going to see what it is.' He could tell Puniya's brother was excited, or nervous. His breath came fast and shallow. 'Who's there?' he asked. Again, that shuffling sound. Gopal turned. He raised one eyebrow, trying on Puniya's brother that sophisticated English look. 'A girl, heh?'

Kumar shuffled his feet. 'It is not your business, Gopal.'

With immense good nature Gopal slapped him on the back. 'No, of course it is not my business and I do not wish to embarrass you. I am sorry. Now you can go in. Now I have got rid of your one-eyed man. It is time to rid yourself of such primitive superstitions,' Gopal commented loftily. He turned and walked away. As he was about to turn the corner he suddenly realized that the diverting little episode of the girl had culminated in his forgetting to chastise Kumar for yesterday's disappearance. He turned. His brother-in-law was still hanging round the doorway, watching him. Vaguely uneasy, Gopal went on to the corner then waited just out of sight. When he edged forward again to where he could see without being detected, Kumar was still moving nervously from one foot to the other, looking down the alley. Gopal moved frowningly into a better position and settled his back against the wall.

It was a long time, perhaps half an hour, before Kumar Singh could be certain that wretched, interfering husband of Puniya had gone. It would have been so much better if he had been able to confide in Gopal. After all, it was he Kumar was here to help by getting rid of the girl. But the Begum had insisted that Puniya's husband should not be told. 'It might disturb his conscience,' she said. If only the Begum knew, though, how difficult she had made it for him! He went into the building, feeling his way along the wall until his foot touched the body. He leaned down and lifted it, slinging it over his shoulder. Then he felt his way back to the door and peered out. There was no one in sight.

An automatic uprush of movement shot the horrified Gopal out of his hiding place as he tore down the lane almost before he had taken in what was happening. The Sikh had gone round the corner and was making for the field. Gopal sprinted after him, heart in mouth. He was lighter, and he had no burden. Besides, his legs were flying on shock waves from within. He could see the long fair hair swinging from the body over the Sikh's shoulder, and he knew. Kumar heard him coming and took to his heels, but it was not easy to run with a tall girl hanging lifelessly down one's back.

Gopal caught up, grasped the Sikh by the shoulder and swung him round. The burden fell with a sickening thud to the ground. 'Jane!'

'It is for you,' Kumar whined in distress. 'You must stay away.'

Gopal had dropped to his knees. 'Jane! Jane!' She was blindfolded, gagged, and her hands and feet were tied together with the rags Kumar had bought at the cloth shop for just this eventuality. He knew if the opportunity came to capture Jane in daylight she would have to be hidden until dark because the crowds who were using the grass fields as public lavatories would see him carry her through. Jane moved and Gopal's breathless shock turned through relief to a flash of animal fury. He leaped savagely to his feet. 'You son of a grass snake and a worm! You were going to kill her.'

'For you. For you, brother, and for Puniya,' Kumar whined.

Gopal's hurled insult was very obscene indeed. He hoped the bandage that covered Jane's eyes also precluded her hearing. Convulsed with rage, he shouted, 'How dare you interfere in my affairs!'

Kumar saw then with astonishment and outrage that he was not going to be allowed to cut the girl's head off, after all. The primitive savage in him reared up at his brother-in-law's ingratitude, at his insults. One hand flashed automatically to his hip as his blood lust scorched through. He drew his sword. Gopal leaned back. The blade unsheathed, gleamed in the half light. First, he pointed it ferociously at Gopal, then, as Gopal retreated, down at the girl.

'No,' screamed Gopal. Jane was Helen's cousin. Puniya's brother could not do such a thing! But Kumar, his black eyes blazing, was slowly, tauntingly, mercilessly, bringing down that terrible blade. There was nothing he could do unless he, also, was to be killed. Jane, without seeing, sensed what was happening. She gathered up all her trussed strength in a spasm of blind terror, a shuddering defence reaction aimed at throwing herself out of the way. She failed. So this was it. Brutally, mercilessly, death had to come. Gopal would not be able to stop this savage from killing her. Dear heaven! Do I have to die this way? Time extended to allow the past in, running in slow motion. Louise, her pretty face only faintly lined with the years, came up before her. Waiting? Then Ashley. But Ashley was not dead! Reality was receding. Had it actually happened without her feeling anything? Was she already in another world? Then Ashley's face came up side-by-side with their mother. Ashley, who was still alive along with the dead! She sensed some divine error and dragged herself back. She screamed. The sound burst suffocatingly against the scarf round her mouth.

Gopal did not want to do it. He was ill-prepared for a situation where he had to kill Puniya's brother. None the less, it was Kumar or Jane. He drew the revolver and aimed at Kumar's right arm. If the Sikh had not jumped to avoid the shot, Gopal might have been successful in his precise intention, but he did jump. He leaped to the right, forcing Gopal, who would never willingly kill a fly, to commit murder. The bullet hit him where it was never intended to go, right in the heart.

Chapter Twenty-two

'It was the Begum,' said Jane shakily. She was sitting on her sleeping bag drinking the hot, sweet tea that a distressed Tsring had produced. 'It was the Begum all the time. She must have rushed off that very first day when I met her at the palace, told the swami, and arranged for Kumar Singh to be waiting outside. She knew the Rajah would send me home in his jeep. The Sikh had tampered with the brakes. He told me. They weren't very good in the first place,' she added wryly. 'He didn't have to do much. Then Gopal and I played into the Begum's hands by going to the ashram to borrow the camping gear.'

'He told you all this?' She nodded. Clive was grimly silent wondering what further obstacles were secretly in store for him. The tears broke through and trickled down Jane's cheeks. She brushed them away. 'It's the shock. I'm a mess. Oh Clive, it was the most dreadful, dreadful experience.'

'I know. Try not to think about it.' He put an arm round her, drawing her close against him.

Gopal was sitting with knees tucked up under his chin, his beautiful black head in his hands. 'Ay-i-eee! This is a terrible thing I have done. I have killed my wife's brother. I will never be able to face Puniya again.'

And that seemed at least to sort out one facet of his problems, Clive thought sardonically. He said, 'I'd better go to the headman and say I've seen someone lying apparently dead up there. I'll get Gopal to show me the spot. I don't suppose Kumar carried any identification.' Gopal's burning conscience would evidently see that he informed the family. It was not the business of the people of Tarand. He said, 'Let's change the subject. I have some brighter news to tell.

The jewels are in the holyman's cave. I've seen them. Rubies, emeralds, diamonds, sapphires. Enough to fill a flower pot.'

Jane could only gaze at him in disbelief. 'D'you know,' she managed at last, 'I never really believed in the jewels. Only in the necklace.'

'The necklace is there, too.'

'So Ashley hadn't – hadn't—'

'Yes, Ashley did. He changed places with a chap called Eesh Nohal who was one of the goldsmiths designated to go into the cave and collect the god and the three pieces of treasure we saw on show with him in the temple yard.'

'But how did he work it? The swap?'

'The Begum had given him an introduction to the gold-smiths. You'll remember they are relatives. That was his way in. Then, by a fluke of circumstances, the rest turned out to be comparatively easy. This goldsmith, called Eesh, who incidentally was given shelter in the cave along with the real victim, had recently fallen in love with the victim's sister. As you know, the men who go into the cave, by tradi-tion, die the following year.'

Jane nodded. 'It's true. The Rajah told me that after the last Bhunda one of the goldsmiths who went into the cave died of cholera, one fell off a cliff, and one died of something mysterious.'

'Pure chance,' asserted Gopal, smiling self consciously.

'The fact remains,' Jane countered, 'they all died. If I were a Hindu, I think, like Eesh, I'd be only too happy to by-pass the honour if an opportunity to do so came my way.'

'So Ashley was lucky.'

'Ashley was always lucky,' Jane commented and Clive gave her a sharp look.

'He wasn't so lucky when he tried to get off with the necklace and the bag of jewels,' Clive continued. 'The gold-smiths saw him. However, he reminded them of his original story. He'd told them he'd come to represent the Rajah of

Kodapur. Now he added that he had been sent to collect the jewels. The goldsmiths evidently knew about the jewels — I suppose, when you think about it, one of them must have deposited the package in the cave when they were brought here originally. Even if the original participants were not involved, the story would have been handed down. It's only thirty years ago. Anyway, they were quite happy to give up the package, but they insisted the necklace belonged to the god.'

'Ashley had violated the cave,' Gopal pointed out gravely, 'by taking away what actually belonged to Situ-Rama.'

'That's right. Then Ashley had another bit of luck. Young Rafiq Tankha, the son of the holy man, had been chosen months ago as the victim and until recently had been enjoying the run-up. Apparently they have hi-jinks in the fields when the grass for the Bhunda rope is gathered to the sound of music. Then he'd spent three months making the rope. All this time he'd been a VIP. The victim, by the way, has to make the rope so he can be sure there's no skullduggery in the way of weak patches and knots, since, by inference, he is to ride across the valley on it.'

'They take the pretence the whole way?'

'Even the onlookers convince themselves the victim is going down the rope,' Gopal interposed. 'So when they switch to the goat at the last moment,' he shrugged, 'in the excitement the illusion is there, at least for the susceptible ones.'

'They're abiding by the law and satisfying their bloodlust at the same time.' Jane repressed a shudder.

'That's right. Now, you'll remember that Jullunder Cariappa our schoolmaster guide told us the holyman's wife, who is also the victim's mother, is in a religious retreat.' Jane nodded. 'It seems she dreamt the sacrificial goat was trampled to death during the festival. This was construed as an ill-omen. Neither the victim nor his family were very happy any more about his continuing in the role. So Ashley, as an Englishman untrammelled by the local superstition, saw his opportunity. He'd already done what was easily construed as a good deed by taking the place of the victim's future brother-in-law in entering the cave. So he offered, in view of Rafiq's cracked nerve, and also no doubt in view of the fact that he needed a guard for his jewels while he thought of a way to deal with this new problem of getting off with the necklace, to take the victim's place for the final ceremonial.'

'And he was accepted?'

'Yes. He was put in the lower temple with the rope, and incidentally that was why the five guards were outside, just in case word got out and some indignant Hindu stirred up trouble. And the two chaps, Rafiq and Eesh, thinking it might be tactful to keep out of the way, went off to join Rafiq's father in the cave, taking Ashley's booty with them for safe keeping.'

'Now what's to happen to the necklace?'

'The necklace! Ah! That's the problem. The jewels are there for the taking but they want the necklace to go back into the cave when the god is returned tomorrow night. They're terrified of Situ-Rama's wrath.'

Jane eyed Clive speculatively. 'And how do you feel about that?'

He ran a finger along the edge of the groundsheet, his eyes hidden. It was one thing to disapprove of these Hindus' appallingly wasteful habits, it was quite another for him, a Christian, to meddle in their religious affairs. He said at last, reluctantly, 'There are enough jewels there to build a dozen hospitals.'

'You said they're for the taking.'

He nodded. 'In a manner of speaking only. Eesh and Rafiq are guarding them for Ashley.'

A mountain of silence lay between them. At last Jane said in a small voice, 'After the final ceremony, I could talk to Ashley.' Gopal and Clive stared hard at the ground. They knew that a man who has gone through all Ashley had tackled to get the jewels was not going to hand them over simply because his sister pointed out he was being dishonest.

Someone had to say something. Jane asked, 'What sort of cave is it?' By talking round the subject, they might find a way.

'Tiny,' Clive replied. 'There is one small partition to sleep in, and one where the sadhu sits. The village people bring him food. They believe they will gain redemption for themselves by looking after him.'

'He walks for exercise? Clive,' she exclaimed excitedly, 'all you have to do is wait for Eesh and Rafiq to leave – as they're bound to do as soon as it's safe to go – mightn't they even creep quietly out to watch the rope ceremony? After all, they're not going to have another opportunity to see it for twelve years. You could be there, near the cave, Clive, watching for the sadhu to take his exercise.'

'Yoga,' broke in Gopal gloomily.

'What?'

'He need never leave the cave until he is ready to die. He would practise yoga for exercise.'

'Ready to die?' Jane asked.

'As a holyman, he would know when death is coming.'

Jane looked unhappily away. They were back to Ashley and Clive again. After a while she asked bluntly, 'So what are you going to do?'

'Play it by ear.'

Later, unable to sleep, Jane crept out of her sleeping bag and draping it round her back left the tent. Tsring was curled up in his blanket beside the dying fire. Quietly, she added some logs the porter had gathered, went down on hands and knees to blow them to flames, then huddled close by, knees beneath her chin, gazing miserably into the coals. The night was brilliant with stars, the moon so bright she could see the outlines of the towering mountains that hemmed them in. Across the valley the white post to which the Bhunda rope would be hooked the next day glimmered like a malignant wand in the moonlight. A movement behind Jane caused her to swing round. Gopal was emerging from the tent he shared with Clive.

He gave her a wry, sad-sweet smile. 'I, too, cannot sleep.' He sat down beside her, pulling his anorak round his shoulders. 'It is a terrible thing I have done, Jane.'

She put a comforting hand on the Brahmin boy's arm. 'You did it for me, so I must carry the blame. I'm very grateful, Gopal. It was the second time he had tried to kill me. You did not know, did you?' Gopal's eyes widened. 'We thought it better not to tell you.'

His face fell. 'You did not trust me.'

'No,' she replied sadly. 'We did not trust you. It isn't easy to trust anyone in the circumstances in which we find ourselves. I don't trust Clive. He will kill my brother tomorrow, if he has to.'

Gopal lifted her fingers and held them gently in his. 'As Ashley will kill him, if Ashley has to. Men will do anything when a fortune is at stake.'

'Gopal, we must think of something.'

'That is why I am not sleeping,' he replied disarmingly. 'I have come out here to think of something. But what?' They chewed the subject to pulp. They came up with ideas and discarded them. Gopal was too lightly built. He hadn't a hope against Ashley. They built up the fire and sat in long silences staring into the flames. At last, leaning one against the other, they dozed fitfully as the moon came nearer to the western horizon and the eastern sky grew pale. They were no nearer to a solution and the dreadful day had come.

Later, Gopal, lurking miserably in the shadows, watched his brother-in-law's funeral pyre being built, then watched the flames consume the body. The heat and flies made the disposal of even a murdered man in India a hasty affair. Or particularly a murdered man. They would not take time off to dig a grave for a Sikh on such a day. Overhead a flock of vultures, portents and shadows of death, wheeled elegantly and fearsomely across the sky. Today they had been deprived of their human carrion, but tomorrow India would provide once again.

The final rite of the festival was to begin early. Jane and Clive breakfasted in silence, each wanting to ask the other what they would do, each one retreating. Tsring was clearing away the tin plates and porridge pot. Jane rose. She walked slowly towards the little stone wall that ran beside the lane. Clive followed. The air was cool, the sun burning. She heard his footsteps and paused, then turned and as he came abreast of her she saw the shape of the gun at his hip. His face was tense, the skin pulled tight over the cheekbones, the mouth grim. There was something to be said between them at this eleventh hour. They both knew it, but neither knew how to start. The only words that came to mind were pointless, argumentative. They both knew Clive had to get the jewels. He knew she loved Ashley. It was no good asking for pacts or promises.

He said, 'If I disappear—'

'Don't,' she replied convulsively, the pent-up emotions in her breaking through. 'I'll help you. You know I'll help.' He put a hand through her arm and held it close against his body. 'I just want you to know – it's not the right time – but I want you to know I love you, Jane.'

She swung away from him, eyes wide and pain-filled. 'How can you say that, at such a time! If you loved me—'

And so she killed what may have been between them. His face closed, he withdrew his arm and strode away towards the centre of the village. She did not know she was crying until a gentle, diffident voice behind her said, 'Memsahib!' She turned but she could not see the little Tibetan porter for the flooding tears.

'Doctor Sahib good man,' Tsring told her gently. She mopped her eyes with the filthy bit of rag that her handkerchief had become. 'Memsahib wished to see procession?' Tsring asked shyly.

She said, 'Tsring, you're awfully strong.' He was small, not more than five feet four inches, but he looked to have immense strength in his arms and short, muscled legs. He nodded, his white teeth flashing, his smile broadening. The words suddenly came tumbling out, falling over each other, ill-chosen, as the plan formed in her mind. 'The victim, after he comes away from the sacrifice ceremony – do you understand?'

The little Tibetan nodded. 'Sacrifice, yes.'

'He will go down into the valley to a holyman's cave. We want to stop him.' Tsring looked puzzled. 'I haven't any right to ask you this,' she went on in a rush. 'He may have a gun. But could you, do you think you could tackle him? Gopal and I would help, but we're both so light. We want to stop him going down into the valley.'

The porter was baffled. 'Why, Memsahib? Is Hindu religious ceremony.'

'But he's not a Hindu, Tsring. The victim is not a Hindu. He is my brother. An Englishman.'

'No, Memsahib.' The little man shook his head. 'I see victim yesterday. He Hindu.'

'He isn't, Tsring. I assure you, he is an Englishman. I should know. He's my brother. I know he looks dark, but that's the sun. Or maybe even a stain, used as a disguise. But he is English.'

The porter's smile seemed fixed. 'Memsahib have bad time yesterday,' he said sympathetically.

Jane's spirits slumped. 'All right. Let's go to the procession.' It was not fair, anyway, to ask the little porter to tackle Ashley.

Chapter Twenty-three

Feeling was running high in the square. Three or four hundred men, tenants of the temple, were lined up ready to carry the Bhunda rope across the valley. Jane and Tsring edged their way through the jostling mass of Indians until they were stopped by the tightly packed crowd around the temple. Suddenly the gates began to move. A murmur of anticipation rose, ran round the square, grew in volume until it became a primitive convulsion that ebbed and flowed. The temple gates swung wide and the crowd fell back as the two Hindus emerged carrying one end of the rope. The band on the eastern side of the square began to crash out rowdy, triumphal music. The two men who were to head the rope procession marched ahead and then, two by two, the rest of the temple tenants took hold. Jane found herself pushed to and fro, buffeted, elbowed and knocked as she fought her way towards the corridor that had been cleared between the gates and the exit from the square. The rope snaked through the gateway and, gathering its bearers like legs, marched off down through the village, a quarter mile long centipede of a rope. The band grew more boisterous, the crowd more turbulent. They pushed and shoved, lively, disorderly, rampant. Hot, bruised, often despairing, Jane made inch-by-inch headway. Here near the entrance by the time the end of the rope emerged the crowd was well nigh beyond control.

Then Ashley came and silence fell, a silence that hung over the square, eerie, strange. Even the band had stopped playing. Ashley, white-clad in a long, shirt-like garment, came soberly, half a head taller than the small Hindus. He was flanked by the temple *Pujaris*. He looked directly ahead, as though the strange events of the night had taken the fun out of his escapade and replaced it with something dark, deeper than apprehension.

'Ashley!' Jane's scream was lost for, as the tall figure in white was led forward, suddenly the crowd came alive again, roaring, stampeding. Buffeted this way and that, losing her vantage point, she found herself receding as the rampant Indians surged into the centre, squeezed out, sliding backwards until suddenly she was on the outskirts and Tsring was saying concernedly, 'All right, Memsahib?'

She pulled herself to rights. 'Yes, I'm okay,' she gasped. 'Tsring, you saw him. You can see he's an Englishman?'

The porter shook his head. 'Hindu, Memsahib. You make mistake.'

'He's my brother. Hell!' she exploded. 'I should know.' The porter turned unhappily away.

Clive, from his vantage point against a wall on the opposite side of the square saw the blonde head like a golden beacon in the sea of black ones. God! She ought not to be here. Anything was likely to happen. She was fighting for position, trying to get to that cleared channel down which the victim would walk. She was not more than thirty feet away, now. The suspicion, the dread that was always with him rose like a snake, coiling and shifting inside him. She was going to get up to Ashley and somehow tell him, warn him that Clive was after the jewels. That Clive had a gun. No matter what she wanted, in her heart, to do, she was in the end on Ashley's side.

His doubts and his fears took over. He had to get those jewels now. He had nurtured this dream for too long to take a chance. Situ-Rama, dressed in sumptuous green and red silk, appeared alone in his little *palki*. The seething excitement of the crowd charging to and fro drowned out the lively band as the god went by on his way to some vantage point where he could watch the sacrifice. And then the white goat came running, bleating unhappily, tugging at his rope. Clive swung grimly away and headed off into one of the little lanes. He was going to hate himself for the rest of his life for what he had to do now. Don't think about it. Just concentrate on the fact that one Englishman with a gun ought to be more than equal to an elderly sadhu and two lightly built Hindus. He began to run.

The Rajah of Kodapur, very much against the host's advice because he wanted his honoured guest to have the best view of the sacrifice which meant going to the lower temple where the goat would arrive at the climax of its ride, was waiting at the white post on the opposite side of the valley. He saw the long procession descend to the stream, cross the little bridge then wind up the steep path beside the precipice. The main section of the crowd had gone to the temple on the village side, but the younger, more agile ones, rowdy as a pack of caterwauling hounds, streamed down through the terraced fields below the village, splashing through the water, scrambling up the grass slopes, and even, some of them, up the perpendicular cliff beside the precipice. The victim came more sedately, still flanked by the temple *pujaris*. The Rajah watched him through narrowed eyes.

The goat was climbing ahead, the crowd swarming round it like flies. The band had gone with Situ-Rama's entourage to the temple at the lower end of the village where the other end of the rope had been attached to a hook on its wall. A group of officials was here now ready to fix the top end of the rope to the white post. The Rajah's waiting look returned to the victim, striding up the track. Then suddenly he saw a head of golden hair, a pale skin. Jane? She was scrambling up the steep slope just outside the crowd that hemmed in the victim. And then she disappeared. The Rajah moved forward, strained his eyes, but he could no longer see her.

Jane had missed her footing. She was not as agile at the unaccustomed height of seven thousand feet as the young Hindus. Whilst their excitement seemed to give them wings, her apprehension made her clumsy. Whichever way she turned now, she could make no headway. Those who had arrived at the white post would not relinquish the splendid position they had striven to gain, so those behind could climb no farther. Frantically, she turned this way and that. The young men jostled her goodnaturedly, advising her in incomprehensible Hindi and Urdu to stay where she was. But with the Tibetan porter's help she slid through and at last, free of the shouting, swaying bodies, scrambled breathlessly higher. It was very steep, but there were dry little plants to pull on. Here was a rocky outcrop, the summit of which moved like an ant heap with jostling humanity. Those who had managed to get on to it were above the post and obviously they were going to have a good view. They were already taking over, dancing with excitement, hurling advice down on the officials below. She came round the top and, holding the porter's hand, slid down the slope beside the rock. She could now look over the heads of the seething crowd. Where was the goat? She could not see it, and neither could she see Ashley. 'Tsring, I'm going to slide.'

'No, Memsahib. Dangerous. Break leg.'

Ignoring his warning she took a step forward, lost her footing on the dry, slippery grass and grabbed at a rough little outcrop of foliage. It gave, and with a gasp of dismay she slid on a protruding piece of granite she had meant to avoid. It was not until she was hurtling towards them that she saw Ashley, and the goat beside him. She was going in the right direction, but she was going too fast. She shrieked, but her cry was lost in a sudden uproar from the crowd as it surged forward. She flung out both arms, grabbed a pantalooned gentleman in an untidy turban and went down with him as her knees buckled beneath her. 'Sorry. I'm so sorry.'

He had swung round on her, fists raised, a cry of rage on his lips. Then he saw, and fell back in astonishment. She jumped to her feet. She was unhurt and less than ten feet from the post, now. She was slim, and she was strong. She pushed two of the swaying bodies apart, insinuating herself determinedly between them, then pushed again. They were so taken up with the excitement of the moment that they scarcely seemed to notice her. As they swayed, she pushed further in until at last she was within a few feet of the post. The goat was nearby. She could hear its pathetic bleating, but she could not see it. Nor Ashley. Then suddenly he was there, towering over the small Hindus.

'Ashley?'

'Hills!'

At the two familiar voices, Ashley's head came round. Ashley's black head with the stained features that made him as dark as the smaller men round him, and as like them.

'You see, Memsahib. Hindu.' The porter's voice in her ear was like the opening of Pandora's box and the shock of it seemed to turn Jane's muscles to jelly. The breath seemed to leave her body as the realization came to her of why Ashley was here. Tsring had been right. Her half-brother was also half-Hindu. The jewels, he could assume, in a manner of speaking, to be his birthright.

In that inexplicable way that had been happening since the temple door opened, the crowd went quiet again. Faintly, the cymbals from the opposite side of the valley came through. Ashley smiled. It was an arrogant smile, but in a way, kindly. He said, 'You can't use them. But I can.'

The Rajah's face changed. Dismay converted to anger and then a deadly venom. His features twisted barbarically until he was a devilish caricature of a man. There was a bleat of terror. The goat was being lifted towards the saddle.

And then it happened. The Rajah leaped forward with an inhuman scream. 'Moslem! Kill that Moslem impostor,' he cried in Hindi and Urdu and, for Barry Hills who had done this dreadful thing to him, in English. His black eyes blazed with a savage malice, more deadly, more brutal than spite.

A startled shout flew through the crowd. 'Moslem!

Moslem!' The cry went up. Thirty years of repressed hate burst out of the Hindus who thought they had forgotten what the Moslems had done to their friends and relatives who were trapped at Partition in Pakistan. Pandemonium broke loose in a senseless lust for blood. The goodnatured stamping and hooting changed to a ferocious uproar. They dragged and kicked brutally at each other as they fought to get near the Moslem who had defiled their Hindu festival by his presence. The goat disappeared. The crowd went mad. They fell upon Ashley, lifted him and flung him into the saddle.

Oh no! Jane leaped forward and fought her way towards the Rajah. She could see him now, his animal face contorted with rage, his black eyes burning with triumph and the bloodlust that had swept through the crowd. Ashley was fighting like a madman but the small men who had converged furiously upon him had produced a thousand hands and they were pressing him down into the saddle, tying the ropes.

Jane reached the Rajah. He saw her but he took no notice. 'Kill the Moslem! Kill the Moslem!' And they were doing just that, their fists raining down upon him, winding the ropes carelessly in their haste, making a mess of things because they were maddened by the Rajah's obscene lie.

'He's not Barry Hills,' Jane screamed over the din. 'He's your son. Louise's son and yours. My brother, Ashley. Your son.'

'Moslem!' screamed the Rajah, looking beyond her at the glorious sunrise of revenge.

'He's your son! Oh God! Stop them,' Jane sobbed. 'Don't you understand? He's Ashley, your own son. Louise's son.'

He heard her. His hands that were lifted in barbarous triumph fell to his sides. He looked at her with the shocked face of a man condemned. 'Ash—'

'Louise's son. Your son. Stop them, and save your son.'

He would have stopped them. He tried. He rushed in, screaming to the murderers and to the gods. But it was too late. He had drawn from them a convulsion of primitive savagery that was as unstoppable as the Ganges in flood. The rope jerked, the crowd went mad, the saddle with its human victim went flying down towards the temple on the opposite side of the valley. The crowd went silent. The whole valley went silent. With sick despair Jane stood with one hand to her heart, and then she closed her eyes.

Clive, hurrying down the valley towards the sadhu in his cave heard the silence and swung round to look back. He saw the saddle and its rider part, saw the human form spread-eagled, come flying through the air towards him and towards the rocks below. For a moment he was too stunned for thought, then a vague awareness seeped through that he need not continue his journey. He turned and walked back towards where the body had fallen.

Jane said numbly, 'You killed him.'

The Rajah's acceptance of the truth was in his face and eyes. The scorching agony, the regret. He did not get up from the ground because he could not. The crowd had trampled him in their rush to the valley.

'You killed him,' Jane repeated, her voice a broken sob. She could not stop saying it. 'You killed him. You killed my brother. You killed your son.' It seemed to have become a tortured treadmill in her mind. 'You killed him.' She said it again. 'Your son.'

'Ashley!' said the Rajah brokenly. 'Ashley!' And then he covered his face with his hands.

Gopal, having battled his way through against the raging tide of his fleeing countrymen, hurtled toward them. He had expected Jane and the Rajah to go to the temple and realized too late that they were not there. 'Are you all right? Are you all right, Jane?' She went numbly towards him and they clung together in silence. The Rajah looked across to where the goat lay spreadeagled on the ground. It was quite dead, trampled to death in the horrific climax to the day.

Chapter Twenty-four

Ashley of the Indian brown eyes, the outrageous charm, was dead.

'It had to be. It was in Ashley's karma to die today,' Gopal said. 'Nobody could change that. Someone had to be the instrument of his destruction. It was fitting that it should be the Rajah. There's a pattern to life. Look back, Jane, and you'll see how it all fits, leading up to this.'

Jane had told him about Louise saying as the goat flew down the rope, 'It seems to be happening to me.' Louise, standing with one hand clasped, apparently, to her waist but in fact lying over the womb where the seed of the half-Hindu child lay. Clive was silent beneath the weight of fatalist India. Jane wanted to say, in the moment of Kumar Singh's murdering hand descending, she had seen Ashley's face along with the dead face of Louise, but she was afraid to put into words the undoubted fact that India had pushed itself too far into her subconscious.

Clive had known all along. 'The Rajah's Christian name is Ashwani,' he told her gently. 'A dead give-away. I realized you didn't know, but how could I tell you?' And then Jane recalled the Rajah's sharp reaction when she mentioned Ashley's name. She had thought his surprise was due to the fact that the child had not been called after the British Resident whom Jane assumed to be his father.

She felt hollowed out. She said, 'Let's go now, shall we?' She wanted to kick the dust of this accursed village from her feet. What remains there were of Ashley had been buried quickly and quietly. In a way, it was perhaps fitting that he should lie here. The Rajah had wanted a funeral pyre. But

Ashley had lived as an Englishman and his dying had changed nothing.

'We've got to collect the jewels,' said Clive.

'Will the sadhu give them to you?'

'It won't be necessary to upset him, now. I'll march the Rajah down to the cave. The sadhu knows they're to go to him and will hand them over. Then the Rajah and I can have our little talk. He can't use them. I'll have to make him see. I hope there won't be any trouble. If there is,' said Clive quite straightforwardly, 'I shall know how to deal with him, or rather, the Indian government will. I am sure he's an intelligent man. I've no intention of telling anybody who put the jewels away, or even where they came from, if the Rajah co-operates.'

'What about the necklace?' He gave a wry little shrug. In one part of his mind lay anger for the flagrant waste. In another, an unwillingness to meddle. 'Gopal says he doubts the Begum would trust Ashley to return the necklace to her. Why should she, when you think of it?'

Clive nodded. 'That has been at the back of my mind all along. It depends upon what sort of relationship there was between them, and how much the Begum was prepared to pay Ashley. She must live on a pension, too. If it was not a big sum, then yes, I think Gopal's right. It's likely she would have him tailed.'

'That means, if the "tail" is astute, he'll tackle the Rajah. And the Rajah will certainly tell him we have it.' Jane's hands began to tremble. 'Give it to the Rajah to put back into the cave. There's been horror enough. Put it back.'

Clive pondered for a while, then he said, 'I have the answer. Let's hand it over if we're approached, attacked or whatever. Why not let the Begum have the necklace again, for a day? She's done us no harm and life hasn't treated her kindly. It can't be easy to drop from such a height. It could save a lot of unpleasantness all round.' Jane's eyes misted over. 'Don't cry.'

She brushed the tears away. 'I'm not. I'm thinking how incredibly kind you are.'

'I couldn't hear it from a nicer person. I've something to say to you, too, but here's Ashwani Kodapur coming over the stone wall. I can see his eyes glittering with avarice even at this distance. I fear I am not going to get such compliments from him.'

There were no good-byes to be said. When Clive arrived back they took the tents down quickly and quietly and were on their way. There was a long, hard journey before them, not only concerned with the heights and the leopards, the bears and the bad tempered *pujari*'s wife at the sacred lake, where she had learned a little of what made India tick. She wanted to go back but she did not know why. There was no reason to hurry now, but they wanted to get started before the great Hindu exodus began.

Jane was numbed to walking as she was numbed to feeling. They wound in and out of the little stone walled fields, crossed the chattering water courses and then came up on to the bare hillside. As they climbed higher and higher into the hills there was an emotional moment when they paused to look back at Tarand far below. It had begun to empty and they could see the swaying ant tracks of pilgrims trailing back to their home villages. Gopal said as they climbed slowly on and up the foothill that was thimble high in the vast Himalayan range, 'I shall have to go back to England very quickly now, once I have seen my family. It will not be safe for me to stay, for the moment.' His burning conscience was to be his enemy. 'One day, I hope I shall be able to come back.' So he, too, had become entwined in their lives.

They reached the sacred lake on the second night. The *pujari* greeted them like old friends, invited them to the *puja* in the temple and commented they had lost one of their party. 'We left him at Tarand.' So they disposed of Kumar Singh with shocking ease.

That evening as the sun went down Jane and Clive

climbed to the rim of the magic basin. It was indescribably beautiful with the green downs and forests spread out before them, the white capped mountains in the distance and the strange, wild sky. They sat in silence for a long time, too overwhelmed to talk.

'You're staying, aren't you.'

She turned to him, blinking in surprise at the unexpectedness of Clive's statement. He had spoken with quiet certainty. 'Yes,' she replied. She had not thought to put it into words. 'Yes, I think I am.'

He smiled at her, his eyes quizzical. 'You say that as though you don't know why.'

'I don't think I do know why, yet. When I first met you I asked you what you were doing in India and you said: "It's not as simple as that." It's how I feel. I'd like to help you. May I?'

He said, still smiling at her, 'You could help me with the Rajah. He sees Louise in you. Perhaps you could capitalize on that, in the interests of his less fortunate countrymen. He may be deposed, dispossessed, fairly poor etcetera, but he's still a person of importance in the town. I'd like him on my side.'

'Was he angry?' She had not wanted to ask before, when Clive returned with the jewels.

'Very. Then despairing. Then resigned.'

She nodded. She did not want to know the details. She knew Clive had not got the necklace. Even feeling she never wanted to see the Rajah again, Jane had a premonition their lives, for better or worse, were going to be irrevocably intertwined, and she was mature enough to accept the fact. 'Gopal is still determined to go back to England,' she said. 'I think I must help him. He saved my life. And, would you believe it, he wants to earn enough money to send Puniya to university. He thinks that's a good solution. I'm glad. Somehow, it would have been callous to simply hand her back like an unsolicited gift.' Nothing had been resolved with regard to Helen. Perhaps it never would be. Jane shrugged the problem away. She had never felt it was her affair.

Clive slid an arm round her. 'It's time for us, now. You know what I want, don't you?'

'Yes, and I want it too. But I'm too bruised to accept it, yet.' Bruised in mind and spirit. Needing time.

He said, 'I loved you the first moment I saw you standing over that poor fellow's grave in the British cemetery in Kodapur.' He gave her a lopsided smile. 'It wasn't always evident, I know. But I can make it evident any time you say the word.'

She rested her blonde head on his shoulder. 'Let's stay here for a day or two. We agree it's Shangri-la. Perhaps it's the sort of place where bruises heal. I think we need breathing time before we return to Kodapur. Gopal, too.'

Beyond, the ridges were filling up with that soft blue mist, and beyond again, the sunset flamed into a wild sky. The strong, strange colours above the horizon darkened to reflect the many coloured soils of India. The hills crept nearer, swallowed the sun, and night encircled them.